THE DARKEST LIE

THE DARKEST LIE

PINTIP DUNN

KENSINGTON BOOKS
www.kensingtonbooks.com

This book is a work of fiction. Names, characters, places, and incidents either are products of the author's imagination or are used fictitiously. Any resemblance to actual persons, living or dead, events, or locales is entirely coincidental.

KENSINGTON BOOKS are published by

Kensington Publishing Corp.
119 West 40th Street
New York, NY 10018

eISBN-13: 978-1-4967-0359-0
eISBN-10: 1-4967-0359-6
First Kensington Electronic Edition: July 2016

ISBN-13: 978-1-4967-0358-3
ISBN-10: 1-4967-0358-8
First Kensington Trade Paperback Printing: July 2016

10 9 8 7 6 5 4 3 2

Printed in the United States of America

For my brother Pan, who shares with me
the loss of our beloved mother

Acknowledgments

This book was my first foray into the YA contemporary genre. While it felt different in some ways, in many more ways, it felt like home.

Thank you to my literary agent, Beth Miller, for encouraging me to try a contemporary story—without you, this book may never have been written. You are amazing in so many ways, I can't list them all. But I appreciate every single one of them.

My heartfelt thanks to my editor, Mercedes Fernandez, for the brilliant insights into character and story. This book is so much better because of your input, and it has been a true joy to work with you. Thank you to Kristine Mills and Wild Empress Photography for the beautiful cover. Thank you, as well, to my publicist, Lulu Martinez, and the rest of the team at Kensington for turning this book from a manuscript into a reality. Thank you to my new editor, Alicia Condon, and my outside publicist, Jen Halligan.

Thank you to my wonderful critique partners, Kimberly MacCarron, Vanessa Barneveld, Denny Bryce, Danielle Meitiv, and Holly Bodger. I value your thoughts on my writing so much, but I value your friendship even more. Meg Kassel and Stephanie Winklehake, we may be flung to different corners of the world, but your friendship is always constant, always true. To the rest of the DoomsGirls—Romily Bernard, Natalie Richards, and Cecily White—thank you for being here. Thanks to Michelle Monkou, and thanks to the Waterworld Mermaids—Masha, Carlene, Alethea, Kerri, Dana, and Susan.

I'd like to thank my other writing groups for being SO supportive. Seriously, you guys blow me away with your collective awesomeness—the Firebirds, the YA Story Sisters, Waiting on 2016, and the Writers House Army.

Special shout-out to my DreamWeavers. Back when it was titled *Carlie in Crisis,* this manuscript was a finalist in RWA's

2014 Golden Heart contest. Because of this, I met my Dream-Weaver sisters and also connected with my wonderful editor, Mercedes. So, thank you, RWA, and the other local chapters of which I'm a member: WRW, MRW, YARWA, and TGN.

I adore taking writing classes to improve my craft, and I'd like to thank Laura Baker for her input and guidance. I conceived of the idea for this book on the morning her "Turning Points" class began, and that is where I brainstormed the initial outline. Thank you, as well, to Margie Lawson, whose lecture packets I read while writing this book.

Thank you to the Star Vista Crisis Intervention and Suicide Prevention Center, in San Mateo, California, where I volunteered as a call counselor.

I've said this before, and I'll say it again: I have the best, most supportive, most wonderful family and friends in the world. I am truly blessed to be surrounded by so much love. You have moved me to tears with your thoughtful gestures that go soaring miles above what is necessary.

Thank you, from the bottom of my heart, Anita, Sheila, Aziel, Mahira, Kai, Bo, Peter, Francis, Amy, Josh, Grace, J. D., Aruna, Nick, Steph, Gaby, Shani, and Monique.

My family. I don't even know where to begin. Among them, they have bought enough of my books to open a small bookstore—and that's a mere example of the love and support they show me every day. Thank you to my dad, Naronk, who is without doubt my biggest champion. Thank you to the rest of the Hompluems: Uraiwan, Pan, Dana, Lana, and P. Noi. I would be lucky to have any one of you—to have all of you is like winning the family lottery. Thank you to the Dunns: Donald, Catherine, Chantal, Franck, Quentin, and Natasha. I'll never be able to express how much I appreciate each of you.

Thank you to the joys of my life, Aksara, Atikan, and Adisai. You taught me what unconditional love truly means.

And finally, to Antoine. Without you, none of this would be possible.

Prologue

It's time to view the body. Family first.

Well, technically, me first. There was always only three of us in the nuclear unit, and Dad's been locked in the den for the past seventy-two hours. I've only seen him once, when he shuffled upstairs like a pajama-clad zombie and asked me if I'd eaten.

That was it: Did you eat?

Not: I prefer the cherry wood casket. Or: Let me make your grandma's travel arrangements. Or even: I know this was Mom's favorite dress, but isn't the neckline a little . . . low?

Did I eat?

Yes, Dad. I had soup from the can and microwaved pizza rolls and a bowl of cereal. The food sloshes in my stomach now as I walk down the runner to the casket I picked out because of its mauve tint.

Calla lilies pile in urns around the viewing room, and the air-conditioning wars with the sweat along my hairline. My mom smiles at me from a portrait erected behind the casket. Her eyes are hesitant and a little wary, as if she knew, somehow, some way, she would wind up here. Lifeless. Pumped full of formaldehyde. About to be gawked at by a town full of gossips.

This was only going to end one of two ways—with Tabitha Brooks dead or in jail. I never thought I'd say this, but I'd give anything to see my mother behind bars.

I wade through the dense, chilly air and stop a few feet from the body. Behind me, my grandmother and aunt sit, a box of tissues between them, blowing their noses like it's a sport. They're the only relatives we have. Mom's parents have both passed, and Gram's husband—my grandfather—took off when my dad was a kid.

"Look at our Cecilia," Gram sniffs. "So brave. Not a single tear shed."

If she only knew. I'm not brave. Fifteen minutes ago, I was retching into the toilet bowl. Five minutes from now, when the doors open for the visitation, I'll be long gone, leaving Gram to shake people's hands and deal with the bit lips, the knowing eyebrows, that inevitable speaking-in-a-funeral-parlor whisper. I can hear the titters: "Is it true? Tabitha's heart stopped while she was boffing the high school quarterback? Why, she must've been twenty years his senior!"

Twenty-three years, to be exact, and a high school English teacher to boot. But she didn't actually die during sex. Instead, a few days after Tommy Farrow came forward with their affair, my mother took her own life.

What could be a clearer admission of guilt? She might as well have been caught in the act. The investigation was shut down before it even began.

I take a shuddering breath. Two more minutes. A hundred and twenty seconds and then I can leave. I steel my shoulders and walk the final steps to my mother's body.

Oh god. It's even worse than I thought.

The room whirls around me, and nausea sprints up my throat. My hands shoot out to grab the casket, stopping short of actually touching the corpse.

This . . . this thing . . . can't be my mother. She never smiled like that, all serene and peaceful-like. She never wore this much makeup; her red hair was never chopped so closely to her head. My mother was chaos and passion, devastation and joy. Dad used to say you could reach deep into her eyes and pull out a song.

Well, her eyes are closed now, and I'm not sure there'll be any music in my life, ever again.

I stumble backward, tripping over a ripple in the carpet. So that's why they call it a "runner," I think hysterically. For all those brides fleeing the altar. And me.

Sorrow drags at me, the current threatening to pull me under. My limbs feel weighed down by rocks; my throat floods with tears. One way or the other, I'm going to drown.

I barrel out of the room and through the tasteful lobby, with its startling white sofas and oversized flower arrangements. As if grief can be subdued by clean furniture lines. My knee smacks into the coffee table, knocking the decor out of alignment, and I burst out the back door into the alley beyond.

I'm not alone.

A huddle of teenage boys breaks apart. For a moment, we all freeze, like someone's pressed the "pause" button on a video.

The boys, perhaps because they mistake me for a crazed mortician.

Me, because I'm looking at the broad shoulders and square jaw of Tommy Farrow.

I become aware of each and every compression of my heart. Notice the graying mortar between the bricks, the Dumpster that smells of embalming chemicals, the fists shoved into the boys' khaki pants.

"What . . . what are you doing here?" I stammer.

"I'm sorry," Tommy says, running a hand through his boyish curls. "I had no idea it would turn out like this. If I did, I never would've . . ."

"What?" My voice is as dry as sandpaper. And just as harsh. "Slept with my mother? Or came forward with the truth?"

His mouth opens—and stays open. As if he can't come up with an answer. As if all rationality, logic, and reason fled with my mother's death. And maybe they did. Because I haven't been able to make sense of a single thing since I found out she's gone from this world.

Least of all the boy in front of me.

I take off down the alley, my feet spraying up gravel, my heart pumping like a metronome. Every step takes me farther from the boys. Every stride puts more distance between me and her.

How could she do this to me? Take her own life, sleep with that boy. The mother I knew would never do those things. The mother I knew converted her office into a studio so I could sketch my portraits in natural light. She set her alarm for three a.m. the entire week before my big art show, so she could keep me company during my bouts of insomnia.

But maybe I never knew her, after all.

I run out of the neighborhood, skirt around the park, and head to the lake for which our town is named. I run until my legs melt like butter and my lungs whistle air. And when I finally collapse, a heap of bones in a graveyard of buried grass and muddy shore, a single thought worms its way to the surface. A thought that's been niggling at the corner of my heart ever since the police officer rang our doorbell, his cap clasped against his chest.

If this is who my mother really was, I'm not sorry she's dead.

Chapter 1

Six months later . . .

I stand rooted to the linoleum tile, my stomach clenched as tightly as a steel trap. The first day of senior year and it's happening already.

Only this time, I'm not the victim.

Like every other student in the locker corridor, I swivel my head toward the entrance of Lakewood High, where a skinny sophomore sprawls amid a bunch of flyers, her stick-like legs encased in green and yellow stockings.

Standing above her, ample hip cocked and a bored look on her face, is the school's reigning princess, Mackenzie Myers. She's got more money than anyone in school, as well as the biggest ass.

"The crisis hotline?" She picks up a flyer with two fingers, as the sophomore scrambles on the floor for her papers. "Don't tell me you're a call counselor. How can you advise other people on their social lives when you don't have one?"

Mackenzie drops the flyer. And then steps on it with her Jimmy Choo sandal—strappy, wide, and more expensive than my entire wardrobe.

I wrap my arms around myself. I should do something. Say something. I can't leave the girl there, crawling around Mackenzie's feet like a rodent.

But I do.

First, because it's the crisis call center—the same hotline my mother founded and coordinated.

And second, because that could be me on the floor. In fact, it was me. For the last couple months of junior year, I couldn't get through a day without being tripped by an errant foot, one of Tommy Farrow's pals approaching me and unzipping his pants. "Oh, sorry, is that my dick in your mouth? Guess I must've mistaken you for your mother."

But now that Tommy and his buddies have finally graduated, this is my year to have the reputation I want. That is to say: no reputation at all.

Wallflower. Nondescript. Flying so far under the radar I might as well not exist. I don't care if I'm forgotten, so long as they leave me alone.

"What's your expertise? Fashion advice?" Mackenzie taunts. "Not unless we want to look like Strawberry Shortcake. This is high school, not kindergarten."

I rip my eyes away, and my gaze collides with a guy I've never seen before. Which is saying a lot, since Lakewood, Kansas, only has a population of 10,000. He's tall, totally built, and wears a pair of wire-rimmed glasses.

I can't figure out whether he's a hottie or a nerd. Maybe both. On the one hand, he has the kind of pecs Mackenzie would be all over like buzzards on a carcass. On the other, his jeans are an inch too short, the color unfashionably faded from too many washings.

As I stare, he nods in my direction—why? what did I do?—and crouches down next to the sophomore. The jeans hitch up even more, and I can see three inches of skin.

Something inside me lurches—and I don't know why, but I bend down and pick up the flyers closest to me. I assemble a small pile and hand it to the sophomore.

"Thank you," she mouths, too terrified to talk.

I retreat to my locker, my heartbeat reverberating in my ears like a tornado drill.

They finish gathering the flyers, and the new guy glances at Mackenzie and places a protective hand on the sophomore's shoulder. "Come on," he says to the girl. "I'll help you hang these up. There's nothing for you here. Nothing worth your time, anyway."

They turn their backs and walk away. Right in front of everyone. Half the senior class. A gaggle of Mackenzie's cronies. Oh, and the captain of the varsity tennis team, the boy everyone says is a shoo-in for Homecoming King. Him too.

Mackenzie's cheeks flame red and then burn down to ash. Never, in her long reign over this school, has she been snubbed so thoroughly.

For an endless moment, no one speaks. And then Mackenzie pulls herself together, buttoning up her features the way one might fasten a coat.

"Eat some food!" she squawks after the couple.

I blink. Is that what this is about? Not the hotline, after all. Mackenzie's harassing the sophomore for being . . . skinnier than her? Seriously?

Before I can digest this sickness, the new guy and the sophomore walk past me. The guy's gaze finds mine again. And then he winks.

He *winks*. As if I'm somehow complicit in his snubbing. As if I've plotted with him to bring Mackenzie down.

I whip around and pretend to rummage in my locker. Books, schedule, and an oversized sweater I can throw on in case someone makes a suggestive comment about my outfit.

But the weight of someone's stare prickles my skin. I peek to the side, and my heart nearly stops. The school princess glares at me, her hands fisted on her hips. If I thought the new guy's gaze was piercing, Mackenzie's hauls me up and pins me to the wall.

No! I want to shout. *I don't even know him. I picked up a few papers. That's all. I wasn't trying to snub you.*

But my voice burrows itself under the lump in my throat, and before I can find it, Mackenzie shakes her head disgustedly and stalks off.

So much for flying under the radar.

Chapter 2

"Ooohh, Alisara! Over here! I saved you a seat!" Raleigh squeals, her streaked golden tresses bouncing as she completely ignores me. I've known her since she was six, when her mom used to bind her mousy hair into two braids.

Still, Raleigh's not trying to be cruel, even though Alisara and I walked into the classroom together. It's just that Alisara is her friend, and I'm not. Or at least, not anymore.

There was a time, before, when I ran around with that whole group of girls. They didn't cut me out or anything—they're way too nice for that. I just kinda waned.

Alisara gives me the kind of smile that makes little creases on her cheeks. Out of my old group, she's the only one who still tries to continue our friendship. "I'm glad you had a good summer, CeCe. I'll catch you later, okay?"

I force a fake smile onto my own face. "Of course. Later."

I walk down the aisle and sit where I always do. The middle seat in the middle row. Too close to the front, and I'd be called a gunner. Too far in the back, and I'm a slacker.

The middle is exactly where I want to be: invisible.

Invisible doesn't silence an entire room when you walk in. It doesn't leave a trail of whispers in its wake. Maybe it means nobody will ever squeal your name from across the room, either, but that's a trade I'm willing to make.

The seats on either side of me are empty, but five minutes before the bell, someone plops down next to me. The new guy.

My hands clench around the black-and-white composition notebook I've been carrying around all summer—the one that's a prerequisite for our Intro to Psych class. Before I can pretend to be terribly busy with the course syllabus, he turns to me with an easy grin.

"Hi. We didn't get the chance to be properly introduced before. I'm Sam Davidson."

"Cecilia Brooks," I mumble. "Everyone calls me CeCe."

"I'm new here." He shifts closer to me. As in, his chair moves an entire six inches in my direction. All of a sudden, I can see the freckles sprinkled across his nose, turned cinnamon by the morning rays of the sun. A thin scar snakes across his forehead, almost hidden by his hair, and his dark eyes puncture me through his glasses. I feel like I'm plunging down a roller coaster, weightless and free.

I look down, but his bare ankles mock me. Reminding me of my role in this morning's debacle.

"I thought I was going crazy this morning," he continues. "Everyone stood there and watched that poor girl being bullied like it was some YouTube video gone viral. But then you gave us a hand, and I realized I hadn't entered some freaky fifth dimension after all. So thanks for that."

I blink. It was a few papers. Less than nothing. And also more. Because it was a lapse in judgment. A failure to be unremarkable, before the school year even begins.

"I hear we have open lunch periods here," he says, oblivious to my turmoil. "And I don't know where to go. Maybe you could show me?"

Despite everything, my stomach flutters. Because the way he looks at me, it's like a blank slate. He doesn't see the girl everyone's been gossiping about for the last six months. He doesn't see my mother's ghost lurking behind each of my features. He sees me.

I open my mouth to say "yes," when I notice the people staring. Girls, primarily, and from the looks on their faces, it has nothing to do with Mackenzie—and everything to do with the new guy talking to Cecilia Brooks.

"I can't," I say.

He looks at me expectantly, as if waiting for the rest of the sentence. I can't because I have a yearbook meeting. Or: I can't because I have a boyfriend.

But I don't want to lie. He's been more genuine with me in five minutes than some of my classmates have been in their entire lives.

"I'm sorry." I stare at my notebook, my lifeline this past summer. The thing that kept me from reliving, over and over, how my mother looked in her casket.

"Wow." Sam's voice, light and gracious, pulls me back to the present. Smoothing things over even as I'm shooting him down. "As far as pickup lines go, I thought that was pretty good."

I can't help but smile. "I've heard worse." Much, much worse, on an almost daily basis, but he doesn't have to know that.

The warning bell rings, and students begin drifting to their desks. The psych teacher strides into the room, wearing a blazer over his Captain America T-shirt. I face the front, ready to put the conversation behind me.

"Okay, class. Settle down." Mr. Willoughby perches on the edge of his desk, next to a gilded picture frame. "That means you, Mr. Brinson. You and Mr. Taylor can discuss football plays after class. And no need to check your eye makeup, Miss Stevens. This is high school, not a fashion show."

Raleigh blushes and twirls a lock of hair around her finger, looking up at him through her eyelashes.

My stomach rolls. Ew, ew, ew. Raleigh probably thinks she's being cute. I'm sure she doesn't see any harm in flirting with the psych teacher. I mean, he's nice-enough looking, and he dresses youngish in comic book T-shirts.

But he's not young. And it's not cute. In fact, Mr. Willoughby is a widower, and we all know he's never gotten over his wife's death. She's been buried over twenty years, and he still doesn't date.

After the scandal with my mother, I don't know why anyone—much less one of my old friends—would think it's appropriate to trifle with a teacher. I guess that's why Raleigh isn't my friend anymore.

"I'm so pleased to welcome you to a year of examining the human psyche," the teacher says. "Which means, first and foremost, we'll be studying ourselves. To that end, please pass forward your summer assignments, the self-examination journals."

I jerk. Wait—what? NO. No, no, no. This wasn't part of the plan. We're not supposed to turn in our journals.

All around me, students pull out their black-and-white notebooks. Unfazed. As if this were any other homework. Even Sam has one, so whenever he moved to town, it was recently enough to complete the assignment.

The girl in front of me holds out her hand for my notebook. I stare as if it's a severed, floating appendage. Then, the hand drops and actually *touches* my speckled cover.

I snatch the journal off my desk. "Sorry! There's been a misunderstanding."

My misunderstanding, at least. If I'd known, I wouldn't have taken the assignment to heart. I wouldn't have bared my soul and drawn my mother in all the ways I remembered her. Heaped on the snow in a tangle of limbs the first—and only—time she went skiing. The sunset-red hair bouncing on her shoulders after her monthly visit to the salon. Rolling her eyes but not saying a word when Gram taught the six-year-old me how to play poker.

My classmate's brows crease, and the journals pile up behind me.

"Is there a problem, girls?" Mr. Willoughby approaches us.

"You said no one would look at our journals," I say, my voice low and raspy. I don't talk in class, as a rule, and it's like my voice is punishing me for speaking up so early in the year. "You said to fill the pages with whatever we wanted and not to worry because no one would ever see them."

He frowns. "I'm not going to *read* the entries, Miss Brooks. But I do need to flip through the pages to make sure the work was done. Why else would I ask you to bring the notebooks to class?"

Why, indeed. The explanation I gave myself—that flashing the speckled covers would be sufficient to earn us credit—seems stupid now.

"I promise I did the work, Mr. Willoughby," I say. "But I can't let you flip through the pages."

"Why not? Don't you trust me?"

"It's not that. What I put in my journal—they're not words."

The room is silent for two heartbeats. And then the whispers begin. I can't make out the words, but I can guess only too well what they're saying.

"What's in it, then? Photos from Tabitha's private collection?"

"Maybe it's drawings of her and her mom naked together!"

"Or a collage of all the guys they've slept with!"

Snickers fill the air. I fix my gaze on the Captain America shield on my teacher's chest and pretend not to hear. Pretend not to care. Pretend I never had a mother.

"That's enough, class," Mr. Willoughby says sharply. "Turn your psych textbooks to chapter one." He lowers his voice. "Miss Brooks, please stop by my office after school."

I nod meekly. The whispers from my classmates circle around my head like a dog chasing its own tail, never tiring, never stopping.

It's the first day of school. And already, I'm in trouble.

Chapter 3

Mackenzie's waiting by my locker after school. She sticks out her designer-jeans-clad butt, taking up half the hallway, so that the foot traffic has to diverge around her.

As I approach, her eyes flicker over my gray hoodie and black canvas high-tops, clothes designed to make me disappear. I think about walking past her and out the double-glass doors, but I need to face her sometime. And if I look like the coward I really am? She'll find some way to use it against me.

"Excuse me," I say. "You're in front of my locker."

Her eyebrows raise. "Oh, is this yours? I didn't realize."

She shifts languorously to one side. "How was your first day, CeCe? Make lots of new friends?" Her voice arches like a worm on a hook, daring me to say the wrong thing.

"It was all right." I spin the dial on the lock, but my fingers fumble and I flub the numbers. I try again. And then again.

Sweat pools at my neck, and the hair sticks to my forehead. This is ridiculous! I've got more important things to worry about—like my meeting with Mr. Willoughby. I can't let a simple conversation bother me.

I try the combination one more time, but the FREAKING LOCK WILL NOT OPEN. It spins and spins, and clearly this isn't the right set of numbers. Clearly, the right combination doesn't exist anywhere, and they've given me the one faulty lock in the ENTIRE school . . .

The dial clicks. Mackenzie smirks.

"Nervous much? You wouldn't have something to hide, would you?"

Um, yeah. The senior class has been buzzing about nothing else all day. But Mackenzie couldn't care less about my self-examination journal. She's got more pressing concerns: herself.

"I saw you getting cozy with the new boy this morning," she says.

"No, I wasn't. I hadn't even met him yet."

The "yet" slips out, and her eyes narrow. "Listen, CeCe, you and I, we've always been okay. I would hate to see some guy get in the way of our friendship, wouldn't you?"

This is both truth and lie. Sure, we've never had a problem with each other, but a guy did come between us. Or more precisely, between her and my mother.

Tommy was Mackenzie's boyfriend when the scandal broke, and the school princess has never forgiven me for being my mother's daughter. I don't blame her. I haven't forgiven my mom, either.

"Watch yourself. You don't want to get on my bad side." Mackenzie looks pointedly at my locker number, as if committing it to memory, and then sashays down the corridor, her ass jabbing the air with every step.

I take a shaky breath. I'm okay. As far as harassment goes, that wasn't bad. Just a warning. I can handle a warning. That's nothing compared to a group of boys walking past me while I'm eating a banana, smirking to one another and whispering, "Suck it, baby."

I open my locker door, and a folded piece of paper tumbles out.

Oh god. I was wrong. It's not over yet.

With trembling fingers, I unfold the paper. It's a flyer from the crisis hotline, pleading for volunteers to staff the phones. The same flyer the striped-tights girl was hanging up this morning.

Did Mackenzie stick this in my locker? Or is it from another bully, intent on reminding me my mother may be dead, but her memory is still very much alive?

The last time my locker was stuffed, a hundred copies of my mom's faculty photo from the yearbook spilled out, scrawled with one epithet after another. Pedophile. Slut. Predator. The crumbled-up papers filled an entire trash can.

Maybe I should be thankful that this time, there's only one.

I turn the paper over and see handwriting on the back.

Sorry if I made you uncomfortable this morning.—Sam.

I read the message again and then a second and third time. So, not harassment, after all. But what is it, then? A nice gesture?

I'm still staring at the paper a few minutes later when Alisara comes up.

"Are you thinking of volunteering at the hotline?" my old friend asks, her black hair pulled into a long ponytail, a volleyball at her hip.

"What? Oh god, no." I shove the paper into my pocket, the warmth traveling up my face like mercury in an overheated thermometer. "I'd never do that."

"Why not?"

"Alisara." I break her name into four distinct syllables. "My mother died at the hotline. It's where Tommy said they rendezvoused for sex."

She passes the volleyball from one hand to the other. "It's just a place. Besides, didn't they move the call center, once the police blew the secret location?"

I turn to my locker and begin color-coding my folders, alphabetizing my textbooks. Anything to show Alisara how uninterested I am in this conversation.

"I mean, it's not like the hotline itself is a bad thing," she persists. I grab my pens and lay them, alternating ball point and clicker, in my plastic case. "No matter what your mom did, the hotline helps people. It always has."

"Oh, please," I scoff, glancing over my shoulder. "Does anyone even call?"

"I did. Last year, when my dad died and we almost moved back to Thailand. We didn't, of course, but for a while, things were really tough for me and my mom." A smile ghosts across her lips. "I used to call the hotline when I knew your mom was working. I had her for sophomore English, and she was one of my favorite teachers. Calling her was a way to continue our bond, even if she didn't know it was me. Up until the day she died, she was so kind to me. I'll never forget that."

A twinge of guilt stabs my stomach. Alisara lost a parent, too, and I haven't been there for her the way she has for me. I'm a terrible friend. An even worse person. But as always, my mom's death pushes its way to the front, demanding precedence above everything else.

"You talked to my mom that last day?" I ask, hating myself. Hating the self-absorbed person I've become. The selfish girl my mother made me. "When?"

She fiddles with the volleyball. "A few hours before she, um . . . you know."

My throat closes up. I can't believe this. My mom worked the phone lines that day. Hours before she took her own life, she had enough left in her to counsel other people's children.

But what about her own daughter? I got nothing. No note. No good-bye. No final wisdom about how to live my life. That's what gets me the most about my mom's suicide. She was leaving this world forever. And she didn't even bother to write me a letter.

I throw the plastic case into my locker. It hits the wall with a metallic twang, and I slam the door closed.

"I'm sorry, CeCe, I shouldn't have said anything—"

"It's not your fault." I look at her, this grown-up version of the girl who used to play at my house. We once baked a coffee cake in a mixing bowl and then wondered why the batter wouldn't cook. If only that were our biggest problem now. "It's not your fault my mother didn't love me."

I hurry away. That's all I seem to do these days. Run.

At least this time, I have a destination. Mr. Willoughby's office.

When I arrive, Mr. Willoughby's stretched out on a worn beige sofa, reading a comic book and chuckling to himself.

I hover by the doorway. It's weird seeing him like this. I know he's supposed to be some kind of comic book fiend. Supposedly, he even wrote his college thesis on The Dark Knight. But still, he's a teacher. He belongs in a classroom, pointing things out on the whiteboard. He shouldn't be kicked back, reading a Spider-Man comic, for god's sake.

"Cecilia, come in." He sits up and waves at a folding chair next to the coffee table, which holds, predictably, yet another photograph of his late wife. There's no desk in sight, and that adds to the weirdness. But it's not like Mr. Willoughby is a traditional guidance counselor. Due to budget cuts, we had to let go of "nonessential" staff. If Mr. Willoughby hadn't volunteered, the student body would be without any career advice whatsoever.

Not that I need much. At least, not anymore.

"We haven't talked much since last spring," he says as I perch on the chair. "How's your portfolio going for your application to Parsons?"

I won't meet his eyes. "I decided not to apply."

"Oh?" His eyebrows leap up his forehead, even as his voice remains perfectly calm. Too calm. "When did this happen? It's all you've talked about for the past three years."

"That was . . . before." Before my mom died. Before my dad stopped looking at me. Before he would forget to change his clothes unless I place a freshly laundered outfit on his dresser every morning.

Attending Parsons School of Design was always my dream, and even back then, New York seemed like a whole other world. Now, it might as well be in a different galaxy.

"It's across the country," I mumble. "And I can't leave my dad right now. He . . . he would completely fall apart if he had to fend for himself."

"I see." The lines around his eyes soften. "And have you discussed this with him?"

I give a short laugh. "My dad is a man of few words. The only thing we talk about is what I ate for dinner. If it doesn't fall into one of the four food groups, then forget it."

"May I suggest you submit an application, then? You can always turn them down. No harm done."

I close my eyes. He's wrong. Deciding not to apply severed the connective tissue around my heart. As it is, that organ's holding on by a few strands. If I have to clutch an acceptance letter in my hand and then say "no"? I think my heart would float away altogether.

"I know you haven't stopped drawing," he says. "In fact, I'm guessing that's why you won't turn in your self-examination journal. Because it's filled with your sketches?"

"Yeah," I whisper.

"I understand, Cecilia. I really do. And I wish we could leave it like that. But if you slide by without consequences, then nobody would bother doing the assignment." He places his hands on his knees. "So let me put it this way: If you don't turn in your journal, I'll have to give you a zero. Do you stand by your decision?"

This is bigger than you think, a little voice whispers. *The decision you make now could impact your GPA—and, in turn, the rest of your life.*

But I can't give him my journal. Once upon a time, I displayed my artwork for everyone to see. The bigger the audience, the better, since that meant my drawings had a life outside the visions in my head. But ever since my mom died, it seems like they all want a piece of me. The reporters who camped out on my lawn. The boys who raked me over with their eyes. Even my girlfriends who pumped me for every bit of gossip. They gobbled me up and spit me back out, and I can't give them any more of myself. I just can't.

So I give Mr. Willoughby the only possible answer: "Yes."

He sighs. "That's what I was afraid of. But although you're too stubborn for your own good, you've always been a good student. So I'm going to let you do extra credit to bolster your grade. I've spoken with Principal Winters and gotten his approval. You may choose any community service activity you wish to make up for not turning in your journal."

My eyes widen. He's letting me off easy. A little too easy,

given his strict classroom policies. "You mean I just have to work in the outdoor classroom? Or pick up trash by the lake? That's it?"

"Whatever you wish."

Okay, now I know something is really off. When I had him for freshman English, I once lost a daily homework assignment. He made me write a fifteen-page paper on Jane Austen to make up for it. And now I fail to turn in an entire journal, and all I have to do is clear a few weeds? Doesn't make sense.

"Why are you being so nice to me?" I blurt out. Stupid, stupid. I should leave this golden opportunity alone. If he's giving me a free pass, I should grab it before he changes his mind.

"I know your mom's passing hasn't been easy for you." He lowers his voice. "But you can't stop living just because she has. You can't give up just because life has gotten too hard."

His tone is appropriately mournful and wise—but there's something else there, too. Some hard undertone that almost sounds like anger. But that doesn't make any sense. He and my mom were colleagues, but he barely knew her. At least as far as I know.

"I haven't given up," I say, watching his face. Trying to understand where the harshness is coming from.

But he gives nothing away.

"Good." He stands and ushers me to the door. Our meeting is over. "Think about what I said. Talk it over with your dad, and you can let me know which activity you pick in the morning."

I open my mouth, to argue or question or protest, but he doesn't give me the chance. He pushes me the rest of the way into the hall and closes the door.

I'm left where I always am. Alone.

Chapter 4

A few hours later, I grip the pencil so tightly my hand begins to cramp. The tension shoots up my neck, but I keep drawing anyway—bold, dramatic slashes that bring my mother to life again.

Today, she is a serpent eating her own tail. I shade the underside of her belly and draw flames flickering up her scales. There. A circle of fire. Passion that quite literally devours her alive.

All my drawings are like this. Half portrait, half cartoon. It's why I want to be a children's book illustrator. Mackenzie Myers has the elongated canines of a saber-toothed cat, while Alisara drops a worm into the wide-open mouth of a baby bird.

Sam, in the quick sketch I did, rides a majestic horse, his eyes piercing straight into me.

And my mother? She's got more faces than a con man. Whatever emotions I've felt in the last six months, she's worn them all.

My pencil snaps between my fingers when I hear the garage door. I have just enough time to shove the black-and-white notebook into my backpack before my dad enters the kitchen.

"Hi, sweetheart," he says wearily, not looking at me, but I don't take it personally. He never looks at me, and everything about him is weary, from his hair, which turned a shocking white the month after my mom's death, to his faded jeans, splattered with paint and bits of dried concrete from his job as a construction foreman. "How was your first day of school?"

"Fine. Uneventful." I make a mental note to put the last load of laundry in the dryer, and then I hurry to the oven, where his dinner's been warming. "Gram's at her poker night, so it's just us tonight. Are you hungry? I made lasagna."

What else? I only have about five dishes in my repertoire, and we've had lasagna for Monday dinner for, oh, the last twenty weeks or so.

He washes up while I transfer a hefty portion onto his plate. The top layer of cheese is crispy and bubbly, and I mixed cayenne pepper into the filling for that satisfying bit of heat. Pure perfection, if you ask me. It's the only thing my father still compliments me on anymore.

But instead of digging in, like he normally does, he sits down and pushes the plate to the side.

My already-tense muscles twist into even bigger knots. Uh-oh. He hasn't looked this serious since the football team spelled out "S-L-U-T" on our front lawn with toilet paper. They didn't specify whether they meant me or my mother. I don't think they really cared.

"I don't think your day was all that uneventful," my dad says. "Mr. Willoughby called me at work. Apparently, you failed to turn in your summer journal, and you're no longer applying to Parsons?"

I wrap my hands around my tea mug, not answering.

"Your teacher thought you might be acting out to get my attention," he continues.

I snort. "He doesn't know you very well, does he? I'd have smoked pot and shoplifted weeks ago if I thought it would make a difference."

He rubs his chin, where there's a layer of fine dust. If Mom were still here, she'd descend on him with a washcloth and a kiss. But she's not, so the dust stays, as much a part of him as the sadness wrapped around his shoulders. "You think I've . . . neglected you? I always make sure you have everything you need, from new clothes to gas money. I ask you every single night—"

"—if I've eaten," I interrupt. "Yes, I know. Maybe I should leave my dirty dishes in the sink. That would save you the trouble of asking."

He flinches and averts his eyes, and I immediately regret the snotty comment. He needs me, I remind myself. He's not equipped for this, never wanted to be a single dad to a teenage daughter.

But the thing is, I never wanted to be halfway to orphan, either.

"If you got home a little earlier," I say, staring at the steam rising from my mug, "we could eat together. At least once in a while."

"Doesn't Gram eat with you? That's why she moved in with us. So she could help you through your last year of high school."

Last spring, my dad's mother left her glamorous, high-stakes life as a professional poker player and moved to Lakewood, Kansas. For us, she came to this dead-end town in the middle of nowhere, where the nearest casino is three hours away.

And I appreciate that. I do. But her version of parenting consists of cryptic gambling advice like: "Remember, CeCe. Never show your hand unless you have to." And then she'll pat me on the head and float off, her perfume of cigarettes and wild flowers drifting behind her.

"Sometimes, I want to eat with *you*." My voice falters, and I say the rest of the sentence inside my head: *so I can pretend for a few minutes I haven't lost my father, too.*

He doesn't answer, and we fall silent. He eats the lasagna, and I fiddle with my mint tea. Once upon a time, my mother used to make me hot chocolate with whipped cream and crushed peppermint. The treat never failed to make me feel safe, cherished. Clearly, whatever magical powers imbued in the mint have long since faded.

"Why aren't you applying to Parsons?" my dad asks.

"New York's too far from Mom's grave."

He chokes on the lasagna. "You haven't been to the cemetery once!"

He's right. I haven't. I'm still too angry, I guess. Too . . . betrayed. I don't have anything to say to my mother, not when she left me without an explanation. Without even a word.

"You've been to the cemetery enough for us both," I say. "I swear you'd live there if the caretaker didn't kick you out."

"The flowers need tending," he mumbles.

This is exactly why I said she should be cremated and sprinkled on the lake, which she always loved. So both her body and spirit could be free from this earthly world.

More importantly, so *we* could be free. Gram suggested we move to a new town, in order to get a fresh start. I was all for it, if only so I would never have to face Tommy and his pals ever again. But Dad refused. Her body is buried here in Lakewood, and as a result, we'll be tied to this godforsaken town forever.

"So what are you going to do for your community service project?" my dad asks. This has to be some kind of record. I don't think he asked me this many questions all summer.

"Not sure." I trace my finger around the rim of the mug. "I thought I'd do something easy, like work in the garden in the outdoor classroom."

"What about the crisis hotline? That's where your mother would've wanted you to work."

I snap my head up. He never mentions my mother, let alone the hotline. Talking about the flowers or the grave site is the closest he'll come to uttering her name. It's like Tabitha Brooks never lived in this house. Never cooked us pot roast with baby carrots. Never laughed her silvery peal as she sat between us, the glue that held this family together.

If the heavy memory of her didn't seep from every corner of our house, maybe I could believe he'd forgotten her. But every one of my dad's movements radiates her absence; every nuanced expression reveals how much he misses her.

She lives most strongly in the words he cannot—will not—say.

Until now.

"Why would Mom want me to work there?" I ask.

"A few days before she died, she said something strange to me," he says haltingly. "I didn't think anything of it at the time.

It was on the eve of that boy's accusation, and as you know, after that, everything happened so fast. Before I knew it, she was dead." He looks down at his palms. "Later, I had to wonder if it wasn't a joke, after all."

I can hardly breathe. "What did she say?"

"She said: 'Whatever secrets I have, they're at the hotline. If you want answers, look there.' " He shakes his head. "That was it. But she repeated it two or three times, with this forced laugh. I thought she was referring to her callers' secrets. But now, I wonder if she meant her own."

I frown. "She was talking about Tommy, Dad. The hotline was where they had sex. That's the only secret she had."

"Maybe. Maybe not." He shrugs, as lost as the day the policeman rang our doorbell to tell us Mom had passed.

Passed. Ha. As far as euphemisms go, this one's the lamest yet. It's like we're playing some twisted game of Life and Monopoly scrambled together. Do not pass Go. Do not collect $200. Take your game piece and get off the board.

"What exactly are you saying, Dad?"

"Your mother wasn't capable of those things. Having sex with that student. Committing suicide." His voice is raw and scratchy, as if he kept the words under wraps so long they're painful coming out. "I don't believe she did any of it. And you know why? Because her own mother died right before her senior year of high school. She would get nervous whenever she thought about your seventeenth birthday, like she expected lightning or some other freak accident to strike her down."

He looks at me, really looks at me, maybe for the first time since last spring. "She swore to me, over and over, that whatever happened, she would see you through to adulthood. Because she didn't want you to grow up like she did. Without a mother."

My hands shake. My forehead burns. And no matter how hard I try, I cannot swallow the mint tea.

I spit the hot liquid back into the mug. "I don't understand. If you really feel that Mom didn't commit suicide, why didn't you go to the police?"

"I did. I talked to Detective Jensen, the medical examiner,

everyone I could. But they had already determined your mother's guilt. To them, I was a paranoid fool, trying to rewrite my pedophile wife's history." He takes a breath. "After a cursory investigation, the police were more than happy to close the case."

So many emotions boil inside me, I feel like a geyser about to burst. "Why are you telling me this?"

"Because you have to choose a community service project." He drops his eyes, as if he's exceeded his daily quota for looking at his daughter. "And because last night, you had another one of your dreams. The ones where you cry out for your mother." He swallows. "The ones where you plead with her to come back. And beg her for a final letter."

I can't breathe. The space inside my lungs turns solid, and gravity shoves down on my shoulders. I've had the same recurring dream for six months. But I never knew I talked in my sleep. Had no idea anyone else knew about my obsession with my mom's last words—or lack thereof.

"Even if you don't believe that your mother had secrets, there's another reason for you to volunteer at the hotline," he says slowly. "If your mother did write a letter, where else do you think she would hide it? If you volunteered there, you might be able to find it."

I stare at him, my heart battering against my ears. He's probably delusional. He's probably what everyone else thinks—a pathetic widower still pining for a dead woman who never deserved his affection. This is his way to manipulate me into participating in his conspiracy theories. He wants me to investigate a case that doesn't exist.

I know this. And yet, for the first time since I saw her corpse, something stirs in my heart. Hope. I've spent the last six months wishing I never had a mother. The woman in my memory was nothing but a stranger, her motivations unfathomable, her acts of kindness faked. If my father's right, however, and I do find a letter from her, my mother's actions will finally be explained. I'll finally be able to understand why she did what she did. And maybe Tabitha Brooks can finally go back to being who she always was. Who she's supposed to be. My mother.

Something died in me the day I learned my mother committed suicide. No, not something: someone. The girl who believed her mother would protect her from the hurts of the world. The girl who was sure of one thing, no matter what else—her mother's love.

But maybe that girl isn't dead after all. Maybe a sliver of her remains, and all she needed was a shot of her father's passion to jump-start her heart.

"Okay, you've convinced me," I say, pushing images of toiling in the outdoor classroom, undisturbed and uninvolved, to the back of my mind. "I'll do it. I'll volunteer at the hotline."

Chapter 5

"Watch out!" a Rollerblader yells the next morning.

His arms flail, his legs wobble, and he's heading straight in my direction. I dive away from the metal bicycle racks to prevent myself from being bisected like an insect against a car grille.

Too bad blader dude has the same idea.

Oomph. The breath whooshes out of me, and we fall onto the grass. Instead of smacking onto the ground, however, my head lands against something warm and firm and cupped against my scalp. His hand.

"Oh god, I'm so sorry," he moans. "Are you okay?"

There's something familiar about his voice. Something sweet and oddly comforting. And then there's the fact that he had enough presence of mind to protect my head as we dropped . . .

He rolls off me and removes his helmet and sunglasses.

Ah. Sam.

"I didn't break any bones, did I?" His hands hover over my torso, as if he wants to check me for injuries. God help me, I kinda want him to check me for injuries.

I sit up gingerly. "I'm fine. Just a little, um, floored, I guess. What are you doing?"

He plops beside me and pulls off his Rollerblades. He's not wearing his glasses today, but he makes up for the nerd factor with an abundance of safety gear. Kneepads, elbow pads, wrist guards, mesh gloves. He's even wearing a protective headband underneath his helmet.

"These things are way harder than they look." He holds out one of his skates. "Have you ever tried?"

I shake my head. His arms are inches from mine, his fingers a hair's width away on top of the Rollerblade. The early morning rays slide over the high school's cinder blocks, and the front lawn is deserted. It's strangely romantic, like we're secret lovers meeting for a sunrise rendezvous.

And maybe I hit my head harder than I thought.

"You see, I'm doing an internship at the *Lakewood Sun,*" he explains. "They have me writing articles on the school beat. The first one's due on Monday, and if I do a good job, they'll move me up the ranks."

"What's your first assignment? Pedestrian run over by a Rollerblader?"

He grimaces, and his hand moves a few inches, so his fingers brush against my skin.

The most inexplicable chills travel up my spine, as though someone's blowing lightly on my neck. Silly, really, but I can't help it. Back when my mom was alive, casual touches were the norm. She would constantly ruffle my hair, kiss my cheeks, pull me into an impromptu hug. My dad's much more restrained in his affections, and I guess I am, too. It's like my mom was the sun coaxing us to bloom, and now that she's gone, we've shriveled back into tightly furled buds again.

"I really am sorry," he says. "I have to admit, I was hoping to run into you today, but this isn't exactly what I had in mind."

I flush. I thought about him, too. In between questions about my mom and what I might find at the hotline, I thought about his cinnamon freckles and wire-rimmed glasses. I wondered if his pants would be too short today—yes—and if he would talk to me—double yes.

I clear my throat. "You were telling me about your first assignment?"

"Yeah," he says despairingly, stretching out on the grass. "Innovative ways students commute to school. If the article is as boring as it sounds, they'll probably fire me to cut down on costs. And I don't even get paid."

I giggle. "Oh, come on. I'm sure you'll come up with some unique angle. Students do parkour on the way to school, maybe."

"You mean that crazy sport where they vault up walls and jump off roofs? Please. I almost killed myself Rollerblading."

I take in the scrapes next to his safety pads, which also gives me an excuse to check out his body. Well-toned arms, sculpted chest. And something more. A dark greenish bruise blossoms on his upper arm. Several days old and clearly not a result of this morning's activity.

"What happened here?" I ask, gesturing to his arm.

"Oh, um." He tugs on his short sleeve, attempting to cover up the bruise. "Nothing. An accident in the weight room. If you haven't already figured, I'm the world's biggest klutz."

"But then how . . . ?" I start to say and clamp my mouth shut. He's definitely built. Anybody with eyes can see that. But I'm not about to blurt it out.

He grins, as though he can read my mind. "How am I so fit? I run a lot and lift weights. Neither requires much coordination, so I don't have to worry about tripping over my own feet."

"But doesn't it bother you? Being so, um . . ." I rack my brain for an inoffensive word. "Uncoordinated?"

"It used to. I know this is hard to believe, but when I was a kid, I was the ultimate nerd." He waggles his eyebrows up and down until I laugh. "You know the type. Chubby. Coke-bottle lenses. Last kid picked in gym class. I would spend hours reading mysteries and solving any puzzle I could get my hands on. But I wouldn't have it any other way. My childhood made me realize what I truly want to do with my life."

"An investigative journalist?" I ask.

"How'd you guess?" He blinks, and a slow, you-really-get-me smile spreads across his face. The glimpse of something darker, something more troubled, passes like a cloud from in front of the sun.

Not everyone has a secret, I chide myself. *Sometimes, a bruise is just a bruise.*

Except when it's not.

A rusty station wagon rattles into the parking space in front of us, and I jump. Somehow, the parking lot's half-full, and students are beginning to troop around us on the lawn.

"We'd better get to class," I say.

Sam slings the Rollerblades over his shoulder, and we walk toward the building. "Boring's okay for this piece, but I've got to kick it up a notch for my next assignment," he says. "I'm applying for the Winkelhake scholarship. A full ride to the university of your choice, for a student who intends to pursue journalism. It's the only way I'll be able to afford college, and I need a kick-ass article for my portfolio."

"Have you received your next assignment?"

"Yeah, and it's got potential. They want me to do a feature article on the crisis hotline. Apparently, somebody committed suicide there last year, and we just passed the six-month anniversary. Do you know anything about it?"

My skin forms sheets of ice, my blood turns to snow. Could this have been his agenda all along? Feigning interest in me so he can pump me for information?

"I have no idea what you're talking about," I say, my words as stiff as my back. The last thing I need is for him to interview my dad on his conspiracy theories. As if our family needs to be any more humiliated in this town.

"No problem. I'll keep asking around, spend some quality time in the library. Gotta admit, that's more my speed than Rollerblading. At least, I can't hurt myself, right?" He smiles again, and dammit, it makes me want to believe all sorts of things. That he's too new in town to have heard the gossip. That his only agenda in getting to know me is me.

"I'm going to find a hook to this story," he vows. "One no one's heard before. The article's due in a little under three weeks, and it's going to be so good, that scholarship will be as good as mine."

And with his words, I know it doesn't matter. It doesn't matter if he used to be chubby; it doesn't matter if he has more courage and compassion than anyone else at this school. It doesn't matter if he's the first person to capture my interest since my mom died.

Unless I want my personal life splashed across the front page of the *Lakewood Sun,* I need to stay away from Sam Davidson.

Chapter 6

"Hello. Crisis hotline," I say. One week and three training sessions later, I'm finally answering calls myself.

Although not yet on my own. Liam Kessler, twenty-year-old college sophomore and hotline coordinator, sits next to me, a headset over his ears so he can listen in on my conversations. He's worked at the hotline for two years now, and when my mom died, he took over her job. Since he's still a student, however, he reports to Mr. Willoughby, who serves as the hotline's faculty supervisor.

"Can I talk to you?" the young man on the line says.

"Sure." I reach over and close the blinds. The hotline is located at a cabin along the lake. Outside, dusk falls like sooty snow, but I'm not naive enough to think the only nocturnal animals that could be watching are the geese on the water. "That's what I'm here for."

"It's a little embarrassing," the caller says, and I hear a screech that sounds suspiciously like a zipper.

My fingers tighten on the headset. Could it be . . . ? No. Liam said it happens occasionally, but now, on my very first shift? What are the chances?

"I can't get it up when I'm with my girlfriend," the caller continues, and his voice is definitely huskier now. Breathing hard. Oh boy. "Could you role-play with me? Do you do that here?"

What I'd really like to do is fling the phone out the window. But I've had training on this—and my instructor's sitting right next to me. I take a deep breath. "I'm sorry. That isn't the purpose of the hotline."

"But how can I get better if no one will help me?" His voice escalates to a groan. "Please. I'm almost there. Just keep talking!"

Grunt, grunt, grunt. Moan. Moan. Mo-ooan.

Oh. Dear. God.

"I need to terminate this call now. Thanks for calling," I choke out and disconnect the line.

I hunch over, not looking at Liam. The taunts from the boys have toned down this year, but I can't ignore the sexual exploitation like it doesn't matter. Each time is like a fresh animal sniffing around my wounds, threatening to split them wide open again.

When I finally work up the courage to look up, Liam's shoulders are shaking with laughter. "I can't believe you thanked him for calling."

In spite of myself, the corners of my lips twitch. Because this time, it's not about me. I'm an anonymous voice on the line, and if there's a violation, it's directed at every counselor at the hotline.

"The training manual suggested we could let a sex caller finish doing . . . um, what he's doing. And then proceed with the call as normal," I say haltingly. "But I can't do that."

"You're not expected to," Liam says, sobering up. "That's only one option for dealing with a sex caller. You are never under any obligation to let yourself be used. Do you understand?"

I nod. His tone might be soothing, but my stomach always feels tight when he's around. Liam's exactly the kind of guy I normally avoid. Tall and blond, with dimples and a strong cleft chin. The type who's born knowing how to talk to parents. Who's popular with the girls in high school. The very same type who dreams up the cruelest sexual taunts.

The label "DILF" came from one such Liam-type. The nickname "Blow Job Brooks" came from another.

"What you did was perfectly fine," Liam continues. *He didn't call you those names,* I remind myself. *He only looks like the ones who did.* "As a call counselor, your job is to encourage the caller in crisis to come up with his own solution. This guy wasn't allowing you to do that."

Caller in crisis. When he says it with that Midwest twang, it sounds just like "Cahla in crisis." Or maybe: "Celia in crisis." And he would be right.

Because I'm in crisis, too. I've been in crisis for the last six months. From the time I was a little girl, my mother promised me I wouldn't have to do this alone. Life is hard, she said, but she would be by my side every step of the way, helping me navigate the trickiest turns. But she's gone now. I'm lost.

And I have no idea how to find my way back again.

"CeCe, forgive me for saying this, but are you sure you want to volunteer here? You're doing a great job, and god knows, we need all the help we can get. But . . ." He scoots his chair back, the pause so significant it almost has legs. "Won't it bring up too many memories of your mother?"

I open my mouth to do what I always do. Brush him off, shut him down. Answer so brusquely he'll drop the subject forever.

But the words don't come. Maybe it's because my mother once sat where I'm sitting, answering calls from desperate students. Or maybe because there's an understanding in Liam's eyes I rarely see.

"I'm trying to understand her," I say, and the hope bubbles inside me once again. Because if I can find my mom's letter, maybe I'll be able to let go of the rage. If there's more to my mom's story, then maybe she didn't betray me, after all.

Maybe, maybe, maybe. My life is so full of maybes I could drown in them. "When I'm not pissed at her, anyway, for leaving me the way she did. Sometimes, the line between love and hate can be very thin."

"You're telling me," he says. "I lost my father two years ago. He was a difficult man; his expectations of me were damn near impossible. And yet, not an hour goes by when I don't think of him. Not a day passes when I don't wish he were still here beside me."

"What do you miss the most?" I ask softly.

"The times when we would go fishing on the lake. My dad

and I lived in Chicago then, but my grandparents left him a cabin in Lakewood, and we would come for two weeks every summer. We'd get up before the sun, when the only animals crazy enough to be awake were the geese. We never caught much, but when we did, Dad would make a big production of grilling the sucker with rosemary and butter, even if the fish was so small we only had two bites each. It was the closest I ever saw to him at peace. I guess that's why I moved here after he died. 'Cause I'm looking for that same peace." A smile tinges his lips. "What about you?"

I don't share memories of my mother as a rule. That's why I didn't turn in my self-examination journal. But I asked him first, and when I can forget about his good looks, my stomach unclenches. Liam's easy to talk to. But more than that, he doesn't judge. The longer we talk, the less he looks like those cruel guys at school, and the more he looks like . . . himself.

"She used to set up these treasure hunts for me," I say. "Twice a year, on my birthday and Valentine's Day, because she said I was the very heart of her. One coded message would lead to another, and then another, until I finally arrived at my present. One year, she even got the local shopkeepers involved and had me running all over town."

The shadow-smile morphs into a full-fledged grin. "She sounds like a fun mom."

"She was." I could say more. I could tell him how she always gave me the top of her muffin, and I didn't even realize until last year that was her favorite part, too. Or how she used to belt out Broadway musicals in the car, even though her voice was terribly off-key. But I've already shared too much, and my throat's thick with the recollection.

"Is that why you're here?" Liam asks. "Because you want to follow in her footsteps?"

I shake my head, not responding. There are lots of reasons I'm here, the primary one being to find my mom's final letter. But we've both been careful to focus on the positive memories. To stay on the side of love.

"That's what I want," he says. "To be like my dad. I inherited his car, my grandparents' old cabin by the lake. And a bunch of crazy geese that wake me every morning.

"But that's not enough. I was never able to please him while he was alive, and yet, I believe it's never too late. If he can look down at me and be proud of what I've done, I'll feel like my life is worth something."

I find myself leaning toward him, my insides turning warm and soupy at his confession. My tongue tingles, and the words tickle the back of my throat. I want to tell him everything. I want to learn more about his dad, to know what created these feelings that straddle the line between love and hate. To believe—for one moment—that my emotions are natural, normal, and understood.

But then he turns, and his smooth, handsome features catch the light. Liam belongs with the Mackenzies of the world. Too charming, too well-liked. Not an appropriate confidant for someone like me.

I turn instead to the oversized calendar hanging on the wall, filled with the call counselor schedule. "Is it okay if I sign up for Sunday afternoons and Wednesday evenings?" My voice is even and deliberately casual, as if it's no big deal. As if this weren't my mom's old schedule.

Alisara knew when my mom worked at the hotline. Maybe her other callers did, too. Maybe they're still calling at the same times six months later. And maybe they can shed some light on her behavior.

An expression I can't read flits across Liam's face. Oh god, is he hurt? I didn't mean to shut him down. I was just trying to end the conversation before he did.

"No problem," he says. "Go ahead and pencil yourself in."

I bite my lip, not sure how to get back to where we were, but not sure how to move forward, either. "Speaking of my mom, do you know if she left anything at the hotline?" I blurt out. "Some notebooks, maybe? Photographs or knickknacks?"

"I don't think so." He dips his head, and for a moment, I let myself see how attractive he is. How attractive I might find him if I were a different girl. "We had to move here from the old shed when our cover was blown. Most of the equipment was transferred, but I've never seen any of your mom's stuff."

"Okay," I say, trying to sound casual. "Do you mind if I stretch my legs a bit?"

"Nope. Hightail it back here when the phone rings, okay?"

"Got it."

I leave the main room, with the computer, phone bank, and lumpy, burnt-orange sofa, and head down the hallway to the bathroom.

As soon as the door's closed, I kneel in front of the sink. I skim my hands over toilet paper and cleaning products, paper cups and a packet of sponges. And then I see it. The triangle edge of a piece of paper, sticking up from a box.

The saliva flees my mouth. I see, hear, smell everything in crisp, clear notes. The dented corner of the pink box. The hum of the radiator. The acrid sting of pine needles. I tug up the paper and find . . .

. . . the instructional insert of a feminine product.

The breath whooshes out of me, and I rock back on my heels. Great. Super teen investigator, I'm not.

I close my eyes and picture what I'm searching for. A suicide letter. Addressed to me, explaining her actions. Proving my mother loved me, after all.

It's got to be here. It's got to. For god's sake, this is the woman who wrote me a letter every year for my birthday. I keep each one in a packet inside a sandalwood jewelry box. Every few months, I take them out and reread every last one.

My mother knew this. She knew how much her words meant to me. If she loved me even a little bit, she would have written me a letter.

Think! If my mother left me a letter, where would she hide it? Logically, there are only two real options: the caller database on the computer or a storage box somewhere.

During my last session, I logged briefly into my mother's old account when Liam stepped into the restroom. She'd recorded hundreds if not thousands of calls in the four years since she founded the hotline. It would take hours to sift through all those entries—unsupervised hours I don't yet have.

That leaves the storage box.

Determined, I put the insert back and go into the hallway. The phones are quiet, and Liam's pen scratches across paper. I should go back. Prepare myself for the next caller.

Instead, as if pulled by an outside force, my feet turn in the opposite direction. To the end of the hallway, where a set of stairs leads to a basement room. It wouldn't hurt if I take a peek. See if I notice anything out of the norm. I tread down the steps and open the door. A basement room, which Liam has converted into an office. I pause at the threshold and glance behind me. Pen, still scratching. Phones, not ringing.

Was my mouth dry before? It cracks like desert sand now. Quickly, before I change my mind, I cross to the closet at the back of the room and fling it open.

Boxes. Stacks upon stacks of boxes. Tattered cardboard cartons scrawled with black marker. See-through filing crates stacked neatly on top of one another. Pretty storage parcels decorated with paisleys and dots.

I don't know where to start. It's almost as bad as the thousands of call records.

And then my breath catches. No false alarm this time. Because in the corner, practically hidden from view, I glimpse a box papered with a familiar swatch of wallpaper. It has a crisscross pattern featuring a woven basket overflowing with apples, pears, and grapes.

The very same pattern that's on my kitchen walls at home. We had so much leftover wallpaper, my mom wrapped all our storage boxes with the extra sheets. Apparently, at least one of those boxes made it here.

I reach out to tug the parcel closer to me. And then a hand claps onto my shoulder.

My heart leaps into my throat, and my hand flies to my mouth, maybe to catch it. "Liam! You scared me!"

"What are you doing, CeCe?" Liam tilts his head, as though confused.

"Noth-nothing," I stutter. I don't want to lie to him. I don't want to see the hurt cross his eyes again. But I can hardly tell him I'm searching for my mom's final letter, which may or may not exist. I'll sound as delusional as my dad. "I needed some paper for my homework, and I thought I would look in the supply closet. That's all."

"Oh, is that all?" He grins, trusting me completely, and I kinda hate myself. "We have notebook paper in the desk upstairs."

We walk back to the phones together, and the guilt winding through me makes me smile a little brighter and laugh a little louder. Pretty soon, I forget that I'm only pretending to enjoy his company. Liam regales me with stories of the geese setting up camp on his porch, and I double over, clutching my stomach, wiping my eyes. I haven't laughed this hard since before the scandal with my mom broke.

It's not that Liam is that funny. Maybe I just needed to laugh. And somehow, in his presence, I can.

What are you doing? a voice inside me asks. *You're not here to make friends. You're here to find Mom's letter. To investigate Dad's claims.*

For once, I box up the voice and stick it in a far corner of my mind. Everything the voice is saying is true. But there will be other shifts at the hotline. And this Sunday, I'll be completely on my own. Plenty of time to walk around between calls. Plenty of time to peruse a box papered with a certain pattern.

Plenty of time to uncover my mother's secrets.

Chapter 7

"CeCe, wait!" Sam rolls up to me the next day after school, stopping short of crashing into the side of my car, a secondhand forest-green Camry. The radio doesn't work, stuffing's coming out of the seats, and scrapes and scratches riddle the exterior. But it's mine.

More importantly, it wasn't my mother's. And I never have to wonder what did or didn't happen in the backseat.

"You've been avoiding me," Sam pants, and he's right. We haven't spoken for over a week.

Today, instead of Rollerblades, he's on an aluminum scooter, the kind with three wheels and a handlebar. His face is red, and he's decked out in his safety gear. By all rights, he should look ridiculous.

Instead, he's adorable. Like makes-you-want-to-grab-his-helmet-and-kiss-him adorable. And judging from the sideways glances the girls in the parking lot are shooting him, I'm not the only one who thinks so. No doubt he's had plenty of offers to patch up his boo-boos this last week.

"Not that I blame you," he says. "I'm so sorry, CeCe. I was such a jerk. I can't believe I said all that stuff to you about the suicide, not realizing it was your mom."

I wrench my eyes from his lips. "So now you know?"

"Yes." From the way he drops his gaze, I can tell he knows all of it. Not just the suicide, but also the affair with Tommy Farrow.

Hell, maybe he's even lined his locker with Tabitha Brooks's faculty photo, as was the fad among the football team last year.

I turn and shove my key into the car door. "Fine. Apology accepted. You can leave now."

He can walk away from my car, forever, and it shouldn't matter. He was just a momentary blip in my life, nothing more. But sorrow drags at me, and I can't help but think of what could've been. If he weren't writing that article. If he had never found out about my past. If I could have had a fresh start with him, like everyone else.

I wait for his footsteps, for the thud of the scooter hitting pavement. But they don't come.

Instead, he places his palm flat against my car window, keeping the door closed. "CeCe, this doesn't change the way I think about you. Not one bit."

I stare at his hand. Ink stains his fingers, and a callous bulges on his middle finger from gripping his pencil too tightly. Does he mean it? Despite everything he's heard, am I still the "blank slate" girl he met on the first day of school?

Not that it matters. Even if he is sorry, his goal is to write a kick-ass article. A story so big and spectacular the Winkelhake scholarship fund will have no choice but to take notice. So long as that's true, I can't get lost in his eyes, no matter how dreamy they are.

"I said you can go," I repeat.

"If you really accepted my apology, you wouldn't make me leave." He shifts his scooter from one hand to the other and takes a step closer, so that his shoulder brushes mine. "You'd let me stay and hang out. You might even do the citizens of Lakewood a big favor and give me a lift home. I almost gave a woman a heart attack this morning when I swerved into her lane."

The corners of my lips quirk. I can't help it. It's like Sam knows exactly where my smiles have been hiding for the last six months, exactly how to laser in and dig them out.

"Okay," I say, wondering if I'm going to regret it. "Hop in."

* * *

By the time we pull up in front of his town house, with its blue siding and black shingles, I've stared small talk in the face and tried it on for size. To my surprise, it actually fits.

Sam tells me his impressions of the kids at school and how he got his internship at the *Lakewood Sun*. I tell him about the parties at the lake and how all the kids drag Main on Saturday nights. Of course, "all the kids" doesn't include me, at least not for the last six months, but I don't mention that.

"Thanks for the ride," he says, his fingers hooked around the metal door handle.

But he doesn't pull the handle, and he doesn't leave. My heart pounds. His head nearly scrapes the roof of my car, and there's no more than two feet between us. In this enclosed space, our breaths flirt and intermingle in the air.

Kind of like us, if I can remember any tips from the teen magazines Alisara and I used to read.

"I don't know how to say this," he begins.

"Go ahead, Sam." I turn my entire body to face him—my knees, shoulders, wrists—like he is a sun lamp, and I am a flower.

"It's about your mom."

Bam. Make that a wilted flower, whose petals are ripped apart by the gale. Of course it's about my mom. It's always about my mom.

"As you know, I've been researching the story of her suicide. And I came across something in my research that nobody could explain."

"What is it?" I say dully, even though I can probably guess. I mean, there's lots that's inexplicable about my mom's behavior. Tons.

Like: *How could a grown woman be sexually attracted to a boy?* Or more importantly: *Why would she act on it?* And my personal favorite: *Did she have any kind of moral fiber—even a few lost threads—at all?*

But Sam bypasses all the obvious questions and picks up a lock of my hair. I feel the slight tug all the way to my roots.

"Her hair." He rubs *my* strands between his fingers, and I suppress a shiver. "It was chopped off, jagged. One article said it looked like it was lopped off with a butcher knife."

I shrug, but even that simple movement is infused with the awareness of his touch. Still, he doesn't let go.

"They said she was crazy," I say. "Out of her mind. Maybe she was disfiguring herself as a sign of her shame. Who knows what motivated her actions?"

But even as I repeat the explanation the detectives gave for just about everything, my dad's words echo in my mind: *I knew your mother. She wasn't capable of those things. I don't believe she did any of it.*

All of a sudden, my excuses sound exactly like what they are—surface-level assumptions designed to make it easier for the detectives to close the case.

Sam frowns. "I guess I could buy that if I hadn't seen the interview with her hair stylist in one of the local papers."

Oh. One of those. Every newspaper in a fifty-mile radius went berserk when my mom committed suicide. Every day, there was a new article, featuring interviews with her fellow teachers, former students, even our lawn guy, for god's sake. If there was a story on her hair salon, I must've missed it.

"The stylist kept saying your mom's haircut was inconceivable, and I couldn't understand why. So when I was scooting past Cut & Dry the other day, I stopped to talk to her."

"Did she confirm my mom was a natural redhead?" I raise my eyebrows. "Reveal the exact color of dye she used to cover her silver sparkles?"

"Not at all," he says, and something about his tone stops me. The chill begins at the base of my spine and crawls its way up, one long spider leg at a time. "The stylist said she's been cutting your mom's hair for two decades. And in all that time, your mother never let her cut more than half an inch. In fact, she came into the salon two days before she died, and they had the exact same argument. The stylist tried to talk her into a bob, and your mom adamantly refused."

Abruptly, he lets go of my hair, and the strands swing back over my shoulder, loose, unencumbered, and very, very cold.

Sam's eyes pierce right into me. "So what I want to know is: What could've happened in two days that made her change her mind? Unless . . . she didn't."

Chapter 8

The phone's ringing. Of course it is. It's been ringing in my dreams all night, in one form or another. Sometimes I ignore it, and sometimes I pick it up. Sometimes I get my masturbating caller, and sometimes, it's my mother's hairstylist. Sometimes, the phone turns into a Venus flytrap and swallows my head whole.

I snuggle deeper into my sheets and prepare to drift off. The phone rings again. It's not the old-school "briiing-briiing" of the hotline or even the train whistle, guitar strum, or doorbell that my cell phone used to emit on a regular basis. I don't use personalized ring tones for my friends anymore, because, well, I don't have friends. But I've kept the "suspense" tone for my unknown callers, and that's what I'm hearing in my dream now . . .

My eyes pop open. Because the ring is followed by a vibration that rattles my entire nightstand, and my dreams never employ that many senses at once.

It's not a dream.

I grapple for my cell phone and manage to pick it up on the fifth ring. "Hello? Hello?"

Nothing. No words, at least. Just breathing so heavy I can almost feel the fog condensing through the phone lines.

I hang up. It's an automatic reaction. Maybe I'm being paranoid. Maybe it's due to Sam's words whispering in and out of my consciousness all night. But I can't stay on the line listening to that breathing one second longer.

The phone rings again. Same "suspense" shrill. Same chainsaw rattling. I push the button to decline the call.

It rings again. I decline. And again. I decline. And again. I decline. And—

I snatch up the phone. "What?! What do you want?"

A pause. And then a voice, so low I can't tell if it's male or female. "Wrong number. I was looking for the crisis hotline. Sorry."

I hear a click, and then silence fills my ear, my mind, my room. It might as well be liquid concrete. I'm suddenly gasping, choking, fighting to fill my lungs with air.

Why is someone calling my cell phone, thinking it's the crisis hotline? The numbers are nothing alike. NOTHING.

No one's supposed to know I'm volunteering there. When I signed up as a call counselor, I made Mr. Willoughby promise not to tell. All I need is for one student to find out, and it'll spread through the school more quickly than any emergency response system. *Did you hear? Cecilia Brooks is volunteering at the hotline. Like mother, like daughter. Gee, I wonder if she'll start having sex there, too. Who's she going to prey on? A middle-schooler?*

I force a shaky breath, climbing out of bed and dressing for the day. It could've been an honest mistake. Someone could've mistakenly hit "CeCe" instead of "Crisis" when dialing from their contacts.

Except I'm not on people's contact lists. Plus, I can see fat-fingering the wrong number once. But six times in a row? What are the chances?

By lunchtime, I have five more missed calls from five different numbers. Three voice mails, with three different voices. All of which say approximately the same thing: "Um, do I have the right number? Is this the crisis hotline?"

It got so bad I turned off the ringer, but like the Princess and the Pea, I can still feel the vibration through my backpack, where it rests at my feet, against my socks and shoes.

I'm seriously contemplating dropping my phone down a toilet when Mackenzie saunters to my locker. She's impeccably dressed, as always, but even the heavy concealer can't cover the circles under her eyes.

She hooks her arm through mine and leans in close, as if I'm one of her cohorts. "Did you know that new guy Sam is writing an article on your mom's suicide?" The spicy scent of her breath mints assaults me.

"I heard something about that, yeah." I inch backward until I'm practically falling into my locker.

"Well, it took him about five seconds to find out I was dating Tommy when it happened. And now he's contacted me for an interview. Me! Can you believe the nerve of this guy? After what he did to me in front of the whole school?"

You mean, when he helped out a girl you were mercilessly bullying? Like you're trying to bully me now?

I force myself to stand up straight. "Why are you telling me this?"

"Because you need to tell him to back off."

I shake my head. "Uh-uh. I don't tell Sam what to do. We barely know each other."

It's partly true. I've talked to the guy a grand total of three times. And yet, I can still feel the tingle in my scalp from when he lifted the hair off my shoulders. Still feel the tug of my lips at the thought of his aluminum scooter and elbow pads.

Mackenzie's grip relaxes, and she takes a step back. "I can't let him dredge up the drama again. Those boys have finally graduated, and I was supposed to put it all behind me this year."

I stumble, and my elbow hits the locker with a clang. Why, she must have been suffering, too. If I was teased as my mother's daughter, then she must have gotten flak as Tommy's girlfriend. No doubt it was more subtle, but people must have wondered. And whispered.

But just when I'm beginning to feel sorry for her, Mackenzie's features turn to plastic. "Get him to back off, CeCe. Otherwise, I'll tell him exactly what Tommy said to me about your mom. You don't want the sordid details in the *Lakewood Sun,* do you?"

"I . . . I thought Tommy never said anything," I stutter. "You were as surprised as the rest of us."

She sneers. "Sam doesn't know that, does he?"

She turns and stalks off, flicking at a poster taped to the wall. The action dislodges the poster, and I catch the paper as it drops to the floor.

Coincidentally, it's the same flyer advertising the crisis hotline. The one the striped-tights girl was hanging up on the first day of school. But this one's been altered. The space listing the hotline's phone number has been whited out. And a series of digits has been written over it. A very familiar series of digits. My phone number, to be precise.

I stare at the blocky figures written in orange permanent marker. How on earth did my phone number get on this flyer?

I'm cold, so cold, even as my body breaks out in sweat. So that's the reason all these people are calling my cell phone. Not a mistake, after all.

Someone placed my number there on purpose.

Which means, someone is out to get me. But why?

I think again of Sam's words. His insinuation that my mother didn't cut her own hair. His larger implication that somebody else did. Somebody who wasn't my mom's hair stylist. Someone who could've been responsible for her death.

Suddenly, I'm shaking all over, from my knees to my hands to my teeth, and I'm not sure when I'll ever stop.

Chapter 9

A red lace bra dangles on a bush outside a lakeside cabin. The music throbs so loudly I wouldn't be surprised if it were causing the ripples in the lake. Everywhere I look, there are people. Talking, laughing, gyrating. Mostly gyrating.

Alisara steps over a couple in full make-out mode, right in the middle of the front walk, and tugs me inside the house. "Aren't you glad you came?" she shouts over the din.

"Um, sure," I mumble. At least, it seemed like a good idea an hour ago, when Alisara invited me to one of Bobby Parker's Friday night bashes. His parents own a cabin on the lake, a few properties down from the crisis hotline. Normally, I would've declined the invitation, but I'd gotten four more missed calls, and I had to get out of the house.

So here I am. Standing on a hardwood floor sticky from spilled drinks. Clutching a blue plastic cup filled with an unidentified liquid. And having my silhouette and bare legs perused by a couple boys from school.

My cheeks burn. What was I thinking? I wore the dress—a short, black one my mom and I used to share—because it was the first appropriate thing I found. I wasn't focused on how the thin material would skim along my curves. How much this outfit would make me look like my mother.

I resemble her more and more every day. I see it in the way Gram startles sometimes coming around the corner, as if she's encountered a ghost. In the way my dad refuses to meet my eyes. If that weren't enough, all I have to do is look in the mirror. Light brown eyes. Well-endowed chest. No wonder Tommy Farrow's friends can't resist harassing me.

No sooner do I have this thought than I hear the donkey bray of a laugh, one that used to greet me every morning and haunt my dreams every night. In the corner, a beefy, red-faced guy does a handstand on a silver barrel. Justin Blake. Former football player, Tommy Farrow's best friend, and my most vicious harasser. Wherever Justin is, Tommy's never far behind.

Sure enough, holding up one of Justin's legs is a guy with blond curls and a bone structure that's charmed half the girls at Lakewood High. Including, apparently, my mother.

"I've got to get out of here," I blurt to Alisara, shoving my drink at her.

She looks toward the corner and winces. "Sorry, CeCe. I had no idea they were going to be here." She gestures toward the staircase. "Go. Let's meet back here in an hour."

I scamper up the steps, dodging the kids crowded along the railing. There are four doors on the second floor. Four doors with who knows what—or more accurately, whom—inside. Great. I really don't want to be surprised by Mystery Door Number One. But I can't linger in the hallway forever. Can I?

As I shift from one black high-top to the other—yes, I wore the dress, but I draw the line at heels—one of the doors opens.

"Liam! What are you doing here?" My mind whirls. As evidenced by Tommy and Justin, college guys do attend these parties. But I'd thought, since Liam works for the school, that he'd be uncomfortable here.

Apparently not.

He's dressed in the same strategically ripped jeans as the rest of the guys at the party. Same form-fitting hoodie over a plaid shirt. Same muscular chest honed from hours at the gym.

Which I have no business noticing.

He brings a finger to his lips. "Shhh." Glancing furtively around the hallway, he motions for me to come inside the room.

"The geese were driving me crazy, so I was out driving

around," Liam says. "When I saw the house lit up like a Christmas tree, I came over to see what was up. You look very pretty."

As soon as the words leave his mouth, the tips of his ears turn red, and he drops his gaze.

My stomach flutters like a dozen moths are trapped inside. Does he mean it? Or is he just being polite? I mean, I certainly noticed his looks. How could I not? But I'm not used to boys complimenting me, much less boys who are really cute and really nice.

And for some reason, when Liam says it, I don't feel like scrubbing my skin with a Brillo Pad, the way I did when the guys downstairs were checking me out. I feel . . . good.

"If it were any other night, you'd be disappointed," I say, trying to sound casual. Trying to act as though hot guys tell me I look pretty every day. "I had a rough day and wanted to get out of my head."

"Same. Some idiot doctored the hotline flyers with the wrong phone number, so I spent all afternoon replacing every last one of those suckers."

"You did? I could kiss you!" I blurt out and then flush. Oh god. Why did I say that? Stupid, stupid, stupid.

But he takes a step forward, as if he doesn't think I'm stupid at all. And he's got this crooked, dimpled smile on his face—oh god, that dimple!—as if he might make my words come true. . . .

My pulse skitters in a million directions. "That was *my* number on the posters," I babble. "My phone's been ringing nonstop since this morning."

This stops his forward motion. "Why would someone do this to you?"

I lift my shoulders, trying to smile. Not sure if I should be kicking myself for ruining the moment. "Oh, you know. The usual harassment. Nothing more." I aim for light and bouncy, like an inflatable ball at the beach. But the stress of the day punctures a hole in my voice, and the ball fizzles to the ground.

He wouldn't understand. He couldn't. He's probably never been teased a day in his life, much less bullied. And yet, his eyes are soft. "People can be so cruel. Sometimes, they don't even realize how cruel they're being."

"What would you know about it?" I mutter.

"I know more than you think," he says quietly.

We look at each other, and the air crackles with electricity. My every nerve ending comes alive, and he shifts so that his face is hovering above mine. I have time to think, *maybe I haven't killed the moment, after all . . .*

. . . and then I hear a disturbingly familiar voice through the wooden door.

"I know she came up here . . . I saw her . . ." Tommy says.

I freeze and stumble away from Liam. Are they talking about me?

"Look, dude, this is ridiculous," another voice rasps. Justin Blake. It has to be. "You don't owe her anything."

"Like hell I don't!" Tommy's voice rises. "She deserves to know . . ."

He trails off, and try as I might, I can't hear anything else. *What?* I want to scream. *What do I deserve to know?*

"CeCe, are you okay?" Liam asks.

I snap my eyes back to his face, rubbing the goose bumps that have sprung up along my arm. The voices outside wouldn't have meant anything to him. Maybe he didn't even hear them. "Listen, I'm really sorry, but I've got to go. There's something I have to do."

"Take my hoodie. You look cold." He peels his jacket off his arms and hands it to me.

I fumble with the soft cotton, and my hand gets caught in the sleeve. Let's face it. I'm not the kind of girl to whom guys rush around lending their jackets. Stick their tongues through their fingers and simulate gross sexual acts, yes. Do something chivalrous, no.

Without a word, Liam takes the hoodie and helps me slide my arms through. The jacket settles on my shoulders like a flannel blanket, enveloping me with his musky scent, and his hands tighten, just briefly, on my shoulders.

"Thanks, Liam. I appreciate it."

"I'll see you soon?"

His eyes hold mine an instant longer than necessary. They're pale blue, like the sky on those winter mornings when it tries to reflect the snow. Appealing, by any objective measure. But now that I've spent some time with him, I suspect there's much more to Liam than his looks.

Something I think I like. Something I want to get to know a lot better. But not now. Now, I'm focused on one thing and one thing only. Tracking down the person I've been avoiding for the last six months.

Tommy Farrow.

Chapter 10

I trudge through the mud, my sneakers getting wetter and squishier with every step. Thank the stars I have Liam's hoodie, but now I wish I'd thought to wear leggings or tights underneath the dress. The long stems of grass tickle my naked calves, and the wind gusts against my thighs.

Tommy wasn't inside the cabin. Not the kitchen, where opened bags of chips and someone's platform sandal lay strewn across the counter. Or the living room, where a girl was removing her choker, glasses, and retainer in preparation for a handstand. Or even the darkened den, where people stopped being individuals and broke down into body parts—an ass to grab, a pelvis to grind.

That leaves only one option. The bonfire next to the lake.

The moon shines overhead, and clumps of people hover around the flames. Out here, away from the music, the geese chatter nosily to each other, unaware the nighttime belongs to their human neighbors.

I see Tommy immediately, his hair curling at the nape of his neck. As always, the questions slither into my brain and refuse to leave. Did my mother wrap her fingers around those curls as she kissed him? Breathe in the scent of his hair as she pressed her bare breasts against his back?

He faces the fire, his hands shoved into his pockets, deep in conversation with someone hidden behind his broad shoulders.

I straighten my spine and walk toward him. My toes slosh in my sneakers in the same way that my stomach tilts from side to side. Am I really going to do this? Confront the boy who drove my mother to suicide?

The kaleidoscope of emotions hits me at once. The crawl-into-a-hole despair of what my mother did. The white-hot rage that she abandoned me. Even the deep, pervasive knowledge that she will never yank the comforter off my bed, when I've hit the snooze button too many times, ever again.

I let the emotions override the doubt, and before I know it, I'm tapping Tommy Farrow on the very shoulder my mother may have nibbled.

He turns, and the features of his companion come into focus.

Good god, it's Mackenzie freaking Myers. Why is she talking to him? I thought she couldn't stand him.

Her eyebrows shoot into her widow's peak, and her mouth hangs open. Looking at the gap between her front teeth, I realize: She could say the very same thing about me.

Before either of us can speak, Tommy grabs my hand. "I've been looking for you everywhere," he says, not using my name. Does he even remember it? One thing's for sure. I'm the "she" to whom he was referring. There's something he wants to tell me. Something I deserve to know.

"Can we go someplace quiet to talk?" I ask.

"There's nothing I'd like more," he slurs. Without another glance at Mackenzie, no good-bye, nothing, he pulls me from the bonfire.

Mackenzie's eyes blaze. But she's not the only one who's pissed. We haven't gone two steps when we're intercepted by Tommy's watchdog.

"You don't have to do this." Justin spreads his legs, blocking our path. "Your mind is telling you things it doesn't mean. Things you'll regret in the morning. Let go of the girl, and come with me." His voice is slow and deliberate. The kind you use to talk a suicide jumper off the ledge.

"It's past time," Tommy mumbles. "Almost six months past."

Every hair on my neck stands up. I don't care if he's incapacitated. If he wants to talk to me, it has to be about my mother. Right?

Justin rips him from me and shoves him toward one of their brawny friends. "Get him in the car, where he can't hurt anyone. I'll deal with him in a minute."

"But I need to talk to her," Tommy whines as the friend leads him away. "I NEED TO."

"That's not Tabitha, you fool!" Justin shouts after them. "It's her daughter!"

I wrap my arms around my body, squeezing my ribs through the hoodie. Oh. Is that what this was about? Tommy wanted to talk to me . . . because he thought I was my mother?

Too late I remember I'm wearing the dress we used to share. My hair, as dark as hers in the black night, swirls around my shoulders. If she weren't decomposing underground, I could be my mother's much-younger twin.

Justin turns to me. His face is a grotesque puzzle that's been put together all wrong, and I can tell he's going to be mean. Meaner than usual. A meanness that's been saved up, festering on a shelf.

"You girls are only good for one thing," he rasps. "But I don't need you around to pull my dick when I can do a better job myself."

I flinch, and Justin laughs. It cuts me like broken glass.

"Oh, didn't you know that's what your mom did? It wasn't just Tommy, you know. He's the only one who came forward, but she used to go down the row of us guys, giving us whatever we wanted."

"I don't believe you," I whisper. "That story's ridiculous."

He smirks. "Is that right?" His voice is baiting, baiting, baiting me. I'm a helpless fish, unable to avoid the lure because I can't tell where it is. "How well did you really know your mother, CeCe? Did she tell you about her sexual fetishes?"

"I knew her well enough." I lift my chin, but the effect's ruined by my trembling jaw.

He reaches into his back pocket and pulls out a cell phone.

"See for yourself. Apparently, your mother's been a slut her whole life."

He hands the phone to me, and I take it automatically. With the same sick compulsion that draws onlookers to car accidents, I look at the screen.

The Internet browser is open, with the headline "Hotties We Love" blazoned across the top. Underneath, a stunning teenager with sunset hair looks at the camera, her beauty eclipsed only by the glorious orbs of her naked breasts.

The caption proclaims: "Tabitha, at 17."

The phone slips through my fingers and falls into the muddy grass.

"Hey! Watch it!" Justin yells.

But his words are muffled through the roar in my ears. It's my mother, all right. There's no mistaking the classic bone structure, those soulfully expressive eyes that used to be the last thing I saw before I went to sleep. She would croon a lullaby as she tucked me in, and I never felt safer than when I looked into those moon-drenched eyes.

I will always love you, she used to say. *No matter what mistakes you make, no matter how badly you behave, I will always, always love you.*

Too bad I can't say the same about her.

"Where did you get this?" My voice breaks and crackles like the late autumn leaves.

Justin smirks. "I stumbled across it during one of my porn sessions. Imagine my surprise when I realized it was none other than our old friend, Miz Brooks." He turns and shouts at the crowd. "If you haven't already seen it, people, it's www.hottieswelove.com! Go on. You know you want to."

All around us, people pull out their phones. Tap on the keys. And stare at me.

Again. Just like those first weeks after my mom's suicide.

Sweat drenches my body, and I sway on my feet. I can't see anything but a long, narrow tunnel in front of me. Too bad that's where Justin's standing.

He fishes his phone out of the mud and wipes it against his

jeans. "You wanna pose for me, CeCe? Follow in mummy's footsteps? Your rack's not quite as big as the old lady's, but I'll make a few allowances. I'm generous like that."

The whispering increases. I'm trapped in a beehive, and the drones are closing in, surrounding me, sealing off every exit. I'm drowning in their sticky, honey-like gossip, gasping, gasping for a breath. And then, a new voice breaks in.

"Photoshop." Sam strides between Justin and me, pushing his glasses up his nose. "Haven't you all heard of Photoshop? This picture you're all gawking at could be fake. All you need is a head shot of someone, and you can create any image you want."

It's bullshit, of course. The lines in the photo are too clean, too seamless. And I've seen a very similar version of those breasts before, reflected back from my own mirror. But at least Sam's trying.

He looks Justin up and down, from the hair that flops over his forehead to his too-cool loafers. "I could go on Facebook this very second, snag a photo of this guy, and presto, you could be looking at his naked photo. Whether you'd enjoy it is a different question."

The crowd titters. Justin's face turns the shade of a day-old bruise. By outward appearances, the former football player should have the upper hand. Despite his bulk, he could be an Abercrombie model, while Sam's sweatshirt is torn, and his moon-like glasses slide down his nose. But none of that matters right now.

"Come on, CeCe." Sam holds his hand out to me. "Let's go."

I take his hand, and he leads me out of there, away from the sea of unblinking eyes.

Chapter 11

We stride from the bonfire, and at first the adrenaline of what Sam did propels me forward. He faced my biggest bully—and got the best of him. We're walking away, with Justin looking like the fool, not me.

Not me. It's always been me. How could it possibly not be me?

And then the fear settles in, wraps around my stomach, and jumps my heart forward a few beats. Because if I know Justin at all, there will be repercussions. Big ones. Ones I'm not sure I'm ready for.

"I don't have a car," Sam says, pulling me from my thoughts. We've crossed half the lawn, and more mud has mucked its way up my legs, so I feel like I'm wearing tights after all. Sludge tights. "Some knight in shiny armor, right? Whisking you off, without anywhere to take you."

"It's okay." I fish my car keys out of the pocket in my dress. "I drove tonight."

We walk to the long line of cars parked on the gravel driveway. I'm not sure why. I can't leave yet since I'm Alisara's ride, but at least it gets me away from the party.

We reach my car, all the way at the end, and I unlock the doors, grab some paper towels, and begin cleaning the mud off my legs. I finish an entire leg before I realize Sam's staring. My pale flesh gleams in the moonlight, and with my foot propped on the running board, the short dress reveals more than I want of my thigh.

I stiffen, and my mom's topless photo floats through my mind. Her sunset hair, the round, heavy breasts. So this is the way it's going to be, even with him?

Something hot and fierce moves through my body. All I wanted from this year was to be left alone. Maybe meet a guy who likes me for me. No such luck. My mom's in the grave, but she's still here. Still messing things up for me.

I drop my foot to the ground. "So that's why you stood up for me, huh?" The laugh scrapes out of my throat. "You wouldn't be the first. Everyone says we look alike, you know. So if you're wondering? Yeah, I can confirm that's exactly how I look topless."

"CeCe, I'm not interested in you like that." His Adam's apple jumps in his throat. "I mean, I am, but your mom has nothing to do with it . . ."

He trails off, and I yank the hoodie off my shoulders. "Go ahead. Look all you want. Apparently, my boobs are public property, since the whole world's seen my mom's."

To his credit, Sam keeps his eyes on my face. "I saw the photo, but only for a second. I didn't stare at it. I sure as hell didn't get off on it. The only thing I thought was how it would affect you."

The hoodie droops from my hands, and I toss it on the trunk. Sam takes off his sweatshirt, too, and throws it next to mine. I realize how warm I've gotten. Whether it's from the bonfire or the confrontation with Justin, my skin's hot and sticky. Sam probably feels the same way.

The anger flees as quickly as it came. Sam's on my side. He didn't do anything wrong, but I leaped to conclusions. Maybe there are nice guys left in this world, after all. Maybe all the nice ones, I just manage to drive away.

"Why did you help me out back there?" I mumble.

"I may be the new guy at school, but I'm not oblivious." His voice stumbles, as if it's on uneven ground. But like the boy on the Rollerblades, it glides brazenly, unflinchingly on. "It didn't take long to piece together how they've been treating you. You don't deserve that. Nobody does."

I don't say anything. I can't. No one's been this kind to me in ages, except maybe Alisara. In the weeks after the funeral, she would sit by my bed for hours, carrying on a monologue about who hooked up with whom and did I want to try her raspberry lipstick and how she might go to Homecoming with Brian Finnigan. Innocuous gossip in which she only had a mild interest, conveyed in hopes of drawing me out.

But even Alisara has her limits, and after a few weeks of our one-sided conversations, her visits became further and further apart until they stopped completely.

I've told myself I'll be wary around Sam. He's writing an article about my mom, and he's determined to root out every last salacious detail. But I feel myself tipping toward him. A magnetic pull that has me teetering on the edge. Involvement. If there's a way to be around Sam and remain detached, I haven't figured it out.

Maybe I don't need to. Maybe the best way to control what he finds out is to stay near him. Keep my enemies closer and all that.

Except when I look into his face, silhouetted by the moon, the last thing he feels like is my enemy.

"I can't go anywhere because I'm Alisara's ride." I chew on my lips. "But could you . . . hang out with me? I don't want to be alone right now."

I've said it to myself dozens of times over the last year, in different ways, but it all adds up to the same thing. *I'm so lonely. I feel alone. I miss my mom.*

It's funny how I never felt alone before. Even when I was up in my room, studying late at night with only my earbuds for company, I didn't feel alone. I knew I could always find my mom somewhere in the house, and no matter what, she would drop whatever she was doing and have a cup of tea with me. It's not that I sought her out often. I didn't always agree with her advice, and most of the time, I didn't want to hear it. But she was always there, always available. The equivalent of a teenager's security blanket.

I miss her.

The feeling washes over me, and I lean against the car, tilting my head up to the black sky. The stars are hidden somewhere beneath a thick blanket of clouds, but I feel their beauty as an ache inside my heart, even if I can't see them.

Kind of like my mom. I can't see her or talk to her, but she's still here, living inside me, the good parts and the bad.

I turn to Sam, my eyes wet for no reason I can understand, and what I see in his face takes my breath away. A yearning so raw it peels away every layer of myself, leaving me more exposed than my mother's topless photo.

"I'm not going to kiss you," he says in a strained voice. "After the night you've had, I don't want you to mistake a kiss for anything but what it is. But I want you to know, just because I don't kiss you doesn't mean I'm not thinking about it. Doesn't mean I'm not going to dream about it. Doesn't mean I won't want to do it, next time we're together."

My heart sprints, each beat trying to outpace the other. My second almost-kiss in the space of one hour. When I can count my lifetime number of such encounters on one hand. I have to swallow twice before I can speak. "Duly noted."

"Good." He grins, the lens of his glasses reflecting the moonlight. "I just wanted to make that clear. Wouldn't be a very good investigative reporter if I didn't set the record straight."

Chapter 12

I'm late meeting Alisara at the cabin. Like thirty minutes late. She accepts my apology without saying much, and we drive most of the way home in silence. The headlights cut through the darkness, giving us disjointed flashes of the familiar. The worn wooden sign directing us to Lakewood Cabins. The dilapidated playground next to the elementary school, with its creaky swings and peeling paint. The crumbling public library on the way to Alisara's neighborhood.

By day, Lakewood resembles an empty tuna can—plain, rusty, and a little sad, holding traces of something that wasn't all that great to begin with. Once the railroad pulled out of town a decade ago, so did the jobs, leaving the people to make a life out of the leftovers.

At night, though, the town takes on an almost spooky quality, a feeling that makes me grip the steering wheel a little tighter as I navigate the streets.

"I don't mind that you were late," Alisara bursts out when we turn onto her road. "But I saw you walk back into the cabin with that new guy. Are you really not going to say a word about him?"

I jerk, and the car swings toward the curb. "What . . . what do you want me to say?"

"I don't know, CeCe," she mutters, looking out the window. A passing street light paints a stripe over her ear, making her look like the heroine in a slasher flick. "What you two were doing? How hot he is? If he's a good kisser?"

"I didn't kiss him," I say, heat creeping up my neck. "We hung out by the car and talked. But I, uh . . . I think he's cute."

She turns to me, her features softening. She doesn't press me for any more details, and I realize she doesn't actually want the information. Like her running monologues by my bedside, this isn't about gossip. It's about giving her a sign of my friendship.

My throat tightens. Because Alisara is my friend. Maybe, after these last few months, the only friend I have left.

"Alisara," I say hesitantly. "At the party, did they talk about my mom's photo a lot?"

"Yeah." She glances down, but then brings her gaze right back to my face. "The guys were pretending to masturbate to the picture; the girls were saying they always knew she was a slut by the way she dressed."

I pull into her driveway and turn off the ignition. "And what did you say?"

"I said sure, those button-downs and linen pants were *really* sexy. I'm surprised the school board didn't come down with a ban on pearl earrings. Scandalous." She places a hand on my arm. "She was seventeen, CeCe. You don't know why she posed for that photo. You don't understand the context."

"So, what, I'm supposed to give her the benefit of the doubt?"

"She was your mother."

"That doesn't give her a free pass."

Except she wasn't a mother in name only. What about all the times she drove my forgotten homework to school? The years she served as room parent? She had less time after she went back to teaching, but she was just as attentive. Just as loving.

Does that count for anything?

I don't know. Six months after her death, and I'm still no closer to an answer.

My phone rings as I slide my key into the front door. The "suspense" ring tone. I push the button to end the call. It rings again as I tiptoe up the stairs. I switch it to vibrate.

A light shines underneath the door to the guest room—where Gram sleeps. But she's not waiting up for me, no siree.

"Gram, I'm home," I stage-whisper as I push open the door.

She's at her desk, spectacles perched on her nose and laptop in front of her. "I'm not waiting up for you."

"Didn't say you were."

She scowls. "Your father's puttering in the den, doing god knows what, and I've been here all night, losing my life's savings to a bunch of yahoos who can't tell a flush from a straight. I'm not going to ask if you've had a good time. I don't want to know if you've been drinking. And I really don't care if you've climbed into the backseat with any boys."

I smile. "No, no, and not really."

She takes her glasses off and rubs her eyes. "You're a good girl, CeCe."

I bend down and kiss her forehead. Her skin is as soft and warm as bread dough. With Gram, I have a bit of the same relationship I had with my mom. Even though she's my paternal grandmother, she charges headlong into life the way Mom did, and the only time I ever relax anymore is in her presence. "You haven't really lost your life's savings, have you?"

"Nah. I've got that trip to Vegas in a week and a half, remember? Gotta save for that." She hands me a five-dollar gaming chip she won at a Kansas City casino. "Here. For your bank account."

My bank account, as she calls it, is a briefcase under my bed, filled with the clay discs Gram dispenses like candy. "This is an investment in your future," she explained a few months ago. "When you're of age, you can decide if you want to redeem your chips—or if you're going to follow in your Gram's footsteps and gamble it all on a single hand. You could lose it all, or turn a single coin into a hundred. But what is life if not a risk?"

For her, maybe. Not me. Life's hard enough without betting it all on something I can't control.

"CeCe?" Gram says as I turn to leave the room. "Your father tells me you're not applying to Parsons. Is that true?"

I frown. "You're on the verge of hovering, Gram."

"Not even close. In my profession, we can't afford to hover. We have to go all-in with our pocketbooks—and our hearts." She drums her fingers on the laptop. "What I'm trying to say is: If you're staying in Lakewood on account of your father, don't. He can take care of himself. And I'll be around."

"No offense, Gram, but your version of a home-cooked meal is a Lean Cuisine. And you dry-clean all of your clothes, even your underwear. You probably haven't touched a laundry machine in the last decade."

She flashes me a smile. "Made it sixty-five years, didn't I? Life only deals you one hand, CeCe. But how you play it is up to you."

"I'll think about it," I say, more to get her off my back than anything else.

She turns back to her computer. "Good."

I go to my room and lie on my bed, the phone nestled against my chest. It vibrated a couple more times while I was talking to Gram, but I don't bother to check the number now. Probably a random student calling the hotline after the party, wanting to gossip.

Instead, I sit up and type the Web address for the Parsons School of Design into my phone's Internet browser. Once the page opens, I read about the Parsons Challenge, an exercise all undergraduate applicants must complete. This year's challenge is to explore something that you normally overlook in your daily life.

As always, my insides clench as I read the words. Because there's one thing I've been deliberately, systematically overlooking for the last six months. My mother.

Her picture is facedown on my dresser. The clothes we shared are shoved to the back of my closet. Even the sandalwood jewelry box is buried in the mix of old shoes under my bed.

Sighing, I lower my phone. Even if I were willing to share such a personal viewpoint with a random admissions officer, I can't leave my dad now. Maybe he takes the laundry and the meals for granted, but at least he's clean and fed. That's what

Mom would have wanted—if she bothered to think of us at all in her last moments.

The phone pings in my hand. Not a call this time, but a text message. That's different. Must be Alisara, wanting to see if I'm still awake.

I check the number. I don't recognize it, but that doesn't mean anything. I wouldn't be able to call Alisara if her number weren't in my contacts. And then, I read:

Mind your own business. Or you're next.

The breath bursts in and out of my lungs. I throw the phone across the room before I crush it beneath my fingers. I'm NEXT? Next for what? And how exactly am I poking into anybody's business? I'm like one of those turtles who lives her whole life inside her shell, afraid to venture five inches in front of her.

And then I remember I'm volunteering at the hotline. Trying to uncover my mother's secrets. Confronting Tommy Farrow. So maybe not such a turtle, after all.

I cross the floor and pick up my phone, where it bounced harmlessly on the shaggy carpet. Getting back into bed, I type "Hotties We Love" into the browser, and my mother's topless photo pops up.

We look at each other, her seventeen-year-old self and me, and I see something her naked breasts distracted me from before. Her eyes. *Help me,* they seem to implore through the photo, across the years. *Find out my secrets. Don't let them get away with this.*

And before I can think clearly about what I'm doing, my finger flies over the screen and I text back:

Try me.

Chapter 13

Something's poking me in the hip. I roll over to get more comfortable, but it only jabs me more. What on earth?

I crack my eyes open. The sun streams in through the windows, making rectangular rays of light on the floor. I didn't close the blinds last night. Didn't brush my hair or change my black dress, either. I was so emotionally wrung-out I fell into bed, the message from my mysterious texter playing in a continuous loop through my brain.

I shift, and the object digs into my side again. Is it a tag on my dress? One of Gram's poker chips?

I scrutinize the smooth expanse of my paisley bed sheets. Nothing. Which means whatever is trying to drill a hole in my hip is *inside* my dress. Probably ensconced in the hidden pocket.

Of course. How could I forget?

My mom and I both loved this dress, not only for its flattering fit, but also because of the hidden pocket sewn into the lining. We used to leave notes for each other, little messages like "I love you" or "Good luck on your art show." Or, on the night of my sophomore Homecoming dance: "Don't forget—a girl does kiss and tell, especially if the captive audience is her mother."

My fingers tremble like a bird learning to fly, and excitement darts around my heart. I don't want to hope; I can't bear to be wrong. But maybe . . . Could she have . . .

This was always our secret way of communicating. It would

make sense if she left a note in my pocket, in a place only I can find.

Carefully, I peel the dress off and skim my fingers over the lining. Searching for a piece of paper folded in that special triangular way.

Another one of our codes. Silly, maybe, but I've been a sucker for secret codes ever since I was a little girl, and my mother always indulged me.

I don't find any paper, folded or otherwise. Instead, my hands close around a key. A delicate silver key, about half an inch long. I've never seen it before, and I can't imagine what it could fit.

Disappointment swells in my chest. No note. No final words. How many times does my soul need to be crushed before I finally learn?

I squeeze the key in my fist, and when I open my hand, dropping it onto the bed, my palm is creased with the indentation of the metal. That's me—scarred with the traces of my mother's scandal.

Unless . . . my mother left that key for me. Unless this is the first clue in one of her treasure hunts, the very last one she set up for me.

Maybe the most important one of all.

"Holy crap, CeCe. Did you decide to redecorate and forget to tell me?" Gram asks as she strides into the living room. I haven't seen my dad this morning, which means he's already left for the cemetery—or he's locked himself in the den again.

I rock back on my heels. Every paper clip and rubber band has been emptied out of my mom's old desk. The carpet is covered with reams of paper, stacks of dusty photographs, and clusters of faded wedding favors.

The pantry and dining room don't look much better. I'm not exactly sure what I'm searching for. A hidden compartment, a portable safe. Maybe a locked drawer I don't know about.

But so far, nada. Not a single secret keyhole, much less one that fits my silver key.

"Sorry, Gram." I wince at the paper dots from the hole puncher, sprinkled on the floor like confetti. "I'll clean everything up, promise."

She waves off my apology, which isn't surprising. I'm the only one who ever seems to notice—or clean up—the clutter.

"Did you stay up late gambling?" I ask.

"I stayed up late, all right, but it wasn't to play poker." She yawns, covering her mouth with coral fingernails. "One of the gentlemen admired my style. So much that he invited me to chat after the game."

My mouth falls open. "How old is he?"

She shrugs. "He didn't say, but his photo looks like he's in his forties."

"How old does he think you are?"

"Didn't ask."

"Gram!"

"Oh, lighten up, CeCe. A bit of cybersex never hurt anyone."

I grind my teeth. I highly doubt any such thing happened, but that's Gram. Always trying to get a reaction out of me. "What if word gets out? If people hear you're dating a younger man, they'll say you're just like . . . You're just like . . ."

"Tabitha?" Her voice slides into my sternum like a blade. "You can say her name, you know. She's not the devil."

I close my mouth. Maybe it's because she's a newcomer to Lakewood, but Gram has never seemed affected by the gossip. And like my dad, she's always been one hundred percent on my mother's side.

"Besides, the situation isn't even remotely similar," she continues. "We're two consenting adults. Even if people talk, what does it matter, so long as you and I know the truth?"

Truth. Problem is, the word's slippery—too slippery. There's the truth in the police report, the truth the kids at school whisper. Then there's my mom's truth, which I have yet to uncover. And my own truth, which morphs from day to day.

"I found this key," I say, changing the subject. "I'm trying to figure out what it opens. Is there anything in your room it might fit?"

She rakes a hand through her hair, and I glimpse the silver growing in at her roots. "I don't think so. But you're welcome to look."

I grin. Gram may not be much of a guardian, but she has an open-door policy to her life. I thank her and dash up the stairs, two at a time.

Still, I find nothing. I paw through her drawers, tunnel my way to the back of the closet, even tug on patches of carpet to see if anything budges. Zilch.

I turn the key in my hands. It didn't get into my pocket by accident. If my mother put the key there, it must belong to something.

I'm still squinting at the key as if it holds the secrets of my universe when Gram comes into the room. "CeCe, you have a caller."

The key drops soundlessly to the carpet. "I didn't hear the phone ring."

"Not that kind of caller. A young man is at our front door." She leans against the doorjamb, sipping from a mug of coffee. "And he's cute. Very cute."

Chapter 14

Sam's standing on my front porch, fidgeting with an aluminum scooter. As soon as he sees me, he grins widely—and then his smile folds inward like one of those flowers that close when you touch it.

"I'm sorry to barge in like this," he says, as if he's not sure how I'll react to his presence. And how could he? Even I don't know how I'll respond these days.

Behind him, a Pontiac Grand Am backs onto the street. The girl at the wheel honks twice and then drives off, leaving an impression of exhaust and curly black hair. A tuft pokes out the open window, fluttering in the wind as if to say "good-bye."

"Was that your ride?" I tug at my limp ponytail and attempt to smooth my sweatshirt, which looks even more worn in the glaring sunlight.

"Yes. I mean, no. That's my sister, Briony. She's a junior, and apparently, her need for the family car is way more pressing than mine. She couldn't wait two minutes for me to talk to you. No matter. I have another mode of transportation."

He holds up the aluminum scooter, and I burst out laughing.

"Seriously, Sam, I've never seen anyone past the sixth grade ride on one of those things."

"That's about how I look when I ride on it. Like a sixth-grader." He smiles again, clearly more comfortable, and holds up a hoodie. It's the one Liam lent me. "I must've grabbed the wrong sweatshirt last night."

"Thanks. But I could've gotten it from you at school."

"I thought your boyfriend might want it back?" His tone is casual, but I can tell he's asking more than the stated question.

"Boyfriend? Liam's not my boyfriend."

Everything I'm saying is true. Sam didn't ask if I felt a connection with Liam. Or if I ever thought about his winter-blue eyes. So there's no reason for the guilt snaking through my stomach. There's not.

Flustered, I sit on the two-seater swing, and he joins me.

"I wasn't sure." He pushes off the wooden porch slats with his foot, and his arm stretches along the back of the swing. Six inches from my neck. If I leaned against the seat, we'd be snuggling. "The hoodie smelled like fresh cologne, and you didn't have it on when you first came into the party."

"You saw me?"

"You'd be surprised what you can learn by paying attention." He gives the swing another push, and his fingers brush my shoulder. My breath catches. The touch is as light as the graze of a butterfly's wing, and yet, I can pinpoint exactly where his hand landed—and for how long.

"Take my sister, for example," he continues. "You see how she took off like that? She's definitely meeting some guy."

"How do you know?"

He shrugs. "Make-up. Hair. Most days she tosses it in a ponytail and lounges around the house in yoga pants. Did you see the shirt she was wearing? It's a guy, for sure. Weird thing is, she wouldn't tell me anything about him. So I've got to think he's older or into drugs or something."

"Does she usually tell you?"

"Yeah." The word drags out to four syllables. "I know it's not exactly cool, but Bri and I have always been close. Our family situation being what it is, I guess you could say we've always relied on each other. The whole us-against-the-world kind of thing."

I want to ask about his family situation. Everything in me is dying to know. But the pesky thing about conversations is that you're expected to reciprocate. If he spills about his family, then I'll have to dish about mine. And I'm not quite ready for that yet.

"The article's not going so hot," he says, as though reading my mind. "I've only got a week and a half before the story's due, and I'm having a hard time getting any of the key players to talk to me. Tommy Farrow and Mackenzie Myers stonewalled me at the party. Luckily, I'm meeting Mr. W. later. He's my last lead."

"Not quite," I say. "You're talking to me. I'm a key player."

His eyes widen. "This isn't for the paper. Everything you say to me is off the record, I swear."

The swing creaks back and forth. I want to believe him. I want him to be everything he seems to be. But out of all people, I should know appearances are deceiving. He doesn't seem like the type who would lie to me. But my mother didn't seem like the type who would sleep with a high school boy, either.

"That's another reason I'm here." He pushes his glasses up his nose. "We have the same goal. I need an angle for my article. You want to find out what happened to your mom. If we share information, we'd be better off. What do you think about working together?"

I blink. That's the last thing I expected him to say. "I . . . I'm not sure."

"We'd be good together. I'm good at research. I have access to resources at the *Lakewood Sun*. And you have inside knowledge nobody has."

It makes sense. If I wanted an ally, he's not a bad choice. He's smart and inquisitive. And I'd rather not do this alone. But if we keep digging into my mom's past, who knows what we'll find? The reasons for her actions might be as sordid as everyone thinks. How can I share that information with anyone, much less the boy who wants to expose her secrets to the world?

"I've spent the whole morning trying to figure out who posted your mom's photo on that site," he says. "The name listed is an entity called 'PX1990.' But that name led to shell company after shell company, and it was virtually impossible to follow the trail."

"It had to be someone who knew her back then," I say, drawn in despite my reservations. "How else would they have gotten her photo when she was seventeen?"

"Possibly. But this same corporation put up photos of a dozen girls." He pauses. "They had one thing in common: They were all teenagers."

I frown. "You think my mother was part of an underage pornography ring?"

"It looks like she was a victim, at least."

I dig my fingernails into my palms. So many secrets, so many questions. My tongue tingles with the need to tell Sam about the misdialed calls and the text messages. It would be nice to have a confidant for the first time since my mom died. Someone who is just as committed to finding the truth. But can I trust him?

While I'm pondering, my dad pulls into the driveway. He gets out of the car, lugging a half-empty gallon jug of water and a rubber window squeegee.

"That's my dad, coming from the cemetery again," I whisper to Sam. "He's obsessed with washing my mom's gravestone."

Sam jumps up as my father comes up the steps. "Mr. Brooks?" He sticks out his hand. "Good to meet you. I'm one of CeCe's friends, Sam Davidson."

My dad shakes Sam's hand and then stows the gallon jug on the corner of the porch. "Um. Nice meeting you." His voice lilts up, as if he's not used to being introduced to my friends. And he's not. That was more Mom's territory.

He glances at me. "Good morning, CeCe. Have you eat—"

"Bagel and cream cheese," I interrupt. "Glass of orange juice."

"Good, good." He bobs his head. "I'll leave you kids, then."

"How was Mom today?" I ask softly.

He closes his eyes, as if the very question pains him. "A bird had pooped on the headstone, right next to her picture. It was a good thing I was there to clean it."

He goes inside the house, and the air stutters out of my lungs. I shouldn't have asked about my mom. I never have before. But it's silly to pretend she doesn't exist when we can't so much as inhale without breathing her in.

I don't want to live like this anymore. I don't want to skulk around school, hoping nobody notices me, pretending the past will go away if we ignore it.

I want my life back. Not my old life—that would be impossible. But a new life cobbled together from the shards of who I used to be. Maybe the first step is to agree to work with Sam. To talk about the scandal directly and honestly.

"Why didn't you try to interview him?" I ask Sam. "This was your big chance, and you blew it."

"He's still grieving," he says, as if it's the most obvious thing in the world. "I want to write a kick-ass article, sure. I want to learn the truth about what happened to your mom. But I'm not going to deepen anyone's pain. I chose this career in order to help people, CeCe. Not kick them while they're down."

That decides it. There are no guarantees in life. No proof that will ensure you're making the right decision. Sometimes, you just have to hold your breath and jump. And hope you land on your feet unscathed.

"Okay. Let's do it. Let's work together."

"Great." He grins so big his eyes almost crinkle shut. "We can start with my appointment with Mr. Willoughby at the hotline. Maybe we'll find another lead there."

"About the hotline . . ." I knew this partnership would be a risk. I knew I'd have to take a leap of faith. But I didn't think it would happen so soon. "I suppose this is a good time to tell you I'm volunteering as a call counselor."

I hold my breath, bracing myself for his reaction.

His lips arch in a half-smile, and his forehead remains unwrinkled. He doesn't look shocked. He doesn't even look surprised. "Relax, CeCe. You're not telling me anything I don't already know."

Chapter 15

Time slows. The swing arcs from one side to the other. One week passes. A fly buzzes across the porch. A month. Sam holds my gaze, without fidgeting or blinking. An entire year.

"How did you know?" I whisper.

He drops his eyes and studies the patches of dirt on the wooden slats. "It's not like I was snooping or anything. I was interviewing Mr. Willoughby in his office, and the call counselor schedule was sitting right there on the coffee table. I scanned it before I even knew what I was looking at."

"That list is supposed to be confidential." I wipe my palms across my jeans. "If the identities of the counselors ever got out, it would destroy the illusion of anonymity, and the hotline would no longer be a safe place to talk."

That's only half of it. The anonymity also protects me from the Justin Blakes of the world cackling, "Is that call counselor or fuck counselor?" From being a source of amusement for the entire school.

"I'm not going to tell anyone, CeCe. It's irrelevant to the article, and like I said, I don't make a habit of hurting people just because I can."

Everything about his mouth, his eyes, his posture radiates sincerity, but what do I know? I spent my whole life never understanding fully what kind of woman my mother was.

What's more? If he knows I volunteer at the hotline, he

could've doctored the flyers. He could've sent me that text. As unlikely as it seems, Sam Davidson just became a suspect.

I might have just partnered with the boy who seeks to shoot me down.

"When is your appointment with Mr. Willoughby?" I ask, getting to my feet.

He checks his watch. "In half an hour. He promised to give me a tour of the hotline."

I stiffen. "The hotline doesn't give tours. Especially not to newspaper interns. The location is kept as confidential as the identities."

"He didn't want to at first, but I . . . uh, convinced him."

"Define 'convinced.' "

"I gave him a choice. He could either show me the premises, or I would release the names of the counselors." The color fans across his cheeks like a bad sunburn. "I wouldn't have, of course. I just wanted to see the hotline."

I shake my head. If he's willing to bribe a teacher, what else is he capable of? Would he resort to harassment to get a good story? "You'd do anything to get this scholarship, wouldn't you?"

"Nothing illegal. Nothing that compromises who I am or what I stand for. But other than that?" He stands from the swing and faces me. "I want this scholarship, CeCe. And I'm not going to let a few niceties get in my way."

I take a deep breath. I'm not sure what I think of his methods, but maybe that's my entire problem. Maybe I've been way too timid.

Mind your own business, the text said. Clearly, this is sound advice. If I had never volunteered at the hotline, my number wouldn't have appeared on the flyers. If I hadn't confronted Tommy, Justin might not have been so eager to tell everyone about my mom's photo. If I scrambled back into my shell, then surely I would be safe again.

And my dad would still be obsessed with washing my mom's grave. The town would still consider my mom a slut. I can't allow that, not when I'm beginning to suspect that there was more to her death. Much more.

This is my chance to prove it.

"Okay, partner," I say. "Let's go talk to Mr. Willoughby."

It takes twelve minutes to drive to the lake. Number of traffic lights? One. Words exchanged? Zero.

I've never been any good at small talk, and I really don't know what to say now.

So, Sam, I know you have the power to make my life even worse by blabbing to the school that I'm a call counselor. But no biggie. How do you like your classes? Have you started reading Lolita *for Senior English yet? Boy, that Humbert Humbert is something else, isn't he? Oh no, I wouldn't know about that kind of thing. Not at all.*

I sneak a glance at him, only to find he's looking at me. Is he wondering if I'm about to follow in my mother's footsteps? Or is he thinking about kissing me?

My cheeks burn, and I look back to the road before I get us into an accident. Of course he's not thinking about kissing me. He may have said something about it last night, but that was under the cover of a deep black sky, in the midst of a rowdy party, on the high of his confrontation with Justin. That was before we became partners. Before our relationship became . . . if not exactly business, then at least goal-oriented. We're spending time together in order to figure out what happened to my mother. I can't forget that.

I pull into a long, gravel driveway and park behind an orange vintage sports car with two racing stripes down the center.

Sam whistles. "Now that's what I call a nice ride."

I wrench my door open as Liam steps out of the sports car. I stumble on the tiny rocks. Great. I haven't seen him since I took off in search of Tommy Farrow last night. Not since my mom's topless photo got passed around like a bowl of queso fundido. I'm not naive enough to hope that he somehow missed seeing the photo.

Sure enough, Liam hurries to me, his stride long and fluid. "CeCe, are you okay? I didn't expect to see you until tomorrow, during your shift. I've been so worried since I heard what happened."

"You're not supposed to be here tomorrow," I mumble, staring at his chest. It's a very nice chest—any girl would be happy to look at it—and I wish that were why I'm checking him out. But really, it's because I'm afraid of what I'll see in his eyes. "It's my first shift alone, remember? I don't need a babysitter."

"I just wanted to check on you. I heard about that jerk harassing you." He pauses. "But you don't have to worry about him. He'll think twice about picking on girls after spending the night in jail."

My eyes fly to Liam's face. "What are you talking about? What happened?"

"Justin Blake may or may not have been picked up by the cops for a DUI last night. After an anonymous tip that may or may not have come from a certain hotline coordinator."

I gape. If any doubts to his character remained, they're now erased. Liam may look like he could've played football with Tommy Farrow, but he's not one of those guys. Maybe he never was, and it was my own insecurities that made me see him that way. "You did that? For me?"

"I'd do a lot more than that for you." He steps closer, those ice-blue eyes gleaming. I think of arctic waters and snow-covered mountains. And then Sam clears his throat.

Liam looks up, as if noticing him for the first time. "Who are you?" His tone is not quite hostile, but it's not friendly, either.

"Sam Davidson. I'm writing an article about the hotline, and I have an appointment with Mr. Willoughby. Nice car, by the way."

"Thanks. What do you drive?"

"Me?" Sam laughs. "I don't drive anything. Unless you count my trusty three-wheeled scooter."

"I don't."

We look at each other, and an awkward silence descends. I

hurry to my car and grab Liam's hoodie from the backseat. "Thanks for letting me borrow this last night," I say, handing it to him.

Sam's mouth drops. "Wait a minute—that was his?"

I push down the foolish urge to explain: *I already told you. He's not my boyfriend.* But I can hardly say that in front of Liam. He might get the wrong idea about what's going on between me and Sam.

Which is what, exactly? a voice inside me whispers.

The sun ducks behind the trees, casting us in long-fingered shadows. The remains of last night's bonfire drift by on the wind. We stand around like actors who've forgotten our lines. Can this get any more uncomfortable?

Finally, Sam gestures toward the top of the drive. "Should we go? I don't want to be late."

We trudge up the loose gravel, not speaking. The tension is so thick I can feel it pushing into my lungs and expanding, slowly but surely, until I'm taking short, quick sips of the air. Finally, we round the corner, and the log cabin comes into view. An old pickup is parked in front, the bed of the truck filled with boxes. Stacks upon stacks of boxes. Tattered cardboard cartons, see-through filing crates, pretty storage parcels.

My throat works, trying to swallow something that isn't there. Because I've seen those boxes before. Three days ago, they were stacked in the storage closet of the crisis hotline.

"Why are all those boxes in the truck?" I ask.

Liam slows his pace, so that he can match his steps to mine. "Mr. Willoughby thought it was time for a spring cleaning."

"But it's the fall."

"These boxes have been around since before we moved locations. He wants to go through them, and either file away the papers or toss them."

Sam lifts a lid, peering inside as if he might find a wild animal. "I can help."

I know what he's thinking. There's a potential gold mine inside. Fodder for his article and information about my mom. All we have to do is find it.

"Not on your life." Mr. Willoughby strides toward us, wearing a Green Lantern T-shirt. He has a box tucked snugly under his arm. A certain box wrapped with fruit-basket wallpaper. My mother's box.

My mouth goes dry.

"I agreed to a tour, Mr. Davidson," the teacher says. "I didn't give you license to snoop into the hotline's confidential documents."

Sam holds up his hands, and Mr. Willoughby stashes the box in the front cab of his truck. In another second, the door will close, and I may never see it again.

"Wait. That's my mother's box." I lunge forward, but Mr. Willoughby turns, blocking my access to the open truck door.

He pushes the box further into the cab. "Why do you say that?"

"The wallpaper. It's the same as our kitchen's. My mom used the leftover paper to wrap our storage boxes."

"Tabitha papered the kitchen walls herself?" His voice softens, as if I've given him a gift he didn't expect. I think, all of a sudden, about an arrangement of flowers from my mother's wake. All-white roses, lilies, and carnations clustered in a glass cube. The card was signed, "I will never forget you. ~W."

Guess whose job it was to write the thank-you cards? Me. And guess who nearly ripped her hair out trying to figure out who "W." was? Yep. Me again. It seemed like the entire town showed up at my mother's funeral. She was well-liked, sure, but I'll bet most people came not to pay their respects, but to catch a glimpse of Tabitha Brooks's poor widower and daughter. Hell, maybe even Mr. Willoughby and Liam were there.

Could the glass cube arrangement have come from Mr. Willoughby? If so, why didn't he sign his name?

"She wallpapered our living room and bedrooms, too," I say. "In fact, she redecorated my room every few years, because she said a girl's room should reflect her mental state."

"She would say something like that." The sun reappears, highlighting the deep crevices around his eyes. "Your mother was one of my students, you know. When I started teaching twenty-odd years ago. And when she came back as staff, we reconnected."

I stiffen. His tone is too hazy, too emotional for the reminiscence of a former student or colleague. Did they have another connection?

Whatever their relationship, he doesn't open the truck door. And the box stays out of my reach. "If I find anything that belonged to Tabitha, I'll pass it on, okay?"

"But—" I sputter. "Can't I look through it?"

"These boxes are the property of the hotline." His tone shifts from hazy to authoritative. "The contents belong to the organization. As the executive director, I don't have to release them to anybody, much less a volunteer call counselor."

"On the contrary," Sam interjects, "if that box belonged to Tabitha Brooks, I would think the contents should revert to CeCe."

"We have no proof of that. Just Cecilia's assertion that she has the same wallpaper at home. It's a common pattern. Anyone could've picked it up at the hardware store."

Mr. Willoughby takes the keys out of his pocket and gets into the car. I rack my brain for something to say that will change his mind. But he reverses the truck a few feet on the gravel, and it's clear he's not in the mood to listen.

"Liam, would you give Mr. Davidson a tour?" he says through the open window. "Make it quick and make sure he doesn't touch anything." He nods at us. "See you kids at school."

Before we can respond, he continues reversing and drives away.

With my mother's box next to him.

Chapter 16

The next day is Sunday and my first shift alone. I tried the basement door when I first arrived, but surprise, surprise, it was locked. Kinda hard to snoop when I have no access.

The tour provided frustratingly little information. I kept my eyes peeled for a keyhole that would fit my silver key, especially in the basement office. But true to Mr. Willoughby's orders, Liam kicked us out of the hotline five minutes after the tour began. The only thing I learned was he uses vanilla-scented air fresheners in the closets.

I sign in to the computer to log my latest call. As I type, my scalp tingles, and a cool, invisible breeze blows against my neck, under my ponytail. Someone's watching me. I can feel it. If not the computer, then the abstract art on the walls or the floor-standing lamps with their too-realistic limbs.

Cre-eak.

I bang my knees on the underside of the desk. Was that a footstep, or is the cabin just settling?

Stop it! Buildings shift. That's what they do. I sit down and try to relax. Just this past Wednesday, I couldn't wait to have the place to myself. But now my mom's box is gone, and there's nothing to search. I long for Liam's company. He's friendly, warm. And, you know, alive. That counts for a lot right about now.

I could start sifting through my mom's call records, but there are so many of them, I don't even know where to start. It would be like looking for a needle in a haystack—where the needle could be any shape and may or may not even exist.

Instead, I flip to the back of my spiral notebook and begin to sketch the places I visited yesterday, after our tour of the hotline. Maybe if I keep my hands busy, my skin won't feel like it's about to slough off and crawl away.

The safety deposit boxes at our local bank. The lockers at the YMCA. I struck out at both places. Where else would a key belong? Some cabinets in my mom's old classroom? I can check with the school secretary tomorrow. Where else?

I stare at the exposed wooden beams in the ceiling. Maybe Tommy Farrow has some ideas. If he was close with my mother, maybe she told him about a secret cabinet or locker. It's worth a try.

Impulsively, I look up his phone number in our online school directory, which includes alumni information, and dial it. He answers on the second ring.

"Tommy, this is CeCe Brooks—"

Click. Dial tone.

I can't believe it. That's *my* move.

I'm still trying to make sense of the long, monotonous beep when the phone rings. Not my cell this time, but the crisis line. I snarl at the black box, showing my teeth, and then remember I'm on duty.

"Hello, Crisis hotline."

"Bea?" a girl's voice says incredulously. "Is that really you? I thought you'd left."

"No, it's not Bea." The prickles on my neck are back full force. Not because someone's watching me. But because Bea used to be my mother's nickname.

As the story goes, when I was six months old, we were having lunch outside when a bee landed on my arm. Without a second thought, my mother reached out and pinched the bee between her bare fingers, squeezing it to death. When her lunchtime companions gaped, my mother explained calmly, "It was about to sting my baby."

Coincidence. It has to be.

"This is Annie," I tell the caller. Each counselor picks a nickname to use with callers, to preserve our anonymity. Mine is in honor of Gram's favorite poker player, Annie Duke.

"Oh. Sorry about that." Disappointment spreads through her voice like a grapevine. "I haven't talked to Bea for a while now, and you sound just like her."

My stomach tightens, and I wind the old-fashioned phone cord around my finger. No, not a coincidence. The caller has to be talking about my mother. After I hang up, I can check the pseudonym chart to confirm.

"What would you like to talk about today?" I curl my fingers to keep from reaching for the resource binder. My first duty is to the caller. Freaking out over personal issues has to wait for my own time.

"It's too much to explain in one phone call," she says. "I was hoping to talk to Bea. She helped me end my last relationship, see. Being with him . . . changed me. The only person who understood was Bea. My life was one big secret, and she knew all about secrets. But then she disappeared. I really want to talk to her again."

"She's not here anymore." My heart pounds. Secrets. This counselor named Bea knew all about secrets. "Like you said, she hasn't been here for a long time."

"I know that. But I call the hotline every once in a while, hoping I'm wrong. Stupid, isn't it?"

"No. That doesn't sound stupid at all." I swore I wouldn't put myself out there. Whatever happened, I promised I wouldn't let anyone infiltrate my shields. But she sounds so lost, so much like me, I can't help myself. "If there were a number I could call to get her back, I'd dial it, too. Ten times a day."

She laughs, but it's not so much amused as it is sad. "Thanks for saying that. What was your name again?"

"Annie."

"Maybe I'll call back and talk to you, Annie. Would that be okay?"

"Sure. What's your name?"

She pauses. "Bea used to call me Lil. I thought that was

lovely. A bee and a flower. Like we were meant to have a connection."

The call ends, and I leap for the resource binder. Near the beginning, there's a table of counselors and their nicknames.

The breath rattling in my lungs, I run my finger down the list. Sure enough, there's an entry for "Bea." And the corresponding counselor is none other than Tabitha Brooks.

The blood sings in my ears, so loud I can't hear the whir of the computer, much less any footsteps, real or imagined. Lil referred to my mother's secrets. Maybe she knew something. Maybe my mother confided in her. This is the break I've been looking for. A way to sort out the irrelevant entries. To pinpoint a particular bale of hay where the needle might be hiding. And maybe—oh please, oh please, oh please—a message for me.

I log in as my mother. When prompted for a password, I put in my birthday—the same password my mom used for everything. Thousands of records pop up, and I add the keyword of "Lil." Just as I thought, the field narrows to nine manageable entries.

I open the entry with the earliest date. My mom's tone is clinical, relaying the facts in short, declarative sentences. Yet, as I sink into her words, I can almost feel her presence beside me.

Lil was involved with an older man. Although the relationship started innocently enough, he soon talked her into posing for explicit photos. Pretty soon, that's all she was doing. Taking off her clothes and contorting her body into acrobatic poses to please the camera—and her so-called boyfriend. She was fourteen years old.

The tingles along my scalp sharpen. Sure, the report itself is disturbing, and I'm reading the words of a dead woman. But it's more than that. There's something disconcerting about this entry, something that strikes me as not quite right.

And then I get to the final sentence, and the prickles turn into a thousand needles stabbing my skull. I reread the final few paragraphs:

He calls her his darling. "If you love me," he says, "if you are who I think you are, you won't waste time reading this situation. You will do as I say."

Lil couldn't remember the rest of his words. Something, something, she said. But it doesn't matter. The message is clear.

Oh dear god, it's happened again. Only this time, it's not to me.

Chapter 17

The air turns solid, and no matter how much I gasp and pant, I can't draw a proper breath. I want to run and scream. I want to shout to the world that they have it all wrong. My mother wasn't a slut. She was a victim. She was wronged.

But I still don't have any proof. I still don't have a clear picture of what happened. So I do the only thing I can do: I hit the "print" button.

The call entry is not directed at me. I don't even know what the message means. But dammit, these are my mother's words, and I won't take them for granted, ever again.

I tuck the printout into the front pocket of my backpack, but snippets of the entry continue to circle my brain.

Dear god, it's happened again. Again. *Again.*

What's happened? I'm guessing it has something to do with Lil's explicit photographs and her own. But was my mother involved with an older man, too? Was she also coerced into posing for explicit photos?

At the end of my shift, I gather up my car keys, iced tea, and extra sweatshirt and sling my backpack over my shoulders. I'm just about to leave when Liam comes into the room.

"Oh, hi." My voice is stiff. I don't mean it to be, but I can't help it. Yesterday, he treated me like he didn't know me. Like we never had a connection. "What are you doing here?"

"Oh, come on, CeCe. Don't be mad." He shoves his hands in his jeans pockets, as sheepish as a kid caught sneaking TV past his bedtime. "I'm sorry about yesterday. I shouldn't have been so . . . abrupt."

I raise my eyebrows. "Abrupt? You couldn't have gotten rid of us fast enough. It's like we were these annoying little gnats disrupting your day."

"Not *you*. Him. I don't like that guy. Asking all these questions, trying to peer into drawers. He was just so nosy."

"That's his job! Sam's an intern for the *Lakewood Sun,* and he's writing an article about the hotline."

"Well, this is my job." Liam squares his shoulders. Not for the first time, I notice how his muscles stretch out the thermal fabric of his shirt. "I have a duty to protect the privacy of my counselors, and I'm not going to let some bozo come in here and jeopardize it."

I soften. "I appreciate that. Truly. But that's not Sam's intention, I promise." Even as I say the words, however, I wonder. Sam threatened to broadcast the call counselor list in order to get a tour of the hotline. What else would he be willing to do to get his story?

"At any rate, I'm sorry." Liam takes a step closer to me, and the air between us comes alive. Kind of like when I thought somebody was watching me, but different. Better. "I have something for you that I hope will make up for yesterday. A present, you could say."

Before I can respond, the door squeaks, and a junior boy named Stanley walks into the cabin. He's got the school record for the fastest one-hundred-meter dash, and he's the call counselor for the next shift.

Liam and I say "hello" and "good-bye" to Stan, and then we amble out of the cabin. Outside, the sky shines blue and clear, and a slight breeze keeps the temperature from being too hot. In the distance, I hear the faint song of geese honking. The perfect fall afternoon—bright, sunny, beautiful.

Once upon a time, I believed that nothing could go wrong when the sun kissed your skin just so and the leaves seemed to laugh as they fell from the trees. Now I know better. My mother died on a day just like this one. So instead of tilting up my face to catch the rays, I scan the sky for rain clouds. I've experienced how quickly the weather can change. How absolutely your world can turn inside out.

"How about a drive out to East Rock?" Liam asks as we approach his orange car. "I could show you my favorite spot to sit and think."

"So long as I get my present," I say, smiling because both the day and Liam deserve it. It's neither of their faults what shadows lurk in my past.

We drive east out of the town limits, heading toward the hill where families like to go to barbecue and hike. I sneak looks at him, picking up on details I missed when we first met. Like the deliberate, thoughtful way he moves. Or the way his lips quirk, as though he's always laughing. Or the chain hanging around his neck, with a pendant that displays an ancient-looking symbol with wavy swirls and dots. All of these things suggest he's way more than the popular jock I'd initially dismissed.

Eventually, we pull into a clearing at the foot of the hill, a good distance from the picnic tables and well-populated trails my mom, dad, and I used to frequent not even a year ago. Back when we were still a family.

"Come on." Liam turns off the ignition. "It's a short hike from here, but the view is worth it."

He takes a package wrapped in brown paper out of his backpack and sticks it in the pocket of his hoodie, the same one I was wearing the other night. My present, I assume. It's about the size of a small stuffed animal. All of a sudden, curiosity hums through me.

"Can't you give it to me now?" I eye the bulge in his hoodie.

"I could." He walks to my side of the car and opens the door. "But I think I'm going to make you wait."

I stick my lower lip out. "That's mean."

"Actually, it's selfish." He holds out his hand and helps me out of the car. "I want to remember your face when you open it. And I want the backdrop to be as beautiful as you are."

I flush. A line. It has to be. Someone as good-looking as Liam probably has dozens of lines stashed in the pockets of his well-worn jeans. Yet, when he looks at me like that, I believe he means every single word.

We enter a thicket of trees, where there is a barely visible trail—a path that was created by the tread of feet rather than a machine, with the worst of the bramble shoved to the side. Liam goes first, so that he can hold back low-hanging branches while I pass. I'm wearing torn jeans and dirty sneakers, an old sweatshirt and a loose ponytail, but I feel cherished. Special. I haven't felt this way since I was folded in my mom's arms.

We slowly make our way up, up, up. And then the man-made trail opens into a creek next to the hillside. A thin but constant stream of water runs down the rock wall.

My mouth falls open. "Is that a waterfall?"

"Yep." Liam beams. "It might be the world's smallest waterfall, but it's the only one I know of in all of Lakewood. Sometimes it's a trickle, and sometimes it's a stream, but it's always here. What do you think?"

"It's perfect," I say. Just like the sun peeking through a gap in the leaves. Just like—I'm beginning to suspect—the boy in front of me.

And then he takes the package out of his hoodie and hands it to me, and I forget everything else.

Carefully, so I don't rip the brown paper, I unwrap the present. It's a snow globe. Three figurines are inside. The mom and grandma are drinking hot cocoa with their arms linked, while the little girl builds a snowman.

My eyes widen, and it's like someone turned up the volume on my heartbeat. I feel and hear it everywhere—in my ears, at my throat, on my chest. I gave this snow globe to my mother when I was eight years old. On the anniversary of my grandma's death, I caught her sobbing in her bedroom after she thought I was asleep. The next day, I broke open my cupcake bank and asked my dad to take me to the corner store, where I bought the snow globe.

"I don't want you to be sad anymore," I'd said to my mom when I gave her the globe. "I know you miss your mom, but I want you to know she's still here with you, the way you're with me. You see." I'd pointed to the mom and grandma under the snow. "You'll always be together, no matter what."

I haven't seen—nor thought about—this globe in years. If pressed, I would've guessed it was somewhere in the back of my mom's old closet.

"Where . . . where did you get this?" I ask Liam, my heart tight, my mouth dry. All the moisture must have fled to build up in a wet, hot pressure behind my eyes.

"It was in your mother's box," he says slowly. "The one wrapped in the wallpaper. After our tour yesterday, I went to Mr. Willoughby's house to help him sort through the boxes, and I saw this. Your mom used to keep it on her desk at the hotline, so I knew it was important to her. I stuffed it in my bag when Mr. W. wasn't looking."

I hug the globe to my chest and blink, blink, blink. There's so much heat inside me, so much condensation that's about to burst into a storm. If only my eight-year-old words were true. If only this globe meant that my mother were with me still.

"Was there anything else in the box?" I manage to say.

"Just a bunch of papers. Hotline documents you wouldn't care about." He twists his hands together, as if suddenly unsure. "Was this the right thing to do?"

"Yes. A thousand times yes." The globe digs into my chest, cold and hard. And yet, I don't let go. I don't ever want to let go again. "This is the best thing you could've done for me. Thank you."

He stares at the tiny waterfall. The sun hits the water just right, and all of sudden, it looks like rays of diamonds are cascading down the rocks. "It belongs with you, not in some moldy old box. Your love for your mother is evident. Even I can see that, and I never even had a mom." There's a harshness in his voice that might be pain or sorrow. Maybe both.

I'm not sure what to say. Not sure what to do. So I put my hand on his arm, wanting him to feel a fraction of the comfort that his present gave to me.

He looks at my hand for a long moment. "Clearly, I had a biological mother. But she only stayed long enough to give birth to me before taking off. She never wanted a baby, but my dad did. He wanted someone to whom he could pass his life's lessons, a son who wouldn't make the same mistakes he did." He squeezes his eyes shut. "Of course, that meant I was never good enough for him. He died considering me to be a disappointment."

"Oh, Liam." I tighten my grip on his arm. "No matter what he may have thought, you're not a disappointment. Not to me, and not to all the people you help at the hotline." I lick my lips. "You're . . . you're a hero. For giving me back this snow globe. For being a good friend."

"I'm trying," he says softly. "I'm trying, in the aftermath of losing my dad, to find myself. But sometimes, the grief is just so large it eats away at everything else. And I can barely remember my name, much less figure out who I'm supposed to be."

"Yes," I say, sliding my hand down his arm until our fingers intertwine. "I know exactly what you mean."

And we stand like that, holding hands, watching the droplets sparkle in the world's smallest waterfall, until the sun drops below the trees.

Chapter 18

The next morning, I hunch in a toilet stall, drawing on a piece of paper as if my life depended on it. I thought I could do this. I thought, after everything I've been through, after spending a magical afternoon with Liam by the waterfall, I'd have the strength to face the student body this Monday morning.

Guess not. I spent five minutes giving myself a pep talk in the parking lot. I even came in the school's back doors to minimize contact with the other students. Yet, I beelined for the restroom the moment I crossed the threshold.

The snow globe is at the bottom of my backpack. I wish it could be enough to give me the confidence to walk into school with my head held high. But the printout of my mom's words is also tucked in the front pouch. *Oh dear god, it's happened again.*

Damn right it's happening again. Of course, *this* wasn't what she was talking about. Walking into school for the first time after a major scandal. A moment of absolute silence when all eyes descend on you. And then, the whisper-scurry-whisper of the gossip mill cranking its sails. But the feeling underlying her words matches mine: stark terror.

The final bell rings. I'm officially late. My hand relaxes on the pencil, and I stash the drawing in my backpack. At least now, there won't be anyone in the halls to look at me.

I move to the sink, wetting a paper towel and pressing it to my forehead. Rivulets of water slide down my face and drip onto my black tank top. I check the damage in the mirror. Not quite as ugly as streams of black mascara, but close.

The door bangs open, and Mackenzie Myers bursts inside, sparkling like the waterfall I saw yesterday. Jewelry winks from every part of her body—her fingers, wrists, ears, and neck. If I lift her shirt, I'll probably find a belly ring.

"Oh." Her mouth forms a cartoon circle. "You saw, huh?"

I dry my face with a paper towel. "Saw what?"

"Nothing." For the first time since kindergarten, when she insisted on playing Goldilocks and forgot her lines, Mackenzie looks like she wants to flee. Instead, she crosses to the mirror and reapplies her lipstick. "I hear you're trying to get in touch with Tommy."

I flush. Did she talk to him? Or overhear Alisara's amateur sleuthing? Late last night, after I shook the snow globe for the hundredth time and relived my afternoon with Liam for the thousandth, I'd asked Alisara to find out what party he's attending next.

"Yeah," I say, trying to sound nonchalant. "He won't take my calls. Any other ideas?"

Her hand slips, and the lipstick paints a bloody red line across her cheek. "Like I'd tell you. Why do you want to talk to him?"

"None of your business."

"Like hell. If you ask him about your mom, if you start digging into the past, sooner or later, it's going to come out—"

She stops and scrubs at the smear on her cheek.

"What's going to come out, Mackenzie?"

She shakes her head. "Bottom line, you don't need to talk to him. Leave the past alone."

I keep patting my face, although it's long since dried. Mind your own business. Leave the past alone. Different words. Same message. Could Mackenzie be my mysterious texter? "What's my phone number?"

"What?" She shuffles back a couple steps. "Who cares?"

"I'm serious." I run my eyes over her outfit, trying to figure out where she might hide a cell in those skin-tight pants. "Let me see your phone."

"Um, no, weirdo. I was going to help you take down the posters because they're blocking our flyers for the literacy auction. But not if you're going to act like a freak show."

"Posters? What posters?"

My heart taps in my chest, a steady drumbeat that begins to crescendo. Does she mean more hotline flyers doctored with my phone number? She couldn't mean another topless photo of my mom . . . could she?

"I guess you really haven't seen them. Lucky me, I get to be the first to witness your reaction." She shoves her beauty tools into a makeup bag and crosses to the door. "Coming?"

Taking a deep breath, I follow her out. How bad can it be? I mean, the entire school's already gossiping about my mom. What's one more photo?

We walk down the hallway, and I catch a glimpse of a red-faced, beefy guy rounding the corner. My neck and shoulders tighten, to the point where they might lock up. There's no way that's Justin Blake. He graduated. He has no business here anymore. It's probably just some kid who looks like him. I'm safe here.

And yet, no matter how many times I repeat those lines to myself, I know it's not true. Justin Blake is here, in my high school once again.

I shiver and try to summon the relaxation techniques I learned from the yoga classes to which my mom used to drag me. But who am I kidding? Those techniques have never been a match for Justin.

We reach the corridor in front of the art room, a lightly trafficked wing of the school.

My heart stops. Hundreds of copies of my mom's bare breasts are plastered on every available surface, from the tiled walls to the bulletin boards. A few are even fluttering from the ceiling.

A janitor stands on a stepladder, taking down the flyers. A large pile already lies on the floor next to the ladder.

"There's a copy stuffed into every locker, too," Mackenzie says helpfully.

I ignore her. Because the photos aren't an exact reproduction of the image Justin was waving Friday night. Even from a distance, I can tell something's different.

I rip a poster off the nearest wall. An anchor lodges at the pit of my stomach, dragging it lower, lower, and even lower still. There's no doubt it's the same picture. But that's not my mother's head on top of the body.

It's mine.

Chapter 19

Somewhere in the building, a door must have opened. The posters on the floor fly into the air, whirling as if caught in a tornado. The janitor leaps off the stepladder and grabs the papers.

Caught in a tornado. That's exactly how I feel—swept up, turned upside down, holding on for dear life. Or what's left of it, anyway.

"That's not me," I say to Mackenzie, my voice as hollow as the rest of me. The janitor looks at us, and then, as if recognizing my face, hurriedly climbs the ladder. "I mean, that's my yearbook picture, but that's not my body."

I step forward, because that's what you're supposed to do when you make a strong declaration. But my knees give out, and I stumble.

My archenemy catches me, the metal of her rings biting into my elbows. "I know. It's obvious someone Photoshopped your head onto the original image. Just be glad everyone's been staring at your mom's picture all weekend. I don't think anybody thinks it's actually you."

"Photoshop," I whisper, my mind following the rest of me into the tornado.

"Exactly." She lets go of me. "Wasn't that what the new guy was ranting about at the bonfire? Putting your mom's face on some other body? Maybe he did it."

"No." Not Sam. We're partners now. On the same team. There's no way he could've done this to me. "It was probably

Justin. He's pissed at me for embarrassing him at the bonfire. This is his revenge."

"Impossible. Justin's not even in town. He's at a retreat with the wrestling team this week, in preparation for the collegiate season."

I stare at her. "But I saw him. Just now, going around the corner."

She shakes her head and grins slyly. "No way. I saw him off myself, with an extra kiss for luck."

So Mackenzie and Justin are a couple now? More likely, given Mackenzie's continued obsession with Tommy, they're just hooking up. I suppose it doesn't surprise me. They're only my two favorite people in the world.

"He could've had help," I say, wondering if I'm going crazy. If I'm seeing things—and people—that aren't there. "Maybe it was you."

"Now you're really grasping." She shoves a poster into my hands. "Everyone knows I can barely turn on a computer. I wouldn't have any idea how to do this."

I crumble up the paper, even though I'll never be able to destroy them all.

"You just don't want it to be Sam," she says accusingly. "You're crushing on High-Water Freak, and you can't bear the thought that it's probably him."

"It's not Sam."

She continues as if I haven't spoken. "Who could be out to get you?"

Justin Blake. It has to be. He's the only enemy I have. But even as I think the words, I know it's not true. I have another enemy now: my mysterious texter. *Mind your own business,* he or she said. *Or you're next.*

Could Justin be sending me these text messages? But his harassment was always personal and always about me. Why should he care if I'm digging into the past?

Unless he knows something I don't. Something Tommy was desperate to tell me. Something I deserved to know.

"Be careful who you fall in love with, CeCe." Mackenzie's

voice softens in a way I've never heard. "I fell in love with Tommy, and look what happened to me."

She yanks down a poster with so much force the paper tears in half. The janitor shoots her a nervous look and slides his stepladder down the hall. She grabs another one and repeats the process. Rip, rip, rip. Slash, slash, slash. *That's me,* I want to remind her. *Not Tommy.*

I move next to her, with the intention of helping. But the face from my yearbook picture looms over me. My smile is forced, my eyes shuttered. I had gone straight to the photo session from gym class, where Justin had wrapped a rope around his waist, waggling the extra length at me. "Come and get it, CeCe," he whispered across the aisle. "You know you want me."

And now, that same face is sitting on top of a naked body. My mother's very voluptuous, very provocative body.

"Mackenzie, I . . ." I clap a hand over my mouth, not sure which one's coming first, the tears or the vomit. Not sure which I'd prefer.

"Um, ew," she says. "Get out of here before you puke on my Manolo Blahnik sandals. These are real snakeskin, you know."

She doesn't have to tell me twice. I race back to the restrooms. Only this time, I don't know when I'll be brave enough to come out again.

The first text comes while my head is hanging over the toilet.

I ignore the ping at first. Not hard when you're staring at the concave interior of a toilet bowl. But the phone pings again, insistently, so I rock back onto the linoleum and swipe the sweaty hair off my forehead.

Maybe it's a concerned message from Alisara. Or an annoyed "get your butt out here and help me" missive from Mackenzie. Or words of support from Sam or Liam. I'd be happy to hear from either right now.

But deep down in the pit of my stomach, I know it's none of those things. Because I haven't heard from my mysterious texter since Friday night, and he'll want to know what I think of his latest masterpiece. Or maybe it's a she. An adult or a kid. It could be anybody, really. I tried every "reverse phone lookup" search on the Internet, and the most information I could find was that the number was linked to a disposable cell phone.

Taking a deep breath, I bring the screen to my nose and read:

How did you like the photo?

Beautiful, asshole. A real piece of art. I'm thinking of including it in my portfolio for Parsons, if I ever apply.

But he's not finished.

This is what happens when you stick your nose into other people's business.

The walls feel too tight. The stall's open at the top and bottom, but I can't draw enough air. I lurch to my feet, and the toilets, sinks, and mirrors bleed together.

At that moment, the intercom in the hallway blares: "Cecilia Brooks, if you are in this building, please report to the main office at once. I repeat, Cecilia Brooks, report to the main office."

I press my hands to my temples. I can't stay here, anyway. I came for privacy, but I'm not alone anymore. My mysterious texter has found me.

I make my way to the main office. The halls are empty. Not even a glimpse of the janitor or the flyers.

When I enter the office, Ms. Hughes, our school secretary, is typing on a keyboard with the tips of her French manicure. "Cecilia!" Her nails slip into the crevices between the keys. "Sweetheart, are you okay? Bob's finally gotten all the posters down. There's a bunch of sticky tape all over the place, but it's clear now." She clucks her tongue. "My word, I've worked at this school ten years, and I never would've thought I'd see child pornography plastering our hallways. Principal Winters is in a meeting, but he wants you to wait right here until we can call the police and get this straightened out."

My pulse jumps. No. Not the police. They didn't help my mother, and they aren't going to help me. On top of everything else, I don't think I can handle their relentless interrogation and condescension today. I just want to be left alone. Is that too much to ask? I just want to curl into a ball and be miserable all by myself.

"You don't have to call the police," I manage to say. That's it. Don't sound devastated or destroyed. This kind of thing happens all the time. At least, to people like me. "The picture's fake. You see, they just put my head on another photo. So it's not child porn. It's just a prank. Nothing more."

She frowns. "Are you sure?"

I sigh. "Ms. Hughes, I think I would know if I posed for that photo. Besides, all you have to do is look at the neck. The lines don't match up."

She slips on a pair of glasses and squints at a copy she just happens to have at her desk. Oh dear lord. These posters are everywhere. The linoleum tile might as well open up and swallow me now.

"I can see what you mean," she says finally. "I guess we don't need to get the police involved. At least not yet."

Oh, thank goodness—

"But Principal Winters will still want to see you after school," she continues, before the relief can fully settle on my shoulders. "To discuss what you know about the posters."

"I don't know *anything*—"

She blinks. "You're not under investigation, hon. But whoever did this has violated our student code of conduct, and we need to get to the bottom of it so we can take the proper disciplinary measures."

Now? You're going to take action now? What about last year, when Tommy Farrow's pals whispered obscenities under their breath every time I walked past? Why didn't you do anything then?

I take a deep breath and release it slowly. Clearly, they couldn't address an issue they didn't know about—and I never made a single report. I'm not sure why. There are plenty of people at this school—my mom's former colleagues, my old teachers—who would leap to my defense. But hearing the whispered innuendos made me feel dirty enough. The thought of repeating the words out loud, of having them written down in my file, is more than I can bear.

"You poor dear. What a morning." She pats her white-blond

hair, wrapped in its usual bun, and offers me a purple lollipop. "Here. I know you seniors think you're too sophisticated for a sweet treat, but I say you could always use a pick-me-up, no matter how old you are."

"No thanks, Ms. Hughes. My stomach's a little unsettled." I can't imagine why.

She fusses over me for a few more minutes and then signs my tardy slip with a flower-tipped pen. Forcing a smile on my face, I thank her. I haven't gone five steps from the main office when my phone pings again.

You can stop this any time. Get back in your shell. Stop volunteering at the hotline. Stop digging into the past.

And forget about my mom's secrets? Pretend I never took that phone call from Lil? Not a chance.

I wander back to the art room corridor. As Ms. Hughes warned, tape litters the walls, and strips of paper gather in the corners, casualties from Mackenzie's assault. A freshman girl takes one look at me and tucks her chin deep into her textbooks, as if nudity were a disease.

I lift my phone and text back:

What are you hiding?

Long minutes pass. I pinch the bridge of my nose. Did I make matters worse? Maybe I shouldn't have responded. Maybe harassers are like terrorists, and you're never supposed to engage them. Maybe all I've done is provoke him. It's got to be a "him," right? Probably Justin Blake. But then, Mackenzie's face drifts into my vision, and I'm not so sure. . . .

And then, my phone pings again.

Better yet, what is your new friend hiding? Sam Davidson rides off on the back of a motorcycle with an older woman every day. Did you know that?

And then, an instant later: *I'm surprised at you, Cecilia, associating with this boy. What will people think?*

Every hair on my arms stands up. I hadn't heard anything about Sam's older woman, but this isn't some random harasser. Is Justin Blake perceptive enough to see my deepest fear? *What will people think?*

I wrap my arms around myself and shiver. My classmates already think the worst. My reputation has hit rock bottom. Can it sink any lower?

Apparently.

When I walk into my next-period classroom, every head swivels to stare at me. No, not *me*. Not my eyes, not my face. Twenty-two pairs of eyes bore into my chest.

Even Mr. Swift, the photography instructor and my study hall teacher, gives me a sympathetic look before holding out his hand for my tardy pass.

I pass it over, the bile rising up my throat. So even my teachers have seen—or at least heard about—the poster.

I hunch my shoulders and hurry to my seat, breathing deeply through my mouth. The ceiling fan whirls overhead, but it does nothing to cool my flushed neck, cheeks, and eyes. I've been disintegrating, little by little, and this might be the last puff of air that scatters my ashes to the winds.

Ping.

Think about it, Cecilia. I'm only trying to help.

Chapter 20

"Cecilia, I'm only trying to help," Principal Winters says, tapping his fingers together. "But I can't do that if you don't tell me everything you know."

I can't take my eyes from his hands. Blunt-cut nails. A faded circle of white where his wedding ring used to be. Fingers long, lean, and powerful, just like the rest of him. If you like the type.

I guess his ex-wife, our former school nurse, didn't.

Officially, she was let go because of budget cuts. Unofficially, the entire school knew she was sleeping around on her husband. My mom's affair may have been the biggest scandal to hit Lakewood High, but it certainly wasn't the first.

"I already told you." I shift in the hard chair. It matches the mahogany decor of the rest of the office, but I'm certain this piece of furniture's only here to make students squirm. "I have no idea who's behind the photos."

Oh, I have some idea. Clearly, my texter had something to do with it. But if I share that with Principal Winters, he'll make me stop volunteering at the hotline.

And I can't do that, not when I'm on the verge of getting answers to questions I didn't even know to ask until last week. Questions I should've had from the beginning—but didn't.

Principal Winters wrinkles his nose, as if the smell of leather is finally getting to him. The whole office reeks of it. I wouldn't be surprised if he had a special cologne made so he could bathe in the stuff.

Abruptly, he stands and strides to the bookcase. He faces the bound volumes—leather, of course—as though he were gazing out the window.

"I care about all my students," he says. "But I feel a special responsibility toward you, Cecilia. I remember when you used to come in during your mom's work hour after school. You were such a serious child, quiet, always with your nose in a book. Your mother said it didn't make sense to hire a babysitter for only an hour, but I could tell she just liked having you around. She could never walk by you without stroking your hair or squeezing your arm."

Hot, stinging liquid rises inside me, flooding my throat and pushing against my eyes. I blink and look down. See, this is another reason why I never reported the harassment. Because then I'd have to listen to a well-meaning authority figure reminisce about my mom.

"She was also totally absent-minded, did you know that?" I say. "One time, she came to school wearing one navy pump and one black pump. Another time, she burned the sleeve of her blouse because she was daydreaming and had to keep on her jacket all day."

These stories are supposed to cut Principal Winters down. To show him my mom wasn't some paragon to put on a pedestal. The circumstances of her death prove that. And yet, the memory of the iron-shaped mark on her white silk blouse makes me want to cry even more.

He studies me. I struggle to sit still, but the chair, dammit! It practically begs me to wiggle.

"I want you to know, you're not alone," he says. "Tabitha was very much a part of the family here at Lakewood High, and we look out for one another. When Tommy Farrow came forward with his accusation, I didn't automatically condemn your mother. Did you know that? She told me there was more to the story, and I believed her. We were about to start an investigation into Tommy's claims, but one day later, Tabitha was dead. Out of respect for your father, we felt there was no point in bringing the detail of her philandering to light.

"But don't think for a moment that we've forgotten you. I've had my eye on you these last few months, Cecilia. So even when you think you're alone, even when you think no one's watching, we are."

A shiver skates across my spine. I know he means his words to be comforting. But after the too-intimate messages from my mysterious texter? I don't like the idea of anybody watching me.

The books loom over me, the stink of leather threatening to suffocate me. "Can I go now?"

We look at each other. I could be staring into a mirror. His eyes are as raw and weary as my own. The eyes of someone who's lived through scandal.

"Yes, we're done here." He chews the inside of his cheek, as if debating whether to continue. "But please let me know if you learn anything regarding the posters. I give you my word we'll take care of you. Just like we took care of your mother."

I wade down the hallway as if I'm moving through a murky swamp. A group of girls with bulky kneepads dash into the gym, and a couple makes out by the lockers. At least, I think they're making out. I can't see the girl's upper body, which has disappeared inside the locker, but what else could they be doing, with their pelvises pressed together?

BAM!

I crash into someone, and my stuff goes flying. Notebooks, pens, my snow globe, and the contents of my lunch rain down on us like a violent hailstorm.

"Oh god, I'm sorry!" a girl wails. "I've been wanting to meet you, but my brother's going to kill me if he finds out it happened like this."

I press a hand against my forehead. When my vision clears, I see wild black hair, a cute, upturned nose, and a smattering of freckles. Sam's freckles.

"Briony?" I guess.

She grins, showing me nearly every one of her straight, white teeth. "Sam's told you about me?"

"A little."

"Well, he talks about you all the time. You'd think we didn't have girls at our old school or something."

I sink to my knees and pick up the snow globe. Thank god the glass hasn't cracked. I give it a shake and watch the flakes fall down on the grandmother, mother, and daughter once again.

I haven't seen Sam all day, since I missed first period. More importantly, I haven't seen him since my topless photos were plastered across the corridor. He's not going to judge me. At least, I don't think. But my texter's words drift through my mind, and I wonder how well I really know Sam.

"What does Sam say?" I stick the snow globe back into my backpack, where it will be safe. "That we're working together on his hotline article?"

"He mentioned that. But mostly, he talks about how he'd like to see your drawings. Apparently, you used to win a whole bunch of contests? He said he found mentions of them in back issues of the *Lakewood Sun,* but then, news of your artwork just . . . stopped."

The notebook slides from my fingers. Sam knows about my drawings? My artwork has disappeared from my public life so completely I doubt even Alisara remembers I used to spend all my spare time hunched over a piece of paper.

Before, I had a thick skin when it came to my art. I put my heart into every piece of work and flung it out there for the public to judge. *This is me,* my artwork screamed. *Make of it what you will.*

Ha. So earnest and idealistic, it makes me want to puke. That was before I knew what real judgment was like. Before I had to suffer through Justin Blake's innuendos every morning. Before photos of "my" naked breasts waved from the ceiling.

Briony collects the rest of my possessions. An apple from my lunch, which rolled under the water fountain. Some Post-it notes in a far-flung spot down the hall. And even my cell phone, which flew around the corner.

By the time she returns, I've arranged my face into a blank canvas. "Does Sam always research his friends so thoroughly?"

"No," she says, handing me the phone, apple, and Post-it notes. "Just the ones he likes."

"And, uh, what about motorcycles? Does he often ride off with friends on motorcycles?"

She gives me a mystified look. "Why do you ask?"

"No reason." I flush and thrust the apple at her. "Here. Do you want to eat this? It's only a little bit bruised."

"Sure. I missed lunch today." She takes a huge bite. "Oh, and if you're looking for my brother, he just left. You should be able to catch him if you hurry."

I thank her and walk away, although I have no intention of catching him. Unless "catching" is code for "stalking."

I burst out the front door and see Sam loping across the parking lot, a backpack slung over his shoulder. I count to ten and follow at a safe distance.

He's my partner, I remind myself. *We're a team.* I trusted him enough to tell him I'm volunteering at the hotline. Maybe I should trust him with this. And yet . . . if he's involved with an older woman? I need to know.

He weaves through the cars to the far side of the lot. Once, he glances over his shoulder. The sun glints off his glasses, and I drop onto the pavement behind a beat-up VW Bug, scraping my palms.

This is it. He saw me. How am I going to explain what I'm doing?

But seconds pass, and nobody comes. Cautiously, I peek over the hood of the Bug. The cream paint curls back in ribbons and flakes off where I brush against the car. From the next parking spot, Howie Dorment from physics class stares at me. Any other time, I would've fretted over what he must think. Now, I'm too busy keeping track of Sam as he disappears behind a tree.

I scoot out from behind the car. Sam reappears and shoves his hands into the pockets of his sweatshirt. He walks a block away from school. And then two blocks. Is he going to walk all the way home? Am I going to follow him that far?

Just as I'm about to abandon my tail, a motorcycle roars up. Bleached blond hair flows underneath the helmet, and the rider is clad entirely in black leather. I can't tell her age, but no student at Lakewood High dresses like that.

The adrenaline flees my body, and I duck behind a tree, my arms and shoulders drooping. So my texter was right. Deep down, I didn't really believe it. Never imagined Sam could be another Tommy Farrow. But the evidence is right here in front of me.

Sam picks up the second helmet, but instead of putting it on, he leans over and whispers something in the woman's ear. She says something back. He nods and looks directly at my tree. No, not the tree. At *me*.

And then he walks over to where I'm crouching. "CeCe? Why are you spying on me?"

Chapter 21

My brain shoots into overdrive. Why am I spying on him? Hmmm, good question.

"I'm not?" I say weakly.

Instead of responding, Sam tilts his head and examines my position on the ground, where I'm clearly hiding from someone.

The smell of fresh potting soil perfumes the air, and above us, a bird or some other creature rustles in the leaves. The woman on the motorcycle honks twice—short, light, and friendly—and then drives off.

"You know, CeCe," he says. "If there's something you're curious about, just ask."

"Okay, then." I get to my feet with as much dignity as possible. Which, considering the dirt and dried leaves covering my butt, probably isn't much. "Who was that woman?" I ask and then flush. Now he's going to think I'm really crushing on him. And maybe I am. But he doesn't have to know that.

"Principal Winters isn't keen to have motorcycles on school grounds," I blabber. "Because, you know, of the fatal accidents and all. And he asked me to tell him if I saw any around. That's why I want to know about the woman. I don't want you to get in trouble. Because we're partners and all."

Sweat gathers on my forehead. That's about the flimsiest excuse I've ever heard. There's no way he's going to fall for it.

Instead of calling me on the lie, however, he takes a step

closer, so that we're both shaded under the tree. "That was my mother."

My jaw drops. His mother? Oh god. His *mother*. So mysterious texter was kinda right—and also completely, totally off-base. "Oh wow. She, um, doesn't look like a mom."

"Neither did yours."

Touché. His mom looks like a biker chick, mine looked like a pinup model—so I guess we're even.

"Why is she picking you up two blocks from the school?" I ask.

"Oh, um . . ." He fiddles with the zipper of his hoodie. "You know how I let Bri have the car most days? Some afternoons, I go to the *Lakewood Sun* office, and that's a little far, even for my scooter. I don't have many friends I can bum a ride from. And I don't want to wear out my welcome with the ones I do have." He moves his shoulders. "My mom's more than happy to give me a ride, but I don't really want to advertise that in front of the whole school."

I stare. "But you don't care what other people think. I mean, you stood up to Mackenzie on your very first day, when she was harassing that poor girl with the flyers. You wear pants that are way too short . . ."

"I don't care very much what other people think," he corrects. "But when they look at you and laugh, it always hurts. No matter how thick your skin is." He rubs the back of his neck. A yellow leaf flutters by his ear, and for a moment, he looks just like a portrait. My fingers itch for my sketch pad, so I can record this moment and keep it forever.

"People don't laugh at you," I say. "They're intrigued. The rest of us are carbon copies of each another. Even Mackenzie Myers is a more expensive version of the same old thing."

"Not you," he says.

Maybe not anymore. But before my mom's scandal, I fit right in with the Raleighs of Lakewood High. I wore the same clothes, had the same pastimes. Only my mom's suicide made me different.

Up until this moment, I would've said being a carbon copy

was a good thing. You don't get made fun of when you're the same as everybody else. But now, with his dark eyes looking into mine, I'm not so sure. Is there a way to be different without being ridiculed?

We walk back to school, our pace slow and meandering. The late afternoon sun slants through the trees, decorating Sam's face with dappled light. The air feels crackly and crisp, and colorful leaves litter the sidewalk.

I suddenly feel bad—more than bad—for not trusting him. It's one thing to keep information from Principal Winters. But this is Sam. My partner and ally. No matter what he threatened to Mr. Willoughby, he hasn't spilled about me being a call counselor yet. And I have a feeling, deep down, that he won't.

Besides, what the posters today have shown me is that my mysterious texter is smart. He—or she—knows right where to strike to make me hurt most. If I'm going to even the playing field, I need Sam on my side.

I take a deep breath and tell Sam everything—about the doctored hotline flyers, the misdialed calls, and the text messages I received. I even tell him about Lil and the last sentence in my mom's call log, *Oh dear god, it's happened again.*

I don't have to mention the posters with my Photoshopped head. The way the rumor gale was blowing today, he'd have to be oblivious not to have heard. And newspaper intern Sam is anything but oblivious.

"Do you have a phone number for Lil?" Sam asks. "We need to talk to her again. Maybe your mom told her something."

I shake my head. "We don't trace a phone number unless we feel the caller is at immediate risk for suicide. We'll just have to wait and see if she calls back."

"You wait," he says. "I'll do my own digging."

I open my mouth to argue, but this is what I signed up for when I became his partner. He's supposed to dig. He's supposed to uncover the truth about my mom's death.

And that's what I want, too. It just feels weird to give him explicit permission to rifle through the pieces of my mom's life.

So I don't. "Your mother must think I'm a total freak, skulking around like that," I say instead, changing the subject.

"Actually, she'd like to invite you over for dinner tomorrow. She wants to meet you properly."

"Oh." I scuff my shoe against the fallen leaves. I've never met a boy's parents before. I mean, sure, I grew up with these kids. Most of the moms worked on the PTA with my mom, and a lot of the dads coached our soccer games. But I've never been invited for *dinner.* "Will your dad be there?"

He doesn't say anything for half a block, and I realize how little I know about him. I made the gut decision to trust him, but I don't know why his family moved to Lakewood. I don't even know if his parents are still together.

"No, he won't be joining us," Sam finally says when we arrive at the parking lot. "My parents are separated. He still drops in every once in a while, but for the most part, we're trying to keep our lives detached."

"I'm sorry—"

"Don't be." His voice is as sharp and cold as icicles. "My father's drunk most of the time and always mean. He's been beating up my mom since I was a little kid. And she's refused to call the cops for just as long."

A rock forms in my throat. "Oh."

He turns to me, his eyes glazed. "I told you once that I liked to work out. You didn't ask, but I know it seems strange. A guy like me shouldn't care about muscles. But I started lifting weights a couple years ago, when I was fifteen. I tried to stop my dad from going after my mom, but he tossed me aside like a paper bag. I swore right then and there that the next time he comes after my mom, I'll be ready."

"Is that how you got the bruise?" I lift my hand in the air next to his arm, where his bruise has faded. I want to touch his skin. My fingers ache with the wanting. But ever since he told me he wanted to kiss me at the bonfire, he hasn't made a single move. I don't know if the timing hasn't been right. I don't know if he was put off by Liam.

Maybe he's simply changed his mind.

"Yeah, that's how I got the bruise," he says, rubbing his bicep. "We've gotten into a few scuffles, but nothing major. I think he realizes I'm big enough now that neither of us would escape a full-out fight without major injuries. But one of these days, he'll be so drunk it won't matter."

I curl my fingers into a fist. "I don't want you to get hurt, Sam."

"So long as my mom and sister are safe. That's all I ask."

We arrive at my car. A few students linger in the parking lot, and I can't resist any longer. I bring my hand to cup his cheek, and he covers it with his own hand. The warmth spreads through me like the sun seeping into a stone.

"Bullies think they're all powerful, but they're not," he whispers. "They derive their power from others being weak. They count on us not standing up for ourselves. Not standing up for each other. But the second we fight back, they lose their power."

"Is that why you helped the girl with the striped tights?" I ask. "Why you want to be an investigative reporter? So you can stand up for the vulnerable?"

He steps closer, and the tips of his sneakers bump into mine. I never thought of canvas and synthetic material as good conductors. But the heat zips through me with the speed of an electric current. "I couldn't do anything for my mom for a long time. And I never want to feel that helpless again." He takes another step, and now my shoes are nestled in between his. "I don't want anyone else to feel like that, either. Least of all you."

I look up, and his glasses, his freckles, his mouth are looming above me. And they're getting nearer. And nearer.

My heart tries to punch a hole in my chest, and my breath gets stuck in my windpipe. This is it. The kiss I've been waiting for. I don't know if he actually dreamed about the kiss, but I certainly did.

I close my eyes and lift my lips . . .

And then a horn blares right next to me.

The Mustang pulls out of the parking space and speeds out

of the lot. The air whooshes out of me. I count at least five people in the parking lot. More than I thought. Closer than I thought. They're not looking at us, at least not anymore, but they could be.

I try to curve my lips into a smile. "There's a lot of people here." My voice is thick and cloudy, like honey that's crystallized in the bottle. "Come on. I'll take you to the *Lakewood Sun*."

He clasps my hand and pulls it to his chest. "I don't care about those other people."

"Yeah. But I do."

"Why, CeCe? Why does it matter?"

I wish I had an answer for him. But then, I wish a lot of things. I wish I could back him into the car and press my lips against his. I wish I could say to hell with everyone and what they think. I wish my mom hadn't died.

"You shouldn't care what people think, CeCe. The only person who can make their opinions matter is you." When I don't respond, his hand tightens on mine. "Is this about that guy, Liam? The one who let you borrow his hoodie?"

"No, of course not." Images flash through my mind—a trickling waterfall, a snow globe with three figures inside, and a boy who smiled at me like I was the only girl in the world. I held Liam's hand, but we didn't kiss. We didn't cross any other lines. "Liam and I are just friends." At this moment, I believe that it's true.

"I did research on him," Sam says, a note of jealousy in his voice. One I've never heard before, and one—dare I say it?—that makes me smile. "You know he's a little strange, right? Keeps to himself a lot. All he does is go to the community college and work at the hotline."

"I don't want to talk about Liam." I tell myself it's not because I feel guilty. I tell myself it's because I want to focus on right here, right now. And so I spread my palm against Sam's chest. His heart thump-thump-thumps against my hand. "I want to talk about us. And I want you to know that you can always bum a ride off me. Not just today, but whenever you need one."

"I will." He grins, and my insides flip-flop.

Because we both know that I'm not just talking about bumming rides. What I'm referring to, exactly, I'm not sure. But I can't wait to find out.

Chapter 22

After I drop Sam off, my stomach's all glowy and melty, kind of like the time I ate the chocolate topped with edible gold flakes Gram brought back from a Kansas City casino.

Unfortunately, the feeling only lasts about two seconds.

The "suspense" tone on my phone sounds as I'm driving home. I clench my teeth and ignore it. Since the flyers with my phone number have been taken down, I've received fewer unknown calls, but they're still coming. They're still either misdials or a breathing so heavy it makes my stomach curl. Nothing has been said other than "wrong number"—but it's almost more ominous that way. My imagination fills in the blanks with a dozen different potential threats.

That's probably what my texter intends.

I think about what Sam said about bullies. My texter counts on me crawling back into my shell. Quitting the hotline. Doing anything and everything he or she asks because I'm terrified of what will happen next.

But there's my mom to think about. And Lil. My mom helped her leave a guy who exploited her. What if there are others like her?

Oh god, it's happened again.

I can't walk away. Not when I can make a difference. I haven't been able to stand up for myself recently. But maybe for others, for Lil and girls like her, I can be a little bit brave.

When I arrive home, Dad and Gram are sitting in the kitchen.

Both of them, in the middle of the afternoon, drinking tea out of two of Gram's gambling mugs. This can't be good.

As soon as she sees me, Gram stands and takes her mug to the sink. "Don't lose your temper," she says to both of us. "Remember, in poker as in life, when you lose your head, you lose your money."

She leaves the room, and I try to smile. "For lunch, I had a pita pocket with hummus and some carrot sticks?" I say hopefully.

My dad doesn't laugh, much less excuse me from the conversation. "Principal Winters called. I left a room half-painted so I could come home and talk to you. When were you going to tell me about your mom's topless photo?"

I sink into the wicker chair across from him, and he picks up his mug, which features a group of dogs playing poker. A pink, polka-dotted book that looks vaguely familiar sits on the table in front of him.

"When was I supposed to tell you?" I mutter. "You spent the entire weekend in the den or at the cemetery. I never got the chance."

"That's an excuse. You could've found time. But you never planned to tell me, did you? Just like the posters that were put up at school today. If Principal Winters hadn't called me, I never would've known about those, either."

"I didn't think you would care." My eyes burn, but I'm not going to cry, dammit. Not when I'm stating a fact. Not when I'm saying something we both already know.

He winces, as if the poker-playing dogs have urinated in his tea. "Your mother was the one who always handled these things."

And she did. Whether it was explaining where babies come from, or mopping up my tears because the boy I liked asked another girl to the school dance, it was my mother who sat by my bedside. My mother who listened to my feelings and offered advice.

"Well, she's not here anymore, is she?" The words come out harsher than I intend.

He thunks his mug down on the polka-dot cover, and I remember all of a sudden what the book is. My baby keepsake journal. Except it's more than that. Because my mother continued to tuck bits of paper into it over the years. My first drawings, report cards, essays I wrote in school.

"What are you doing with that?" I ask.

"Oh." He pushes the book away, red tingeing his cheeks. "I . . . I don't have any idea how to do this. Raise a teenaged girl by myself. And your Gram said she always researches the other players to figure out her best move." He lifts his shoulders. "I guess I was trying to understand who you are."

"From a baby book?" I don't know whether to laugh or cry. "Dad, these are just stats. A few random photos. You can't get to know me any more than you can learn about a baseball star from his playing cards."

"This is all I have." His voice is stark, honest—and helpless. As helpless as I feel when I think about my texter. As helpless as we've both been since my mother left us.

The knowledge my dad is looking for is built from years of conversations, thousands of small moments. Something he can't hope to replicate now. So where does that leave him? Where does it leave us?

"You wrote a report in the first grade." He traces his hand along the binding, not looking at me. "You were supposed to write about one of your heroes, and you chose me. Do you remember?"

I shake my head.

"We'd found a family of rabbits in our backyard, and one of them had a hurt paw. I built a house for them out of scraps of wood and wrapped gauze around the rabbit's foot. I even jiggered up a feeding system. It made quite an impression on you." He taps the book. "It's all in here."

Now that he mentions it, I do remember the rabbits. "Yeah. So?"

He looks up, his eyes glossy. I can see the reflection of the chandelier in their sheen. "It's been a long time since anybody's considered me a hero, at anything. Especially you. I was thinking . . ." He stops, as if he has to peel the words from his throat.

"I was thinking, if your mother were still alive, she wouldn't be proud of me."

"Oh Dad." I swallow, and swallow again, but no matter what I do, I can't push away the lump. Like Gram, I've been gambling, too. Betting the lump remains benign. But one day, when I least expect, it'll turn malignant. "She wouldn't be proud of me, either."

For not standing up for myself against the bullies. For allowing rage to blot out seventeen years of her love. But most of all, for not being a good daughter.

Sure, I cook my dad dinner. I do his laundry. But I haven't done a damn thing to ease his pain. I know it's hard for him to talk about his emotions. I know his way of showing he cares is asking me if I've eaten.

But do I make things easier for him? Do I ever initiate conversation, volunteer any details about my day? No. I just wait, closemouthed, for his lead, and when he doesn't take it, I feel justified in feeling sorry for myself.

My mother wouldn't have approved. She wouldn't have approved at all.

"I'm sorry I didn't tell you about Mom's photo." I lick my lips, hesitating. "Did you . . . know about it before?"

"No," he whispers. "This was the first I ever heard of its existence."

"Not a fun way to find out, is it?"

"I've gotten better news." A strained expression flits across his face, and he leans forward. He's trying. We both are. "How was school? Principal Winters told me about the Photoshopped image. Were the kids . . . mean?"

"No meaner than usual."

"CeCe . . ."

I hold my breath. "Yes, Dad?"

He opens his mouth, but no words come out. Not the words I want to hear. The words I haven't heard since my mother died. *I love you, CeCe.* So simple. So easy. And yet, it's too much, too soon. My dad presses his lips together.

"The school says they're going to look into the posters," he finally says. "They're going to figure out who's behind this. In the meantime, Gram's taking me to her poker game tonight. She says it's better than me sitting in the den, counting the carpet fibers. Will you be okay on your own?"

I nod. In her own way, Gram is trying, too.

"What will you eat?" he asks, and I know no matter how far we get, he will always ask me that question. But that's okay. Because it's much better that he's here, asking me something, than not being here at all.

"We have some leftover enchiladas. I'll heat up a plate."

He leaves the room. I hear him and Gram talking, collecting their things, putting on their shoes. A few minutes later, they call "good-bye" to me and go out the front door.

I continue to sit at the table, swirling the tea bag in my dad's mug. *Explore something that you normally overlook in your daily life,* the Parsons Challenge instructed.

I thought the obvious "thing" was memories of my mother. But those memories aren't so much overlooked as deliberately ignored. What I've overlooked in the last few months—what I've *forgotten*—is the girl I used to be. The one who displayed her artwork bravely. The one who never would've allowed Mackenzie to bully the striped-tights girl. The one of whom my mother would've been proud.

It's a good thing I'm not applying to Parsons. How on earth would I explore that in a set of drawings?

But even as I think it, I get some ideas. I pull the snow globe out of my backpack and put it on the table in front of me, so I can look at it as I work. I grab a pen and the closest drawing surface—a paper towel—and start scribbling.

I'm on my third idea and third paper towel when my phone pings.

No. I don't want to look at it. Not now. Not ever again.

I shove the phone under the pink, polka-dotted keepsake book, but it pings again. I turn back to my paper towel, but I can't concentrate.

The edge of my phone sticks out under the book, teasing me,

taunting me. *You know you want to read the message,* it seems to say. *You know you—*

I snatch up the phone. Nothing good can come out of this text, but I have to see. I have to know how bad it is.

Except it's not a written message this time, but an attached photo.

A girl cradles a phone against her ear, her hair swept in a ponytail. One hand wraps the spiral phone cord around her finger, while the other fiddles with the collar of a raggedy sweatshirt. A very familiar sweatshirt.

It's a counselor working at the crisis hotline. More precisely, it's me. Taken yesterday, during my Sunday shift. When I thought I was alone.

The chill begins in my stomach and spreads outward, until my limbs feel as brittle as icicles. One hard slap, and I'll shatter to pieces.

I can't believe it. Someone actually is watching me.

Chapter 23

My pulse thrums in my mouth, tap dancing all over my taste buds. Sharp. Metallic. Bitter. The blood rushes over my eyes, and my vision lists back and forth like a ship on the rough seas.

He found out I volunteer at the crisis hotline. She figured out which shift I was working. He followed me to the cabin. She took a picture of me through the window. He, she, it—I don't know. But this person is out there. Watching me.

No wonder I felt the cool breeze blowing against my neck. I wasn't making it up. It wasn't my imagination running loose. I really am being watched.

I grip the table, looking wildly around the kitchen. Because the feeling's back, stronger than ever. The wind is a gale at my neck, my goose bumps have formed goose bumps of their own.

The faucet drips in the sink. A long-fingered branch taps against the window. And . . . there. What was that? A footstep, a creak? I know I heard something. I know it's not my imagination. I know—

My phone pings again.

I'm watching you now. Run, Cecilia. Hide. That's the only way you'll ever be safe.

My heart shoots up my throat, and I don't think. I don't have time to be brave. I just grab my snow globe and run. I run up the stairs, slam the door, and lock it for good measure. I yank the cord to close the blinds, and darkness engulfs the room.

Shivering, I wrap my arms around myself. Where is he? Is he

in my backyard, hidden in the trees, watching me through a window? Or is he at my front door, about to break it down and come inside?

The back door slams open, so hard the wine glasses rattle in their rack over the wet bar.

I can no longer distinguish one heartbeat from another, and my breath is quick and hot and dry. All the saliva has evaporated from my mouth, and the roar in my ears is so loud I feel like I've stepped inside a vacuum.

It doesn't have to be my texter. It could've been a coincidence. The back door doesn't latch properly. A strong gust sometimes blows it open. Maybe that's what it is. Mother Nature wreaking havoc with my mind.

But then, the floor board creaks. At least I think it does. It's got to be the board on the third step of the stairs, the one my mom tried to fix for ages before giving up on it.

Which means someone's inside the house.

Oh dear lord. I dart my eyes around the room. Cell phone. Where the hell is my cell phone? I need to call the cops, my dad, someone. But it's not here. Crap, crap, crap. Of course it's not here. I grabbed the snow globe, but I left my phone downstairs.

Plan B. Weapon. I don't have a baseball bat, but I put the globe down and grab my paint brushes and a stack of pencils, the ones with the newly sharpened tips. If worse comes to worst, I'll jab them into my attacker's eyes.

I stand by the bedroom door, gripping my weapons, gaze fixed on the doorknob, listening as hard as I can.

I hear someone breathing. I swear I do. A moist puff of air that travels up the stairs, over the floorboards, under my door, so that it skims along the cooled sweat along my skin, whispering words I can't decipher but completely, unquestionably understand.

Fear.

But I don't hear any more creaks, and nobody comes upstairs. I listen, listen, listen. A lock of damp hair falls onto my forehead, but I don't swipe it away. Drops of sweat roll into my eyes, and I just let them sting.

I don't know how long I stand there, waiting, seconds or an eternity. But eventually, my arms, shaky from clenching the weapons, droop.

Maybe no one was actually here. Maybe it was just a combination of the wind and my overactive imagination. Hell, maybe Gram and Dad forgot something, and they just popped in to grab it.

I could call them to find out. But I don't dare go downstairs for my phone. Instead, I burrow into the back of my closet, where I've shoved all the clothes I shared with my mom, and I do exactly what I said I wasn't going to do.

I hide.

And I stay that way, knees pulled to my chest, the snow globe in my hands, until my dad and Gram come home four hours later.

Chapter 24

"CeCe, may I offer you another serving?" Sam's mom asks the next day. This is basically all she's said to me throughout the meal. How do I like the food, could she pour me more water, would I like to add cheese to my pasta?

"No thanks, Mrs. Davidson. But the eggplant parmesan is delicious."

And it is, a step above the lasagna I normally cook for my dad. The silver-dollar coins of eggplant are at once crisp and tender. The tomato sauce has been complicated with roasted red peppers, and fresh herbs add a brightness of flavor.

At least, that's what Sam tells me. I can't actually taste any of the food. Since my texter sent that photo of me, everything seems more dull. The grass faded to dying yellow, and the laughter of my classmates at school sounded tinny and far away. It's as if fear has leached out the vibrant centers of my five senses, leaving hollowed outlines with no texture and depth.

I never called the cops. Hell, I didn't even tell my dad. Sometime between that first rush of adrenaline and when Gram banged into the kitchen, triumphant with her winnings, I convinced myself there was nothing to tell.

I can't prove the door wasn't blown open by the wind. In fact, one day later, I'm pretty sure that's exactly what happened. When I casually mentioned the door flying open, Dad admitted that he had forgotten to secure the latch properly. So what's my proof? My gut feelings? That's the last thing the police want to hear about—they've had enough of my dad's intuition to last a lifetime.

"Mom, you should tell CeCe how you learned to ride a motorcycle," Sam says, interrupting my thoughts.

"Oh, I don't know, honey." She plays with the zipper that slashes across her jacket and smiles wanly, as if Sam's talking about a person she can't recall, or worse, someone she never knew at all. "It was so long ago."

She's shut down all of his overtures in the same way. "Remember the time you served us balsamic vinegar and we thought it was motorcycle oil?" he asked at one point. And then, five minutes later: "My mom's the best cook. She can't make a dish without a secret ingredient. Go on. Tell CeCe about the orange juice in your red sauce."

Mrs. Davidson gives vague, non-responsive answers, while I smile and nod and try to think of something to say. Are all dinners with a guy's parents this awkward? Or is it just me? In the end, I settle for shoving forkfuls of eggplant into my mouth.

"My friend Amber says she wants to ride a motorcycle." Briony looks up from her bright purple phone, where she's been texting nonstop throughout dinner. "But her dad says, no way, José. And Rachel says she'd never get on a bike, even if you paid her."

"What about your boyfriend?" Sam's tone is both biting and protective. "How does he feel about motorcycles?"

She frowns. "I don't have a boyfriend. You know that. No time. I have to focus on my studies."

"Really, sweetie?" Mrs. Davidson says, sounding more awake than she has all during dinner. "You've never felt this way before. I mean, you've had boyfriends since the first grade."

Briony stabs her fork into the eggplant. "People change, Mom."

"You mean circumstances change." Mrs. Davidson stands, her face as pale as the uncooked noodles left on the counter. "Parents who were supposed to set a good example show you how messed up a marriage can be. I tried my best." She walks out of the room, and her words float back to us, strangely disembodied. "But sometimes your best isn't good enough."

Her footsteps pad away, and Sam scowls. "Good going, Bri. Now, she thinks whatever's going on is her fault. When, really, you just don't want to tell us about your guy."

"That's stupid," Briony protests. "It has nothing to do with her."

"Oh, yeah? Then tell us about your boyfriend."

She drums her nails against her phone. "You wouldn't understand."

"I've always understood before." His voice is soft now, and it makes me want to gather him in my arms. "Since when do you keep secrets from me?"

"This is different," she says. "My love with this man, it's on a different plane. It's above and beyond what is felt on this world, so there's no need to share it with anyone else."

Sam glances at me and mouths, "Who talks like that?"

"I saw that." She shoves her chair back. "Like I said, I don't expect you to understand. I'm going to talk to Mom before she does something desperate, like put on a nightgown."

She stalks out of the room, and Sam sighs. "When Mom puts on her nightgown, she drifts around the house for days, like she put down her identity somewhere and can't find it again," he tells me. "The only time she seems remotely like her old self is when she's wearing black leather."

We move the pile of dirty plates to the sink in the kitchen, and I begin to rinse them. Sam hovers by my side so that he can load the dishwasher.

This is my opening. The first time we've been alone since the incident. Hesitantly, I tell him about the photo my texter sent. About the possibility—however remote—that the texter was actually inside my house. Even if my overzealous imagination certifies me as insane, at least one other person has to know. My dad doesn't need any more worries, and Gram's preoccupied with her upcoming trip to Vegas. By process of easy elimination, it has to be Sam.

When I finish, Sam grips my arm and turns me from the sink. "But no one was actually there? You weren't in any danger?"

I dry my palms against my jeans, not looking at him. "I don't think so. Like I said, I think it was just my imagination."

"We should go to the police," he says.

"No way." I back away, so that his hand drops from my arm. "Uh-uh. I don't want to involve the police."

"Why not?" Three creases appear on his forehead. He doesn't get it, and I don't blame him. If his mother were willing to call the cops, they could be rid of his dad, once and for all.

But I have experiences, too. Of the detective who put a cup of hot chocolate in my hands and pretended to be my friend. Of her partner, who proceeded to destroy me with questions designed to expose my mother as a pedophile.

Have I ever seen my mother naked? Did my mother and I ever sleep in the same bed? Did she ever touch me inappropriately? Was I sure? (Because, you know, it's perfectly okay to be honest.) Did she spend a lot of time with her male students? Did she give special tutoring sessions? Was she overly interested in my friends? Did she encourage me to bring them home? Did she talk to me or them about topics of a sexual nature?

And on and on and on.

It didn't matter how I answered. They didn't care how many times I shouted, "No!" Every bit of information was twisted to support the profile of my mom on which they'd already decided.

And the same thing will happen if I go to them now.

"No police. Not until we know this is more than Justin Blake trying to exact revenge." I squeeze my eyes shut. "I know these stupid pranks aren't right, but if we go to the cops, he'll make my life even more miserable than it already is."

He looks at me for a long moment and then nods. "Okay, fine. But if this texter continues to bother you, we call them. Deal?"

"Deal." I pick up a dirty dish to rinse, desperate to change the subject. "Did you hear how Briony referred to her boyfriend as a 'man'?"

"Yeah." He frowns. "Do you think that means she's dating an older guy? An adult?"

"Not necessarily. Briony's sixteen, right? He could be seventeen, eighteen. Older than her, but not a grown-up."

But the words sound forced, even to me. Because Lil from the hotline was also involved with an older guy. And my mother wrote the words, "It's happened again."

Could it be happening now? To Briony? What are the chances?

Sam squints at a bowl and then sticks it back under the running water to get the rest of the soap bubbles off. "What if she's dating a teacher? Someone like Mr. Swift?"

I almost drop my plate. "Why do you mention him?" I can still see his sympathetic smile from yesterday. And I squirm once again at the thought of my teachers seeing my "topless" photo.

"Ms. Hughes told me he asked the yearbook staff for all the students' photos, for a special project. The project never materialized." He shrugs. "Could be totally innocent. But I thought it was a weird coincidence, since your harasser used your yearbook picture to put on the Photoshopped image."

"Yeah." My mind whirls. "There's twenty or thirty students on the yearbook staff. Anyone could've had access to that picture. How'd you get the info out of Ms. Hughes, anyhow?"

"First thing my editor told me. Make friends with the front office. They know everything."

I rinse the last of the silverware and dry my hands, and we move back to the dining room.

"Would you talk to Briony?" He picks up his sister's purple phone from the dining table, enters a few numbers, and begins to scroll through it. I'm not surprised he knows her security code. More evidence of their closeness as brother and sister. "I know she's hiding something about her boyfriend. Maybe she'll talk to you."

"Nope." I shake my head. "I don't get involved. That's my rule for this year. I mind my own business, keep a low profile, and nobody has any reason to single me out."

"I think this will change your mind." He holds out the phone to me, his face as pale as his mother's.

I refuse to take it. "We shouldn't be looking at her phone. It's not our business."

"Normally, I'd agree with you. But not today." His eyes flash through his glasses, bigger, sharper, more magnified. "She's got a text from an email address. The address is just a bunch of random characters, and there's no other identifying information. But whoever he is, he wants her to send him a photo of herself." He stops. The air feels heavy like it's stuffed with the significance of the moment. "A topless photo."

Chapter 25

I stand in front of Briony's bedroom door. Behind the solid wood, the bass of a popular rock song pounds. I can almost see the door vibrate. The message couldn't be any clearer: Visitors not wanted. Stay out.

What am I doing? Why am I about to meddle in the affairs of a girl I barely know?

Because Briony's boyfriend asked her to take a topless photo. It's that simple. I can't let another girl become a victim like my mother. Not if I can prevent it by a single conversation.

I take a deep breath and knock on the door. Nothing happens. I knock louder. And then louder still, until I feel like the bass and I are rivals fighting for a guy's attention.

The music stops. "What do you want?" Briony says from the other side of the wood.

"It's CeCe. Can we talk?" The door gives me the same blank face, clearly unimpressed. "It's about, um, a boy."

She may not want to talk about herself, but judging from the legions of girlfriends she already has despite her status as the new girl, she's always got time for a friend. I may not be the giggly type, but I've got as much boy trouble as the rest of them.

A few seconds later, the door opens. Briony pokes her head out and looks up and down the hall, as if expecting Sam to ambush her. Seeing nothing, she yanks me inside and shuts the door.

"Did my brother put you up to this?" She readjusts her off-the-shoulder sweatshirt. Pink, slouchy leg warmers complete the retro '80s look.

"No," I lie.

She gestures for me to sit on her unmade bed and perches on the desk chair. "I know I'm supposed to be all rah, rah, rah, isn't Sam the best? And I will tomorrow—I promise. But sometimes, he's a little too overprotective for his own good." She sighs. "You won't hold that against him, will you?"

I move a stuffed bear from the bed and sit down. "You don't have to sell him to me. We're not together like that." *At least not yet,* a voice inside me whispers.

"You're not? Did I imagine you sitting at our dinner table, then?"

"We're working together to research his article for the *Lakewood Sun.*"

"You can keep telling yourself that," she drawls.

She's right. Exactly who am I trying to fool here? I like him. I like him a lot. And I think he likes me, too. But it's twice now that we could've kissed—but didn't—and the wait is nearly killing me.

I wet my lips. "Actually, that's what I wanted to talk to you about. I was hoping you could give me some advice."

"Of course." She perks up, like a wilted flower that's just been given water, and I know I've taken the right tactic. Even if it is deceitful. I would never seek advice on a boy from his sister—but that's the first rule of lying. Ground your story in as many authentic details as possible. Gram taught me that in my first poker lesson, and I've never forgotten it.

"Sam's different from anybody I've ever met," I say slowly. "And it's not just his looks. My feelings for him—they go beyond a crush. And I guess that's my question. How do you know when you have something real?"

I drop my eyes to the crumpled sheets as though I'm shy. And that's when I realize my pulse is skittering and my palms are slick with sweat. Holy crap, I'm not pretending. I set out to lie about my feelings for Sam—and spoke nothing but the truth.

"When you fall in love with the right guy, you'll know." Briony's entire face is soft—her lips, her cheeks, her forehead. "It's the most amazing feeling in the world."

Bingo. Falsehood or not, I've maneuvered Briony into talking about her boyfriend.

She hesitates and then pulls a silver cuff out of a jewelry box. "Look what he gave me." She hands me the bracelet. "Go on, read the inscription. It's the most romantic thing I've ever heard."

I turn the bracelet over and read the cursive script.

When I'm with you, I feel like I can do anything. Fly without wings. Breathe underwater. Defy gravity. Your love makes me invincible.

Sounds a little over-the-top to me. But maybe I've just never been in love. "Who is this guy, Briony?"

Her eyes shine. "Only the most wonderful man in the world."

There it is again. That word "man." "Does he go to our school?"

"I guess you could say that."

"Is he . . . a teacher?"

"God no. You mean one of those forty-year-old geezers? No offense, CeCe, but that's disgusting. Not to mention illegal. Men like that go to jail when they're caught. You know that, don't you?"

The breath whooshes out of me. Thank god. She thinks older men are gross. Whatever's happening to Lil is not happening to her. And yet . . .

"If he's so wonderful, why do you keep him a secret?" I ask.

She jams her lips together. "He doesn't want people gossiping about us, that's all."

"Has he ever asked you to do anything . . . uncomfortable?"

She stands abruptly and pats her pockets, scans her desk, and opens the drawers. "My phone's missing. Did I leave it in the kitchen? Have you and Sam been reading my text messages?"

My mouth goes dry. "You must've heard about the topless posters of me they plastered at school. It's never a good idea to give anyone an explicit photo of yourself. Look at me. Look at my mom. She took that picture over twenty years ago, and she still isn't safe."

"Oh. My. God." Her face turns red. It's not a good color with her pink top. "I freaking knew it. You read my texts. Sam put you up to this. If I didn't love my brother so much, I'd kill him."

"Briony, please. Someone took a photo of my mom and put it on a porn site. What if that's what your boyfriend is going to do?

"No." Her voice is certain, flat, and leaves no room for argument. "It's not like that. He assured me the photos would be for his personal use."

"You're not actually thinking about it, are you? No matter what he says, there's no way to guarantee he'll keep the photos to himself."

An expression I can't read flits across her face. The air conditioner hums to life, and even though I can't feel the breeze, I shiver.

"He makes me feel special," she whispers. "Cherished and protected. When I'm in his arms, I feel like nothing bad will ever happen to me again. My life's been a joke these last few years. But he makes me feel like I might have my fairy tale, after all. I need that, CeCe. You wouldn't understand. But after what I've gone through, what I've had to see my mother suffer—" She cuts off, her eyes hollow. "I need that."

Her father. I've never witnessed abuse, but I feel like I understand all too well. In a way, that's what I'm looking for, too. Someone to make me forget, if only for a few minutes, the crap that's being passed off as my life.

"I get that." I touch the ragged edge of her sleeve. "But no matter how special a guy is, he should never ask you to do something you're uncomfortable with."

She jerks her arm, flicking off my touch. "Who says I'm uncomfortable?"

"Briony, you're sixteen. You shouldn't be taking explicit photos."

"I'm not a complete idiot," she says. "You don't have to worry about me. I'll be careful."

"Promise?" I ask, even though I, more than most, knows a promise doesn't mean anything. It's just a word, thrown into the air, easily forgotten in a moment of passion with the captain of the football team.

"Promise," she says.

And that's the closest I'm going to get to ensuring her safety.

Sam's doing push-ups when I arrive at his open bedroom door. Up and down, and up and down, like a metronome. The muscles roll in his biceps, and his back is as straight as a board. He looks like he could keep going forever.

I feel like I could stare at him forever.

My skin sizzles, as if electric sparks are jumping from one cell to another, and I take a huge step backward. Can't let him see me gawking like a groupie, especially since he already caught me spying on him behind a tree. If his sister spills what I said, he'll think I'm really gaga over him.

I knock on the door, and he looks up. "CeCe! What happened? What did she say?"

He springs to his feet, and I venture into the room, feeling like I've grown an extra set of elbows. I'm not nervous, exactly. We've spent hours together. But we're not usually in his bedroom. Alone.

"I'm positive she's not seeing a teacher, or anyone like that," I say. "According to her, older guys are gross and illegal and disgusting."

"That's great! What about the topless photo? Did you ask her about that?"

His restlessness brings him closer to me, and the backs of my calves brush the bed. The only way for me to retreat further is to get *on* his bed—and I'm not about to do that.

"She knows you looked at her phone," I say. "And she's not happy about it."

He comes nearer still. "She'll get over it."

"We talked about the dangers of explicit photos," I babble, for the sake of talking now. "She didn't completely agree, but she did promise she would be careful."

"That's awesome." He scoops me up and swings me around, and all of a sudden, the laughter bubbles out of me and Sam's smiling like I just accomplished something big.

And maybe I did. I put myself out there and talked to Briony. And it wasn't awful. She didn't hate me or judge me. It actually feels . . . good. I've forgotten how good it can feel to help someone, face to face. For a moment, it's like I'm my old self again. Before my mom died. Before I turned so skittish.

Sam leans down and gives me a peck on the lips. "Thank you. I know you didn't want to do it, and it means a lot to me."

Wait a minute. Did he kiss me? On the lips? I think back on the moment, try to slow the memory down. It happened so fast I would've missed it if I blinked. On second thought, maybe I did blink, and that's why I can't remember anything. Were his lips warm? Soft? Chapped? No clue.

I just had my first kiss since my mom died. The kiss I've been imagining, counting down the seconds until, wondering if today was going to be the big day . . . and I didn't feel a thing. Damn.

"What's wrong?" he asks.

"Did you just kiss me?" I blurt out.

His hands drop. "Um, yeah. Should I be apologizing?"

"Maybe. I mean, I haven't kissed anyone for so long, and it happened so fast, I didn't feel anything." The words tumble out. "What am I going to say to my girlfriends? Okay, it's not like I have that many, but Alisara might conceivably ask me. And what about fifteen years from now, when the subject comes up at some fancy cocktail party? Someone will ask about the first guy I kissed after my mom died, and I'll be stuck with shrimp tails in my hand and absolutely NOTHING TO SAY."

I stop to take a breath. He stares at me, transfixed in an awful-car-accident kind of way. And then he bursts out laughing. "You're not like anyone else, are you?"

"I know," I say miserably. Idiot, idiot, idiot. What's wrong with me? Why couldn't I keep my mouth shut and enjoy the moment?

"I like that you're different. I like it a lot."

He closes the gap between us. My heart's got the drum solo on this percussive dance, and I have time to feel and see everything. To smell the Irish Spring soap on his skin. To sense the carpet fibers scratching my socked feet. To travel the infinite space between each heartbeat.

He cups his hands around my face. "I've been thinking about kissing you for so long, maybe I messed that up," he whispers. "But if you give me another chance, I'll try again to give you something to remember."

I can't breathe. I can't even think. My entire being is focused on Sam's mouth. If he doesn't kiss me right now, I might die.

And then, his lips touch mine, gently, hesitantly. They move, parting my mouth, his tongue slipping over mine. Sparks explode inside my body, traveling to the tips of my toes and the top of my head, swirling around my heart.

I tangle my hands in his hair, and we fall back onto the bed. This. This kiss. I feel warmed from the inside out. Like he is the sun, pouring rays of light into me. I'd endure a year of Justin Blake's taunts if my reward were a kiss like this. It's worth a hundred daydreams, a thousand moments of anticipation. I move closer, and then closer still, and yet, I get the feeling I'll never be close enough. I'll never get enough of this boy kissing me.

And then, I can think again. And the only thought in my head is: He's right. I'll remember every last detail for the Rest. Of. My. Life.

Chapter 26

I'm not a hummer. Never was, never will be. I'm not a skipper, either, nor a jumper. But the next morning, I do all three. Not on the outside. On the outside, I probably look the same as I always do. Head down, books clasped to my chest, not looking at anybody. But on the inside, I skip and jump and cheer. I hum and sing and dance. It's a beautiful morning. The sun is shining, the birds are chirping, and *Sam Davidson kissed me.*

The night wasn't as smooth. I had a few bad moments when I woke, drenched in sweat, certain I could hear my texter breathing in my ear. But the wood didn't creak, and the back door didn't open, so I stared at the snow globe, at the white flakes falling over three generations of females, and fell back asleep.

If my texter wanted to hurt me, he or she could've. He took that photo of me at the hotline. He could've come inside the cabin and strangled me. But he didn't. So, at most, his goal was to scare me. Mission accomplished. Doesn't mean I'm going to stop searching for answers.

I push away all thoughts of my texter now as I spin my locker combination. The locker opens—on the first try, no less—and I catch a glimpse of myself in the mirror. Okay, maybe I do look different. It's the start of a day at school, and I'm actually smiling. Crazy.

I grab my psych book and pat the front pocket of my backpack, where the printout of my mom's entry is still stowed. I'm not sure why I'm carrying it everywhere. That last line—"Oh dear god, it's happened again"—isn't a personal communication to me. It isn't. But it's the closest thing I have to a final letter from my mom.

Plus, there's something bugging me about the entry. Something a little off. But I can't quite figure out what.

Alisara appears as I'm closing my locker door. "Hey. How's it going?"

"Good. I mean, not good." Every last poster has been removed from the hallways, but I don't need the physical reminder to know what was there. Besides, I don't think you can ever really be "good" when you've got a harasser breathing in your ear. "But hanging in there. Trying to focus on other things." Like the way Sam's glasses were fogged when he finally surfaced from our kiss. How the flush in his face made his freckles disappear.

She bumps my knee, lowering her voice. "Listen, I've completely struck out trying to figure out which parties Tommy will be at next. He's got tons of friends in our class, but Mackenzie's put out the bulletin. Anyone who gives out info on him will have to deal with her. You know nobody dares to cross her."

And it isn't any wonder. They know perfectly well what Mackenzie's capable of. One of her former besties showed up at prom last year wearing the same dress as her. The princess demanded her friend take it off. The girl refused.

The next day, a video of the girl sitting on a toilet circulated on social media—a video Mackenzie must have recorded long ago, just for ammunition. The girl ran off in tears and never came back. Last I heard, she's attending school in the next town over.

Too bad my problems can't be solved so easily. Even if my dad were willing to leave my mom's grave, I'd have to move out of the state to find a student body that hasn't heard of Tabitha Brooks.

"That's okay," I say to Alisara. "It was a long shot, anyway."

She hooks her arm through mine, and we walk to class, a two-headed entity around which the crowd has to part. I swallow hard. This is how my old group of friends moves around the hallways, in packs of twos and threes. But it's been so long since I've traveled as part of the social Hydra, I stumble as I try to match my stride to Alisara's.

"You know where you could talk to him?" she asks, charging forward, not letting go of my arm. But not letting me fall, either. "At the literacy auction on Sunday. I hear Tommy's going to be the main event, as usual. Graduating hasn't changed that."

I shudder. "I can't bid on him in front of the entire school. Can you imagine what people would say? Besides, the auction is demeaning. Parading around guys and girls like cattle, for sale to the highest bidder."

"It's only a date. For a good cause, no less." We swerve around a couple of guys tossing a football. "But if you're not interested in bidding on Tommy, guess who else is in the auction?"

"Who?"

"The new guy. Sam Davidson."

I stop in my tracks, and Alisara lurches forward, still connected to my arm. She straightens, and I make my voice calm and unruffled. "He doesn't seem like the type to auction himself off. How'd they convince him to do it?"

"Raleigh says he turned them down at first, but then his sister joined the auction committee, and they got her to lay a guilt trip on him, what with supporting the kids and literacy and all." She scans my face, as if searching for a tell. "It seems quite a few girls are wondering if he takes off his glasses when he kisses. Would you know anything about that?"

I flush. "Maybe."

"AHA!" she shouts.

"Shhh. Keep your voice down." I look around the hallway to make sure no one heard.

She creases her brow, confused. "Why? Are you ashamed to be dating Sam?"

"Of course not. It's just with all this gossip going around, I don't want to give them something else to talk about. That's all."

But it's not all. Because even if there were no topless photos, I don't think I'd be willing to trade my invisible status for dating-the-new-boy fame. I can already hear the crude, not terribly inventive taunts: "You go down on Highwater Sam yet? Maybe you can yank down his pant legs while you're at it."

What's more, I don't want to subject Sam to the gossip. God knows, between his showdown with Mackenzie and the inevitable curiosity any new student draws, he's endured enough scrutiny. It wouldn't help to have his name linked with mine.

"Okay," Alisara says. "But you do know you won't be able to keep this quiet for long." She pauses. "Secrets have a way of coming out in this town."

The room is mostly empty when I walk into psych class. Sam's already at his desk, next to mine, and his smile gets bigger and bigger as I approach. When I reach him, I see a paper towel on my chair, covered with an ink drawing.

"Did you draw this?" I ask him.

"Yeah." He pushes his glasses up his nose. "I'm not an artist, like you, but I draw a pretty mean stick figure, don't you think?"

"The best. It might even rival my five-year-old cousin's."

He screws up his face, mock-offended. Giggling, I pick up the paper towel and look at the cartoon more closely. The first frame shows a stick figure on his knees, holding up a square pizza box. A conversation bubble comes out of his mouth: "Will you have dinner with me?" In the second frame, a girl and boy stick figure shove pizza in their mouths. The third frame has them collapsed on a couch, with a banner across the top that reads, "Food Coma."

The glow starts in my stomach and spreads to every limb, joint, and muscle until I feel like I could light up the room. No, make that the entire school.

The drawing is basic. Some of the ink has smudged, and the edges of the paper towel are frayed. I want to frame the cartoon and keep it forever. "Why is it on a paper towel?"

He shrugs. "Isn't that your canvas of choice? I always see scraps with your drawings on them."

Shoved in my locker. In the side compartment of my car door. Tucked in between the pages of my notebook. I can't believe he noticed. "I draw on whatever surface is handy."

"So, what do you say? My mom's taking my sister shopping for new sneakers tonight. You want to come for dinner?" He tosses another scrap of paper on my desk. "Look, I even drew you some flowers. Girls like flowers, right?"

"Yeah, they do." I stare at the bunch of daisies, my heart squeezing. Some girls dream about receiving expensive, long-stemmed roses, the kind Mackenzie gets called to the school office to receive at least once a month. But me? I'd take this inked bouquet any day.

I lick my dry lips. "I have a shift after school, but then I'd love to stuff my face with pizza with you."

"It's a date." He beams and casually drops a hand on my shoulder. Just as casually, I wiggle out from underneath.

"What is it?" he asks.

"Someone might see."

He looks around the room. A couple girls gossip in the first row of desks, but they're laughing and shrieking so loudly they might not notice if the marching band paraded through our classroom. "No one's even here."

"Sam, it's not you." I squeeze his hand before tucking mine securely, safely in my pocket. "Walking around this school is like wading into a pit of alligators. I never know which body part they're going to chew up and spit out. Don't make it any harder, for both of us, okay?"

"It's not hard for me," he protests.

"That's because you haven't lived in Lakewood long enough."

He looks like he might argue, but then he shuts his mouth and nods. "Okay, fine. I can be patient for a little while. But sooner or later, we have to tell them. I'm not interested in a secret relationship."

"Me, neither," I say, but it's not true.

The truth is, I intend to keep my relationship with Sam Davidson a secret for as long as humanly possible.

"Class, we're going to talk about expressiveness in today's technologically advanced society." Mr. Willoughby sits on his desk, next to his ever-present photo of his dead wife, and taps a pointer against his palm. "Our communications on social media are limited by the number of characters, and handwriting seems to have gone completely out of vogue. We can go days or even months without hearing the voices of our closest friends, and emoticons take the place of real feelings. How are we to express ourselves in this kind of world? Anyone?"

Nobody volunteers.

He purses his lips. "Really? You're all so busy you couldn't bother to scan a ten-page article for class?"

I scrunch my shoulders together, trying to make myself as small as possible. Normally, I stay on top of all my schoolwork—a side effect of having no social life—but with the topless photos, the text messages, and the kissing, I've been a bit distracted.

Finally, a lone hand ventures into the air, and the girl in front of me breathes an audible sigh of relief. It's Sam. Of course it is. Newspaper intern and model student. But when did he find time to read the article for class? Before or after he kissed me?

"Yes, Mr. Davidson? What can you tell us about expressing ourselves in the digital world?"

"If we can't rely on voice inflection, we have to find different modes of expression," Sam says. "For example, the *Lakewood Sun* has been looking at fonts as a way of branding ourselves. Times New Roman conveys seriousness, while Comic Sans shows a playful and flexible side."

"Fascinating, Mr. Davidson." The teacher nods his approval. "And can anyone tell me about the furniture study, where the assembly instructions were printed in different fonts? Yes, Ms. Jackson?"

But I'm no longer listening. Sam's words struck something inside me. The feeling that something was off about my mother's call entry turns into full-fledged alarm. I slip my hand into my backpack and pull out the printout.

With shaking fingers, I smooth out the paper and reread the final few paragraphs:

> He calls her his darling. "If you love me," he says, "if you are who I think you are, you won't waste time reading this situation. You will do as I say."
>
> Lil couldn't remember the rest of his words. Something, something, she said. But it doesn't matter. The message is clear.
>
> Oh dear god, it's happened again. Only this time, it's not to me.

I love secret codes. Always have. And my mother never failed to indulge me. Once, she wrote me a letter using a different font for each word. Another time, she sent me an e-mail using two different fonts. At first glance, the words looked like gibberish. But when I isolated each font, two coherent messages emerged.

It was in front of me this entire time, and I never saw it. Until now.

My heart booms in my eardrums, drowning out Mr. Willoughby and the poor student on whom he's called. Quickly, I pull out the words with a different font from the rest of the entry. This is the message I get:

> *Darling if you are reading this something happened to me.*

Chapter 27

My hands don't stop shaking for the rest of the school day. The only time I can keep them remotely steady is when I'm drawing, drawing, drawing. In my notebook. On the backs of old exams. Yes, even on paper towels. Anything and everything I can remember about my mother in the week before she died.

The distracted way she swept through the kitchen, her English muffin forgotten in the toaster. The lines that magically appeared around her eyes when I asked about her day. Even her extra-tight grip when she hugged me good night.

Something happened to my mom. Something awful, apparently, because she's dead. And it's looking more and more like her suicide wasn't as straightforward as everyone would like to believe.

What happened to her? *What happened?*

These coded words are just the beginning. The rest of her message is hidden somewhere in the caller database. I'm sure of it. All I have to do is piece together the rest of her message, and I'll have my answers.

After school, I press down on the accelerator and zoom through the yellow traffic light on my way to the hotline. The tires crunch on gravel, and bits of rock fly in every direction. Kind of like my feelings. Nerves vibrating like a tuning fork. Dread at the pit of my stomach. And underneath it all, the undeniable soaring of my heart.

My mother loved me, after all. She wanted me to volunteer at the hotline, and she left me a message coded in the caller database. A final letter. The one for which I've been searching.

I turn into the driveway, expecting to be alone. Instead, Liam's sitting in his orange sports car, presumably waiting for me.

My face gets hot, and my stomach feels like it's sprouted wings. I haven't seen Liam since Sunday—although I did call him yesterday. I left a vague message about how I'd felt someone watching me, in case my texter was stalking other counselors at the hotline. But we didn't talk. I've barely even thought about him. I've been too busy with my own life, too preoccupied with . . . Sam.

Is it obvious? Will he be able to tell, just by looking at me, that I kissed Sam?

Apparently not. As soon as I step out of the car, he hurries over to me, grinning widely.

"What are you doing here?" I ask. The words are stilted and awkward, and I hate myself. *Stop it!* Stop making this more dramatic than it really is. I don't owe Liam anything. We never kissed—even if maybe I wanted to. Even though—if I'm being really, truly honest with myself—if Sam never moved to our town, I wouldn't mind kissing Liam still.

He raises an eyebrow. "After you told me about someone spying on you, do you really expect me to let you work here alone?"

"Oh." Of course he wouldn't. I wasn't thinking. I didn't mean to create extra work for him. But I should've known. Liam is way too chivalrous to let the information slide. "You shouldn't have gone out of your way—"

"Don't say that." He smiles in that way that turns my insides liquid. "It's not a chore if I enjoy it."

I force myself to return his smile, although my limbs feel both too stiff and too loose. I should really tell him about Sam. Right? It's the decent thing to do.

Except there really isn't anything going on between Liam and me. We bonded over our deceased parents. He got Justin Blake slapped with a DUI for harassing me. He rescued my mother's snow globe, and we spent an afternoon holding hands. I was attracted to him—but who says he feels the same way about me? Maybe he's just a really nice guy, and he couldn't care less what I do with anyone else.

Oh, geez. I have a headache. Why are boys so confusing?

"I like your necklace," I say, sidestepping the issue. Trying to fall back into our once easy rhythm of conversation. I peer at the ever-present chain around his neck. Upon closer examination, I can see the pendant is actually a flat locket, and the design I mistook for random swirls actually forms the wings of a creature. "Can you tell me about it?"

"A present from my dad when I turned eighteen." His fingers close around the necklace. "When he passed, I put his ashes into the locket, so that his spirit will always be here to guide me."

I blink. "You carry his ashes with you?"

"That sounds weird, right? Maybe even borderline creepy. But it's my way of feeling close to him." He grins sheepishly, but it's also lined with sorrow and longing and pain. "I don't admit it to most people, but if anyone could understand, it would be you."

"Of course I understand." Who am I to judge another person's grieving process? I can't even bring myself to visit my mom's grave. I'm tearing the hotline inside out searching for a letter that might not exist. "I think it's lovely."

"Thanks for saying that." He opens the front door of the cabin and gestures for me to go inside. We walk into the main room and sit on the lumpy sofa.

He shifts forward, his knees nudging mine. The heat climbs my neck, and a zip of electricity shoots through me. He's not Sam. There's nothing between us. And yet, the look on his face is so searching, so familiar, I can't help leaning forward, too.

"You and me, we know that grief is a double-edged sword." His voice is low now, and it reaches every aching part inside me. "Everyone was so sympathetic when my father died. Relatives poured out of the woodwork, and I had enough frozen casseroles to last me a year. The attention got to be so suffocating that I had to move here, to Lakewood, to my grandparents' lakeside cabin. Because they didn't know him like I did. They didn't know, as much as I loved him, I hated him, too."

He picks up my hand, engulfing it in his palm, and I can't pull away. I can't move at all. Because he's spoken words I've never dared speak out loud. Not to Dad and not to Gram. And certainly never to myself.

I've been mad at my mother. Given the circumstances, that emotion is justified, even expected. But sometime in the last six months, at some point between my failure to find a final letter and Justin Blake's harassment, the anger twisted inside me. What was loving and good turned ugly, dark—and just as dead as my mother.

That's when I realize why I'm drawn to Liam. I could never show Sam this part of me. He's been through the hell of his father's beatings, but he's a good guy through and through. If he ever saw this hatred inside me, I'm pretty sure that's the last thing he'd ever see.

"I know exactly how you feel." My voice starts out as a whisper, but it gets stronger as I see what's reflected in his eyes: me. "My mom didn't think of me when she slept with Tommy. She didn't care how my classmates might harass me. She only thought of herself when she took her life. Never me. And sometimes I . . . sometimes, I hate her for it."

My lungs balloon with too much air. There. I said it. I laid the deepest part of myself out for him to judge. And his expression doesn't change. His grip on my hand doesn't loosen.

"I could tell you so many stories." He laughs a stuttering-motor laugh, the kind that comes out when there's nothing funny at all. "He used to lock me in my room without food all day, for missing my curfew by five minutes. Wallop me until I was black and blue for not acing a test."

"Liam, that's awful." My throat tightens, and I want to

punch something, preferably his dad. But he's gone now, and we're only talking about the past.

I squeeze Liam's hand, the one I'm already holding, but it feels insufficient. So I pick up his other hand, and we're connected through a circle of our arms.

"It was my fault, mostly," he says. "I was too slow, too clumsy. I made stupid mistakes in school. He knew what I was capable of achieving, and he refused to let me fall short of that. His methods were just a little too rigid, that's all. But I forgive him for that." He lifts his head and looks at the wood-beam ceiling, as though he's addressing his father's spirit. "I forgive him for everything. He always said I would be grateful to him someday, and in retrospect, I am. He raised the bar on my expectations. Because of him, I feel like I can do anything."

"I'm glad, then. But I'm sorry you had to go through his version of discipline."

We sit like that for several minutes, fused together through our hands, and then the phone rings. I turn my head toward the mechanical briing as though in slow motion. "Should I answer that?"

"Of course. Our callers need you, too." He gives me a crooked smile. "You have a gift for listening, and as much as I'd like to be selfish and keep you to myself, I won't."

We pull our hands from each other slowly. My palms are sweaty from being in his grip.

"I'm going to get some air," he says. "You want me to bring you a coffee?"

"Sure." My pulse quickens, and I remember the reason I was so anxious to come here. I need to look over my mother's call logs. See if she left me any more messages to decode. I'm going to dive in—as soon as I'm done with this caller.

"Take your time," I say to Liam. "I'll be right here."

For the next fifteen minutes, I field call after call. A girl who's been struggling with anorexia, a gay teen who cuts himself instead of coming out of the closet, and a woman in the community who's simply lonely.

I ask questions and refer the callers to the appropriate resources. But mostly, I just listen. It doesn't take a lot of involvement. A few murmured words, a sympathetic noise or two. All my callers want is connection, a single point of human contact when they need it most.

I should've started volunteering here a long time ago. It's such a weird thought that my hand tightens on the telephone. A few weeks ago, I wouldn't have been caught dead here—especially since my mom, literally, was.

But no matter what happens with my mom's investigation, no matter what answers I find or don't find, part of me is glad it led me here. The crisis hotline. A place where I can help others even when I feel helpless myself.

When there's a lull in the calls, I hop onto the computer. Just as I finish logging the last conversation, the lights flicker.

My fingers pause over the keyboard. This kind of thing happens all the time. Right? The same way houses settle, lights go on and off during inclement weather.

Except . . . there's no thunderstorm.

I look out the window. The late afternoon sun bathes the trees in a warm glow, highlighting the vibrant colors of the leaves. The scene is as picturesque as a painting. And just as still. There's not even a trace of wind. So why did the lights flicker?

My breath quickens, and every nerve in my body screams, *Run!* But that's silly. I've already overreacted once, two days ago, when I was convinced that the texter had broken into my house. That was just the wind, and there could be hundreds of reasons for the lights to act this way. Thousands, even. And none of them have to do with the weirdo who keeps texting me.

But I feel it again. That unnerving silence pressing around me. The feeling someone's watching me. Oh god. What if I wasn't imagining before? What if I'm not imagining now?

Maybe the texter is out there, snapping more pictures of

me. Maybe he or she will do more than take photos this time. Maybe he'll . . . come . . . inside.

A cold sweat breaks out on my neck. Ridiculous. Even if he is out there—which he's not—he's not going to come into the hotline. He's not stupid. We've got a bank of phones with direct dials to every emergency service in Lakewood. And Liam will be back any minute.

Which reminds me . . .

I glance at the clock. Liam's been gone twenty minutes. Lakewood is tiny, with only one decent coffee shop in town. If I want to look for additional messages from my mom, I'd better stop being so freaking paranoid and get to work.

I square my shoulders and log in as Bea. I pull up the record after Lil's original one, and the breath explodes out of me.

Sure enough, a few words in this entry are set in a different font. And in the one after that. And the one after that.

I was right. My mom's left me an entire letter, coded in the caller database.

The lights flicker again, but I barely notice. I select the entire field and then click the "print" button. And then for good measure, I perform another search for the word "photo" within Bea's entries and print those, too.

As the printer spits out the final document, the power goes out. Just like that. One moment, I'm sitting under glaring artificial lights. The next, the only illumination comes from the sun outside. Every sound shuts off—the computer, the printer, even the air conditioner—and I sit in complete silence.

My mouth goes dry. It's funny. I've never thought much about the background noise before, those faint whirs and hums. But now that it's gone, I want it back. Desperately.

Faulty wiring. It's got to be faulty wiring. There's no other answer. But then, why do I feel like someone's wrapped an icy hand around my throat?

The silence is too quiet. Too eerie. Every sound is magnified. The honking of the geese outside. The occasional splash of the lake. The sound of someone breathing.

My heart stops. The sound of someone *breathing?* But I'm the only one inside this cabin. Aren't I?

I don't care if I'm imagining things. I can't wait another moment. I seize the papers, grab my backpack, and run. I might be the world's biggest fool, but at least I'll be alive.

My elbow slams against the doorjamb, but I ignore the throbbing. My feet slide on the hardwood, but I find my balance and keep going. Are there footsteps behind me? Is he here? Is he here? Is he here?

I don't stop. I can't look. I reach the front door and grasp the handle. It doesn't turn. IT'S LOCKED, DAMMIT. WHY THE HELL IS IT LOCKED?

I fumble at the lever, but my hands are slippery, and I can't grasp the narrow latch. I wipe my hands on my pants and am about to try again when the handle begins to twist.

Oh dear lord. He's not inside the cabin, after all. He's outside, and he's coming in to get me.

I stumble backward, my breath coming in pants. A black haze spreads over my vision, and I can barely see. No. I don't want it to end like this. I don't want to die in the hotline like my mother. Like my mother. Like my mother.

The door opens, and I bump into the wall. I scream, long and loud and never-ending, and then a pair of hands grabs my shoulders.

"CeCe! What's wrong? Are you okay?"

It takes a moment for the voice to register, and then I open my eyes. I didn't even realize I had closed them.

"Liam." Every bone in my body melts. He holds a Styrofoam container with two coffee cups, and the sun shines brightly outside. I have never been so happy to see anybody in my entire life.

He puts the cups down on the hall table and wraps his arms around me. I dig my cheek into his chest, pressing closer and closer. I might be giving him the wrong impression. I might have forgotten to tell him about Sam. Doesn't matter. Because in Liam's arms, I feel safe. The texter can't get me here, and neither can my imagination.

"I thought I heard something," I say weakly. "And the lights were flickering. A lot."

"There's no one here but me," he says, stroking my hair. "I'll get an electrician in to look at the lights. It's okay, CeCe. I'm here now. It's going to be okay."

And for one fleeting moment, with his heartbeat strumming reassuringly in my ear, I actually believe him.

Chapter 28

After my shift, I drive to Sam's house for our pizza date. My stomach rumbles uneasily, but I'm done pushing the feeling away. Damn right I should feel guilty. I was plastered against Liam for a good five minutes. Sam's the one I actually like. Isn't he? I mean, sure, he doesn't understand the ugly parts of me, the way Liam does. But he's the one I kissed. The one I daydream about. The one who eats away at my darkness with his goodness.

The moment he opens the door, I throw myself at him, rising on my toes and pressing my lips against his. I can still feel Liam's chest, warm and solid against my cheek, so I pour myself even more into the kiss.

There. Better. And if that makes me a flirt or a tease, well . . . I've been called worse things, just for existing.

I push Sam against the wall. He touches my face, brushing his fingers on my cheeks, along my earlobes, over the sensitive skin at my neck. I shiver and move my mouth against his until the floor drops and my insides go whirling into space. Until I can barely remember Liam's name, much less the reason why I was ever drawn to him. Until I'm nothing but a jumble of sensations and tastes—hot lips, moist tongue, the silvered remains of a peppermint candy.

I could kiss Sam forever.

And maybe I do. Because it feels like an eternity passes before

I finally, reluctantly, regrettably ease back. “Sorry about that. I, uh, was trying to figure out if I can trust you.”

He takes his glasses off and polishes them on his shirt. His eyes are wide and his breath is short—and dammit, he gets more adorable by the minute.

“By all means, investigate away.” He puts his glasses back on and pretends to leer. “I have it on good authority I’m kinda shady. So, maybe you should check again. Just to be sure.”

I swat his arm, giggling. I don’t think I giggled once in the months after my mom’s death. But ever since I met Sam, it’s an almost daily occurrence. “You’d better not be shady, Sam Davidson, especially when you’ve got a date this Sunday.”

“Oh, geez. You heard about the auction?” He grimaces. “So embarrassing. Please tell me you’re going to bid on me. Save me from having to go on a date with a stranger.”

I shake my head. “You’re on your own, buster. Not my scene.”

“What if I made it . . . worth your while?” He lowers his voice, mock-sexily.

I laugh again, pulling him into a hug. I close my eyes for a moment and breathe him in. “You’re kinda funny, you know that?”

“Kinda? Wow, you really need to dial down that enthusiasm a notch. You’re going to give me a big head.”

I smile, because I can’t be around Sam and not smile, but now that we’re not tangled together, the ice slides over my stomach. I take a few steps back from him. I’m not going to tell him about the lights flickering inside the hotline. Because it’s the second time I may have imagined an intruder. He’ll either write me off as a delusional lunatic . . . or he’ll take me seriously and call the police. Neither option is desirable.

Besides, if I tell him about my crazed run across the cabin, then I’d have to confess where the sprint ended—in Liam’s arms. Don’t really want to do that, either.

Instead, I lead him to the kitchen, and we sit at the square table. I explain how his discussion of fonts in Mr. Willoughby’s class helped me figure out the code. Pulling the sheaf of papers out of my bag, I tell him how I hope there's more to my mom's message hidden in these call entries.

As our socked feet bump under the table, we scrutinize the printouts, starting with Lil's original entry and proceeding through the entire batch chronologically. By isolating the words with a different font, we end up with this message:

> *darling if you are reading this something*
> *happened to me I'm close to getting proof but*
> *he knows it too I've hidden a box for you at*
> *the hotline the key is in the pocket of our black*
> *dress pry up the fifth board from the south*
> *wall I love you Mom*

I collapse in my chair. That's it. The whole message. I've dreamed so often of a final letter from my mother. But I never thought her words would be a set of directions.

"A box at the hotline," Sam says slowly, a crease in his forehead. "Do you think it's the box Mr. Willoughby took away? The one that's wrapped with your mom's wallpaper?"

"I don't think so." The guilt is back, shaking and spinning my stomach like it's a blender. I never mentioned the snow globe or my afternoon with Liam, either. Now's probably not a good time to rectify that lapse. "The hotline coordinator, um, Liam, said there was nothing inside but a bunch of papers. Besides, that box wasn't locked. If there's a key, it has to be locked, right?"

He bobs his head. "Okay. So it's a locked box. Under the fifth board from the wall. When your mom wrote this note, the hotline was in its old location. Which was . . . ?"

"In the old shed by the athletic field."

"Great. So that's where we'll be Friday night. The football team has an 'away' game, and nobody will be around."

"You mean, we're going to break in?" I stammer.

He raises both eyebrows. “I don’t want to ask the janitor for the keys to the shed. Do you?”

The room whirls dizzily around me, but he’s right. We have no idea what we’re going to find inside that shed. And until we do, we can’t go around advertising our excursion.

“Your mother’s been gone six months, CeCe. With every day that passes, the trail gets colder. If she felt desperate enough to leave you a coded note, she’d want you to investigate, wouldn’t she? Even if it means breaking into school property.”

I take a deep breath, pressing my hands against my roiling midsection. I’m not thrilled with breaking and entering, but that’s not the only reason why I’m nervous. The old shed is where my mom’s body was found, her limbs splayed awkwardly, her hair chopped at crazy angles. Lifeless. Broken. Stiff. The poor call counselor who found her the next morning screamed so loudly the janitor heard her all the way back at the school. To this day, if the call counselor catches a glimpse of me, she still squeaks and scurries away.

But I’m not up to reliving those few days after they found my mom’s body. The chaos, the sorrow. The rage that consumed me, nibbling at the stretched-out pieces of my heart until I wasn’t sure if there was anything left.

“Okay. You’ve convinced me,” I say instead. “Friday night. It’s a date.”

My third date with Sam in the space of four days. The thought should make me giddy. Instead, it fills the hollow places inside me with dread.

Chapter 29

"My head itches." I push back the black knit hat on my head two days later. Friday night. At the scene of a future crime.

"But you look cute." Sam grins at me from across the darkened interior of the car. His teeth glint, Cheshire-cat-like, from the passing street lights. Outside, the moon shines, full and round, a spotlight berating us for what we're about to do.

At his insistence, we're both wearing black clothes, like robbers. He's got on black sweats, and I'm wearing yoga pants and a thermal fleece.

"Are you sure we're dressed appropriately?" I ask for the fifth time. "We might as well wear a flashing neon sign. Yoohoo! Up to no good over here."

He runs his fingers down my braid. "If we run into anybody, they'll think we're doing the cute dress-alike thing. We can ask them to call us one of those celebrity couple names. Samcila. Or maybe Cesam. Yeah, I like that. Cesam."

I try to keep my lips still, but I have no more control over my smile than a made-up clown. He thinks we're a couple. He wants to be known by a single name. None of the kids at school know about our relationship—and with any luck, we'll keep it that way—but I know. And that's more than enough.

I park a few blocks from school, and we walk the rest of the way. The parking lot's almost deserted, with only a silver Prius and a tangerine VW Bug in the corner. As soon as we step onto the lot, however, the glass double doors of the building open, and two figures come out.

We slip behind a tree, and I end up crushed between the bark and Sam's pecs. "Did you see who it was?" he murmurs.

"I didn't get a good look." I wet my lips. "But I think they were headed in this direction."

Sure enough, the sound of footsteps and the hum of conversation get louder.

A knot in the tree digs into my neck. Some kind of insect crawls up my arm. And then Sam's lips brush over mine. "In case they see us, we're just a couple of students with one thing on our minds . . ."

I stifle a gasp as he catches my lower lip between his teeth. "You, uh, put a lot into your performance."

"You want me to be convincing, don't you?"

Every inch of his body presses against mine. My mouth is on fire, my nerves smoldering embers. And yet, I'm listening as hard as I can.

The footsteps stop on the other side of the tree. I tighten my grip on Sam's shoulder, and the kiss stills, until our lips are simply resting against one another.

"That was a good session, Amber," a familiar voice says. It takes me a moment to place the smooth, confident tone. Mr. Willoughby. "A few more should do it."

"Thanks, Mr. W," a girlish voice responds. "I think I'm really getting the hang of . . . Shakespeare."

She paused—didn't she? Or was that my imagination?

"Next week, same time?" the girl says.

"If that works for you." I hear the rustle of fabric against fabric. A bag slung over a shoulder? Or bodies shifting against one another? "Your mother doesn't mind the late hours?"

"I haven't told her. I'm going to surprise her with my report card at the end of the semester. She won't know what hit her."

They say goodbye, and the footsteps depart. Engines sputter to life. First one car, and then another, drives away, the headlights cutting a swath through the darkness.

"Whew," I say when we finally separate. "That's got to be the record for world's longest kiss."

"Not even." Sam taps his lips as though they're numb. "People have kissed for hours. Days even. I love kissing you and everything, but man, that's got to suck."

"You wouldn't be able to sleep."

"Or eat."

"Or pee."

"Or poo."

I stare at him for a moment and then burst out laughing. The sound shoots through the night, clear and bell-like, and I clap a hand over my mouth. What am I thinking? We're supposed to be in stealth mode.

I push myself off the tree trunk and begin picking bits of bark out of my braid. "So what did you think?"

He pulls the hat off my head and helps me. As his long fingers work through my hair, taking apart the strands of my braid to make sure he gets every last piece of bark, my stomach executes a slow, liquid somersault.

"Sounds like Mr. W's tutoring the girl. I've heard he does that a lot. Always willing to help out a student in need."

"Especially when she's young and pretty," I murmur. "Isn't it awfully late for a tutoring session? Particularly on a Friday night?"

He finishes undoing my braid and brushes the hair off my shoulder. His fingers linger on my back. Don't think about his hand. Stop imagining his kisses. Must. Focus. On. Task.

"What if Mr. W's the person behind my mom's photos?" I ask. "Maybe this is how he ensnares his victims. I mean, he dresses like a kid, with all those superhero shirts. And he hasn't had a date in twenty-some years. Maybe his dead wife is an excuse. Maybe he's just not interested in other adults." I gasp. "Oh god. That would make him a child pornographer, right? If he's taking photos of underage girls?"

"*If* it is Mr. Willoughby. But we have no evidence of that." He places the hat back on my head and kisses me on the nose.

"And speculating about Mr. W's personal life isn't going to get us into the shed."

I swallow hard. Enough stalling. It's time to do what we came here to do.

We circle to the back of the school and make our way to the athletic field. No one else is around. No guys playing pickup basketball. No overachieving runner loping around the track. Just me, Sam, and that damn spotlight moon.

The hair stands on my arms, and my scalp tingles. There's no wind tonight, but I shiver inside my fleece. Don't be silly. There's no one watching me. My texter's not here. And even if he were, he'd have to get through Sam first.

I grit my teeth and ignore the moon, as much as you can ignore the largest orb in the sky. I place one foot in front of the other until we arrive at the square, squat building.

The shed was updated a few years ago with a tiny bathroom, but no one's bothered to do anything to the outside. The paint peels off in patches, and the wood is rotted through with holes.

The chill creeps inside my gut. Is it me, or is it cooler here? As if the air remembers somebody died. As if the very molecules cling to the remnants of violence.

We stop in front of the door, and Sam reaches for the padlock hanging on the handle. "It's busted."

"What do you mean?"

He hands me the lock. In the light of the moon, I see the shank's been sawed through.

"It's hanging here, useless. But you'd never know until you touched it. Someone's been here."

My pulse skitters. "Who?"

He shakes his head but doesn't answer. He doesn't need to. The possibilities stream in the space between us. My mysterious texter. The child pornographer. The person from whom my mother was hiding. All of whom may or may not be the same person.

"Are they here now?" I whisper.

"I don't hear anything."

"But they could come back. Any second now, they could be back."

We stare at each other for a full sixty seconds. He jams his hands under his arms, and the breath rushes in and out of his mouth, as if he's gearing up for a race. Everything inside tells me to bolt, to get away now before something happens to us. The same something that happened to my mother.

Sam huffs out another breath. "We might as well go inside. We didn't come here to turn around and go home."

"We didn't?" I ask faintly.

He smiles, as if I've made a joke. But nothing's funny when you're breaking into a shed. Nothing's funny when you're about to return to the place where your mother died. In fact, I can't remember anything that was ever funny, at any time.

My legs, arms, feet vibrate with the need to run. But before I can take off, Sam grabs the handle of the door.

"Sam, wait! I have to tell you something." I close my eyes and take shallow, quick breaths. Just do it. Say the words. They won't kill you. "This is . . . this is where a student found my mom's body."

A few seconds pass. He doesn't say anything. I crack open my eyes to peer at his expression. He doesn't look surprised—which is a pretty big surprise. At least to me.

"Oh my god, you knew?" I wheeze.

Reluctantly, he nods. "Newspaper intern, remember? Researching an article on the anniversary of the hotline suicide? It's my job to know."

I double over, grabbing my knees. This isn't a betrayal. It isn't. What he's saying makes sense. With all the research he's done, of course he would know exactly where my mother's body was found. How she looked. What she was holding. Only an idiot would think otherwise.

Well, this idiot, for some reason, thought that the boy she kissed would have confessed that he's been prying into the most intimate details of her mother's death.

"Why didn't you tell me?" I ask. "My god, I've told you everything." Nearly everything. Minus a couple incidents of hand-holding and arms-wrapping. "You couldn't tell me you knew my mother died with a sex toy in her hands?"

He reddens. "I'm sorry, CeCe. I didn't know if you wanted to talk about it. I guess I was waiting for you to broach the subject."

I straighten. Again, reasonable. Again, not a betrayal. He didn't keep his knowledge from me because he was laughing at me. I'm just so used to the taunts and whispers that I automatically leaped to that conclusion.

"Are you okay to go inside?" Sam asks. "If you're not, I could go in, get the box, and bring it out to you."

It is tempting, so tempting. But my mother left that coded message for me. She wanted me to retrieve the box. I'm not about to disregard her final request.

"I'm fine," I say. "Let's just do it quickly before I change my mind."

He grabs the door handle once again.

Screeeeech.

We both freeze, and my pulse thuds in my throat. For what feels like an eternity, we wait. Nothing. Nobody rushes out to clobber us over the head. No pitter-patter of rats scurrying for cover.

"I think we're safe," he says. "No one's here."

"For now."

He nods, waits a few beats, and then walks inside. Just like that, he's swallowed by the darkness, disappearing from view like a coffin being lowered into the ground.

Run! Don't go in there. You don't have to do this.

My muscles strain, but I don't give in to the panic. I can't. These are my mother's final instructions. Sam's in the shed because of me, and I won't leave him. We're a team, and he's my . . . He's the . . .

My mind stutters over the word, and even to myself, I can't think it. But I don't need to. He's Sam. That's all I need to know.

I take a shuddering breath. And then I follow him inside.

The smell hits me first. The cloying scent of dying flowers, sweetness edged with decay. And then Sam switches on a flashlight. I grope in my pocket for my own light, even as his beam dances frenetically around the room.

A couple of rumpled sleeping bags are zipped together on the floor, next to a mountain of jewel-colored pillows. Rose petals mingle with the sawdust, and empty wine bottles and long green stems are strewn across the floor.

Sam bends down and touches the cooled wax that has dripped onto the floor. "Someone's been using this place as a rendezvous. They went to a lot of trouble to make it romantic." His tone is quiet and measured. I can almost see the wheels turning in his head. "Former Hotline Center Hosts Secret Tryst. Not bad. Better than talking about the air fresheners the hotline uses."

He grabs his backpack and takes out a camera and portable LED work lights, which he strategically positions around the sleeping bags. "You mind if I take a few pictures? As long as we're here."

I stare. Maybe Sam should've been a Boy Scout instead of a newspaper intern. "Prepared much?" I say dryly. "Don't mind me. I'll just be over here, following a trail of clues my dead mother left me."

He doesn't respond, already absorbed with setting up the perfect shot, and I roll my eyes and move to the south wall. Gripping the flashlight between my teeth, I kneel in the corner. The wood planks are rough, plagued with splinters waiting to be embedded in my skin. I touch the floor with my fingertips and count over five planks.

This is it. Trembling, I slide my nails into the cracks around the board. No give. I pry my nails up, praying they don't break. There! A little lurch. And then the whole plank lifts up.

"Sam," I croak, the flashlight falling from my mouth. "I think I found it."

"What is it?" He's by my side in an instant.

I retrieve my light and shine it into the hole. At the bottom, partially covered by dirt, is what looks like a small, thin briefcase. Except there's no handle, and the edges are rounded. A metal strip seals the center, culminating in a lock with a keyhole.

"A portable safe." I close my hands around the cool metal just as a loud noise pierces the air.

I dive to the ground, the box clenched to my chest. Oh my god. He's back. The guy who set up the romantic tryst. Or my texter. Are they one and the same? Does it matter?

The noise sounds again, and I curl into a fetal position, moaning. A gunshot. It has to be. I'm going to die in this shed, just like my mother.

I feel a hand on my shoulder and look into Sam's eyes.

"A garbage truck," he says shakily. "Emptying out a Dumpster."

"Are you sure?"

"No."

The air wheezes in and out of my lungs. My heart tries to drill a hole through my chest. Again, we wait, limbs stiff and muscles tight. Not daring to make a sound, but ready to sprint if it comes to that.

One minute passes, and then two.

A full five minutes later, and it's clear that no one's coming. I let out a breath, too on edge to be relieved.

Sam rises into a crouch. "Let's get the hell out of here."

The best idea I've heard all day. Maybe even all year.

Chapter 30

"Call me anytime," Sam says twenty minutes later. I pull into his driveway, and he laces his fingers through mine on top of the black, metal-edged box that's been sitting between us the entire ride home. "If you need to talk. It's not like I'll be sleeping, anyway."

"Too busy working on your article?" It's due on Tuesday, four days away. He's only mentioned the due date once, and I didn't write it down. But I don't need to. The date's ingrained in my mind. What are we going to find before the article's due? And if we don't find anything, what will Sam write the article about?

"Nah. Too busy jumping at every car that backfires. I don't need to lose sleep over the article. I've got some preliminary thoughts." Before I can ask what those thoughts are, he brings my hand to his lips and kisses my fingertips. "Will you be okay?"

"Sure. There's not a bomb in this safe. Or a severed head. Or the chopped-off remains of her hair."

Oh god. Why did I say that? What if there *is?*

We both look at the metal safe. It measures eighteen inches by twelve, and it could hold anything.

"Call me," he repeats. "Unless you want me there when you open it?"

"I'll be fine."

I drive home. Dad's nowhere to be seen, and Gram's still at

her poker night. Surprise, surprise. The way I come and go, you'd never guess I had two so-called guardians.

I take the safe to my bedroom and sit cross-legged on my bed. I clench the silver key in my fist until it turns hot and slippery.

My fingers itch for a quick sketch. Sam, in his midnight-robber gear, untangling my braid with his fingers. The moon shining down on us with its all-seeing gaze. The sawed-off padlock and the pools of cooled wax. I want to draw all this and more, although there's no danger of me forgetting this night. But I know if I take pencil to paper now, I may never stop. I may never open the safe.

What am I afraid of? Not finding the answers for which I've been searching? Or finding them?

I pick up the snow globe, give it a shake, and set it beside me. The snow falls on the girl and her mother and her mother's mother five times, and then another five, and I'm still not ready. No matter. I'm never going to be ready. I just have to do it.

I take a deep breath and slide the key into the lock. Of course, it fits perfectly. Inside, I find not blood and gore, not hair, not brains, not any organic matter. Instead, a slim notebook lies at the bottom of the safe, a notebook with a leather cover and yellowed pages.

No, not just a notebook. I flip through the pages and see my mom's loopy handwriting, dates from over twenty years ago. A journal. From—I do the calculations on my fingers—my mom's senior year.

Why did she go through all this trouble to leave me her journal? Will I find out why she posed for those topless photos? Learn what happened to her a quarter of a century later?

There's only one way to find out. I lie against my pillows and begin reading.

Sept. 10, 1990
Dear Journal,

It's the first day of senior year, and Mr. Willoughby says we have to keep a journal. This is his first year as a teacher, and we're his first class, so he's brimming with all sorts of enthusiasm. He says it doesn't matter how we fill it, so long as we express ourselves.

Yeah, right. You'll forgive me, won't you, Journal, if I don't "express" myself? I mean, we hardly know each other. You wouldn't expect me to spill my secrets to a stranger, would you?

Let's see. What can I say? It's going to be an amazing year. I can feel it in my well-sculpted bones. But don't take my word for it. Take the word of the boy from my art class, who's already asked if I would model for him. Apparently, I have the kind of bone structure that makes his muse weep, whatever that means.

But I didn't ask because I'm not supposed to be the kind of girl who needs compliments explained. I'm supposed to be beautiful and popular and confident, from my lipsticked mouth to my matching red toes.

Nobody's supposed to know that if the sun hits the mirror just right, I can blink and see the girl hiding behind my cascade of hair. It's like those pictures with a million dots, where if you stand back and let your eyes unfocus, the true picture emerges.

This girl has no resemblance to the one who glides through the hallways at school. Nobody sees her. And if I have my way, you won't, either, Journal.

My best friend Audrey always says we can't wait for life to happen. If we want the biggest slice of pie—the juiciest, the sweetest, the tastiest—we have to seize control and take it for ourselves. Well, this is me taking it. I'm going to have a good senior year. No, scratch that. I'm going to have the senior year to end all senior years!

Last year, my life fell apart. A few pieces got swept into the drain, and a few more blew away in the wind, so there was no hope of putting me back together again. After the year I just had, I deserve to be happy.

Don't you agree, Journal?

My chest feels tight, like I've forgotten how to breathe. I read the words of the first entry again. And then again. I want to savor them. No, more than that. I want to swallow my mother's words, make them a part of me so I never have to let her go.

So much hope in these lines. So much excitement. Sure, there's an underlining cloud of sadness, but her overall energy and zest for life shines through.

YES. You deserve to be happy, Mom. You deserve everything.

Back then, the scandal with Tommy was an unfathomable speck in the distant future. Whatever her mistakes or failures, they had yet to occur. My mother was nothing but a girl—a girl who had lost her own mother the previous year. A girl very much like me.

My fear disappears. The uncertainty, the anxiety, even the anger lift like the fog on a sunny morning. It doesn't matter what I find in these pages. Because I now have something I haven't had for the past six months. My mother, back again.

I clutch the journal and keep reading.

September 15, 1990
Dear Journal,

I'm afraid Mr. Willoughby knows what he's doing. There's something about writing on this blank page, which no one will read or judge, that is freeing. Because you won't tell, will you, Journal? Whatever secrets I write will seep into your pages and disappear.

Audrey's pissed at me. She wants me to double-date with her and Cliff, and that's not so bad in itself. But she wants me to go out with Cliff's best friend, Brandon, and that's not okay.

Because I've gone out with Brandon before. All he wants is to pour drinks down my throat and get me in the backseat. If I say "no," he'll call me a cock tease. He'll say I was asking for it because of my clothes, even if I'm wearing sweatpants and a ratty old sweater.

I tried to explain this to Audrey, but she wouldn't listen. She says Cliff will only go out with her if I agree to the double date, and she thinks I'm standing in the way of true love.

What her finding a soul mate has to do with me getting felt up, I'm not sure. But Audrey says I've hooked up with lots of guys before. What's one more?

It's enough to make me want to cut my hair and toss my makeup. But I won't do it. Because my looks are my only ticket out of this town.

Lakewood, Kansas, is like a black hole. Once you're born here, it's almost impossible to leave. You have to be really smart, really talented, or really pretty to get out. I'm not smart. I'm not good at much. But I am pretty. The mirror says so. And if I don't unfocus my eyes, I can almost believe it.

Was that too personal, Journal? I asked Audrey what she writes in her notebook. She says she keeps lists. Of everything she ate that day. The clothes she wore that week. The boys she's kissed this year.

She doesn't mention any similar tug on her inner feelings. The danger a blank page poses to her true self.

I have to wonder, dear Journal. Am I doing something wrong?

September 18, 1990
Dear Journal,

Today was a good day. It's what my mom would've called a "red-letter" day. I wish she were still with me now. We would've parked ourselves at the kitchen table and drank tea and laughed for hours. That's the kind of mom she was. Sometimes, I miss her so much it feels like a switchblade puncturing my lungs.

But I don't want to think about that. All I've done in the past year, it seems, is miss her. And that's not seizing control the way Audrey wants me to.

I met someone today. Oh, I suppose I didn't just meet him. I've known him for years, but I didn't really know *him, if you get what I mean.*

I can't tell you his name. Even from you, Journal, I must keep his identity a secret. But that's okay. His presence is so strong, his spirit so unique, he doesn't need a name.

Unlike everyone else, he sees the real me. He doesn't have to unfocus his eyes. He doesn't have to wait for a trick of the sun. He sees me as easily as he sees flowers or dew drops or rain.

And he promises he'll make the bad things go away. I'll never have to climb into a backseat again. I'll never have to pretend to be someone I'm not. I'll never have to be alone, so long as he's here.

My insides buzz around like a hive of bees, and I can't stop smiling. I'll be in trig class and my hands will brush across my lips, and I'll realize they're curved. Imagine that. Me, smiling for absolutely no reason. Or, rather, for the most important reason of all. Is this what happiness feels like?

I couldn't tell you. It's been so long since I've felt this way, I don't actually remember.

October 2, 1990

It's been a while, Journal, and I apologize. I haven't written because I've been too busy being IN LOVE. I hope you understand and don't hold it against me.

Not like Audrey does. She's annoyed because I don't have time for her hour-long phone calls anymore. And she's beside herself that I keep turning down the dates she arranges. But it's not her fault because she doesn't know. Nobody does, Journal, except for you.

It's like my own delicious secret—OUR delicious secret, mine and his—and somehow this makes what we have even more special. Our love is on a different plane, above and beyond what is felt on this world and so there's no need to share it with anyone.

They wouldn't understand, anyway. They can't because they don't know how he makes me feel.

With him, I feel like I can fly without wings. Breathe underwater. Defy gravity. That's what his love does for me. It makes me invincible.

Alarm bells ring in my head, loud and long and insistent. This isn't going to end well. It can't. I wouldn't be lying here reading my mom's journal if it had. Her topless photo wouldn't be floating around the Internet. Something about her words crawls inside me, something oddly familiar that tangles my stomach with my kidneys and lungs. Something not good.

I want to shout at the journal, at the seventeen-year-old Tabitha. *Run! Run as fast as you can from this relationship. He isn't good for you, not if he makes you keep your relationship a secret.*

But she can't hear me, and even if she could, it's too late. The past has already happened. All that's left for me to do is to find out how bad it was.

My hands trembling with fear, I continue reading.

Dear Journal,

I'm still happy. Still in love. One little incident doesn't change that. I won't let it. This is turning out to be exactly the senior year I envisioned, and I'm not going to ruin it for myself. I'm not.

I'm probably being a prude anyway. That's what Audrey always says. She says I'm so selective about who I let touch my boobs, they might as well be an artifact at a highly exclusive museum. Right. If my boobs were priced that highly, I'd have been out of Lakewood eons ago.

He's older than me. He's used to more experienced women, and I have to respect that. Of course he's going to want to do things out of my comfort zone. I have to grow up sometime.

Besides, if I have to give my virginity to someone, shouldn't it be to the man I love?

October 21, 1990
Dear Journal,

It's not as if I don't like sex. There are moments in the whole sweaty encounter when it's actually okay. These moments, unfortunately, are fleeting. They're gone before I can catch them and hold them close.

What I like best is the part afterward. The part where he holds me and looks into my eyes. He smiles, and I know he likes what he sees. I know I am more than this body and this face. I know I am worth something.

These times, though, happen less and less often. This isn't his fault. He would hold me if he could. But he's so busy. We don't have time for the long conversations we used to have. So we have sex when it's convenient. Where there are no beds. And no time to cuddle afterward.

He tells me again and again he gives me the things I need. He fills up the blank spaces inside me. When he first said this, I thought it sounded so romantic. But now I hear the crudeness behind the words. And I don't like it.

When I ask him to stop saying it, he says I'm being hormonal. And maybe I am.

But you know what? I'm a teenage girl. What did he expect?

October 28, 1990
Dear Journal,

Audrey won't speak to me anymore. I've been a terrible friend. He said she was too immature for me and advised me to cut her loose. I was so in love at the time, I did exactly as he asked.

And now I have no one but you, Journal. I used to think I was lonely before. My mom—my number-one champion—was gone, and the only girl my friends knew was the one on the outside, the one in the mirror. Now, I would give anything for even that level of friendship.

I can hear his voice now: "Don't be so dramatic, Tabitha. If you've lost your friends, it's all your own doing. It has nothing to do with me."

Sometimes, when I'm feeling especially sullen, I want to lash back: Oh really? *You weren't the one who encouraged me to drop my friends? You weren't the one who said they were poison to my purity?*

In the end, though, he's right. It was my decision. But I made the decision for true love. Not for this.

No. *I don't mean that. He is my true love, my soul mate. I've been stressed lately, that's all.*

I guess I'm not sexually exciting enough for him, so he makes me pose for these naked photos. It's not smut, he says, tracing the curve of my breasts, but art. I didn't want to, but he promised he wouldn't show anybody. He promised we would get back to the way we were if I would do this one thing for him.

I hate it. Okay, there, I said it. I really, really hate it. These explicit photos that turn him on so much—it makes me feel dirty. So dirty I can't find those fleeting feel-good moments AT ALL. And when I mentioned it to him, he smiled and said, "Don't worry, babe. I'm deriving enough pleasure for the two of us."

Which made me want to slap him. Is that wrong? I know he's kidding around. He would tell me I have no sense of humor. And so I clenched my teeth and said nothing.

Because in the end, I don't want to lose him, too. He's all I have left.

November 2, 1990

I'm shaking so badly I can hardly write this. I can't believe what I just did. What he made me do. I couldn't even stay at school, I was so upset. I've taken two showers now, and I still don't feel clean.

You won't judge me, will you, Journal? If my dad finds out, he'll skin me alive. Maybe I should let him. So I won't have to think about it anymore.

The lunch hour started normally enough. I was by my locker talking to Billy Cramer. He was sick yesterday and wanted to borrow my notes. So what if he put his arm around my waist? So what if I laughed and dropped my head onto his shoulder, my long hair falling over his arm? Billy and I have been friends since preschool. There's a class photo of us sitting side by side when we were four years old, me in a velvet jumper, him with his trademark smirk. Any flirtation between us can never be more than innocent. It's Billy, for god's sake. Kissing him would be like kissing my brother.

If I'm being honest, maybe I did want a little attention. Maybe I wanted to feel pretty once again, since it's been so long since he made me feel that way. Billy always makes me laugh and smile and I know he had a crush on me in the seventh grade, so maybe I did push the boundaries a little bit. Maybe I held his eyes a little too long. Smiled at him a little too suggestively.

Is that a crime? Is that so wrong?

According to him, the man who supposedly loves me, it is. He stalked up to us and grabbed my shoulder, not noticing who saw, not caring what Billy might think. And then he all but threw me into his classroom.

I was wearing the clothes he likes, these short little schoolgirl skirts, with a thong underneath. I wear these clothes for him, not for Billy or anyone else, but he wouldn't believe me. He called me a "slut" and he said if I wanted to act like a prostitute, he would treat me like one. A moment before the bell rang, he shoved me under his desk, this solid, massive, oak desk that sits right on the floor. And he plopped down in front of me, spreading his legs and shoving my head into his crotch. And then he dug his nails into my scalp, so hard it felt like real metal nails being hammered into my brains.

Right there. In the middle of class. With twenty students on the other side of the desk. He drilled his nails into my head until I unzipped his pants and gave him what he wanted.

I'm so ashamed, Journal. I feel so dirty I could die.

No more. This is it. I can't do this anymore. I won't.

Pray for me, Journal. I'm going to tell him tomorrow.

November 3, 1990

Oh Journal. That didn't go well. That didn't go well at all.

I told him we were done. And he said "no."

I stared at him. I mean, how do you say "no"? This isn't how breakups work. If one person wants out, the relationship's done.

Apparently not in his world.

If I don't keep doing exactly what I'm doing, he's going to tell my dad, the administration, the entire student body that I tried to seduce him. That I walked into his classroom, unbuttoning my shirt, hiking up my skirt, showing him my thong.

And when he turned me down, I got vengeful. Desperate. Actions speak louder than words, he said. And he's got plenty of students who will be his eyewitnesses. Who've seen me leaving his classroom at times when I'm not supposed to be there. Who've witnessed me dressed like a whore.

Did I think my life was bad? He can make it so I can't walk in a room without people hissing. Did I think my classmates saw nothing but my looks? He can confirm to everyone I'm actually the slut they think I am.

That word again. Every time he says it, his mouth twists into an ugly sneer. A rage leaps into his eyes, and it is so deep, so intense and dark, that it makes me shiver. And I know then that I didn't cause this. There's something warped inside him, something that's been there long before he met me. My flirtation with Billy merely brought it to the surface.

I'm trapped. Who are they going to believe? Honestly, who? The well-respected teacher everyone loves? Or the girl who looks like an automated sex doll?

That's what he's thought of me this entire time. An automated sex doll. Everything he said, everything I felt—it was a lie. Nothing but a lie.

"You don't want to mess with me, Tabitha," he warned, his features grotesque. I don't know how I ever thought he was good-looking. "I will ruin you."

And then he yanked up my skirt and ripped off my thong and pushed into me right then and there.

I screamed, but he covered my mouth with his hand. And he said I'd better stop it, bitch. Or next time, he would use duct tape.

I don't know what to do, Journal. I just don't know what to do.

November 17, 1990

There's no escape. I haven't been to school in two weeks, but he found me anyway.

He showed up at my house today, the concerned teacher, and told my dad I was skipping school. The entire administration was worried, he said.

I refused to come out, but my dad let him into my bedroom, anyway. And right there, with my door ajar, with my dad reading the paper in the living room, he made me give him a blow job.

After he left, I told my dad everything. But the concerned teacher was right. He had prepared his story well. My dad didn't believe a single word.

"Now, Tabitha. Be reasonable," my dad said. "Your lies don't even make sense. If what you're saying is true, why would he show up at our house? How could he look me in the eye? He's a good man, Tabitha, and I will not let you ruin his life with your fantasies."

When he said that, I knew. I knew with my mother gone, nobody would believe me. Deep down I'll always be that girl on the outside. The girl everybody sees.

I stood in front of the mirror today. No matter how I let my eyes unfocus, no matter how I tilted the mirror to reflect the sun, I couldn't see her. The real me. She's gone. He destroyed her.

When am I going to learn? Like the fabled phoenix he so admires, he will rise from his ashes.

The phoenix wins. He always, always wins.

Chapter 31

That was it. The last entry. No additional notes to me. No explanation how it relates to her death decades later.

I close the leather-bound journal and push it away. My heart is cluttered, my brain feels soaked. So many emotions crowd inside me I don't know how to react. How to feel.

My gut decides for me. I lurch to the bathroom, barely making it in time to empty the entire contents of my stomach into the toilet. I vomit and vomit, until there's nothing left. Until I move past clear saliva to yellow bile. And still I retch.

Finally, I collapse on the cool ceramic tile. I don't know how much time passes before I crawl back to my room. But when I do, my phone pings. My ribs seize, the way they do every time I hear that sound, but it's only a text from Sam.

U ok?

My fingers hover over the screen, but then I grab the phone and toss it under my bed. I want to talk to him, but I can't. Because this is exactly the angle Sam's been searching for. So much better than a secret tryst. This is the kind of story over which he's been salivating. The kind that will win him scholarships and launch his career.

Which is why I'm not going to tell him.

I open my notebook, instead, and begin to draw. My mother, of course. All those times I saw her sad. The quiet, quiet tears that slid down her cheeks, for no reason at all.

At least, no reason I knew about. Until now.

I draw until my fingers cramp and I feel the ache all the way up in my neck. I draw until the dawn presses around my tightly closed blinds. I draw until I feel sick with fatigue. And still, I don't sleep.

Because there's someplace I need to be. And it's not here.

I grab the snow globe, tiptoe down the stairs, and get in my car. I haven't made this drive since the evening of my mother's burial, but my hands turn the steering wheel almost by instinct. As if there will always be a direct line connecting my mother and me, no matter where—or in which realm—we are.

Inside the cemetery gates, a stream of water shoots out of the mouth of a stone angel, and a center island of tiny tombstones commemorates the lives of babies who were taken too soon. Beyond that, rows of gravestones march across the wide expanse of grass, and tall, lush trees offer shade to the cemetery's permanent residents.

I park the car and walk to my mom's grave. It's not hard to find. More elaborate than the others, and twice as clean. A big, shiny grave marker, devoid of dirt and bird droppings, and a long slab of marble, while most people just have grass. Her picture is set in the center of the headstone, next to the words, "Beloved wife of Peter, devoted mother to Cecilia." Colorful flowers—two of each—bloom in vases anchored by white stones.

Two daffodils, two roses, two lilies.

My mother loved flowers, the variety of them more than a single kind. Her wedding bouquet boasted a dozen different types, with just as many bold, clashing colors. No doubt my father brings her a new bloom every day.

I sink to my knees in the damp grass and set the snow globe carefully on her grave, where my mom's picture can see it.

"Hi, Mom." The words catch in my throat. It's not the first time I've spoken to her since she's died, but here, with her decomposing body a few feet underground, her spirit seems stronger. More alive. "I found your journal. And I want you to know . . ."

My voice breaks. I grip the grass, and chunks of it rip off in my hands. I grab another fistful, but that, too, comes loose. Patches of dirt now show up in the lawn, bald spots on the earth's scalp.

I curl my fingers into fists and try again. "I'm so pissed Grandpa didn't believe you. I hate him for that."

But the emotion is useless. He's long since dead, and there's no point in hating the dead. And yet: How many times did I hate my own mother? How often did I damn her to hell after the scandal broke? How desperately did I wish I'd had any mother but my own?

A sharp pain flares in my chest. Because, in the end, I'm just as bad as Grandpa was. I didn't believe in my mother when it really counted.

I was so angry at her for lying to me, for keeping her affair with Tommy Farrow a secret. But I know now that those aren't the darkest lies. The darkest lie is the one we tell ourselves, the one that makes us forget everything we know to be true, the one that makes us doubt something as simple and basic as a mother's love. This is the lie that changes us, that turns us from someone fearless and strong to someone who cowers and hides and lets others be bullied. This is the lie that's governed me for the past six months.

I know the truth now. Perhaps I've always known it, but I was too hurt, too betrayed, too resentful to recognize it: My mother is innocent.

For the first time since her death, I allow myself to think these words. They've been creeping up on me for a couple of weeks now, and after reading her journal, I know, at the core of my being, what I should've realized from the beginning.

My mom didn't commit suicide. She never slept with Tommy Farrow. She wouldn't have abused a student—she couldn't have abused anybody. In fact, the reason she spearheaded the crisis hotline was to help others in the same position as her, who have nowhere else to turn. Who had no one else to believe in them.

The most important thing to Tabitha Brooks was being a mother. She would've protected me at all costs. Whatever her faults and depression, her passions and mood swings, she never would have left me willingly. Not after she was deserted by her own mother. Not after she had to muddle through the abusive relationship with her teacher alone. She wouldn't have wanted that for me. In fact, she would've done everything in her power to prevent it from happening.

"I'm so sorry, Mom," I whisper. "Can you ever forgive me?"

But my mom's not here anymore, and forgiveness is no longer an option. I can no longer absolve my guilt through my mother's generosity, like I did countless times during my childhood. I need to find another way to make it up to her.

Water sloshes in a steady rhythm, and I glance up to see my father approaching the grave, holding a rubber squeegee, a partially filled gallon jug of water, and two canary-yellow hibiscus flowers.

He stops a few feet away. "You're here."

"Yes. I . . ." I swallow and look at my mother's eyes in the photo, addressing my words to both of them. "I should've been here months ago. But that's going to change now. A lot of things are going to change."

He sticks the flowers into a vase and pours the water over the slab. "You've always been here. In your heart. I think your mother knows that. That's why I bring two flowers every day. One from me. And one from you."

My heart pinches. I've been wrong about so many things. Not only about my mom, but also about my dad.

"Thank you." I pick up the squeegee and attack the marble. "And I think you're right. She does know."

"What's this?" He gestures to the snow globe.

"It was Mom's," I say, my throat tight again. "I don't know if you remember, but I gave it to her when I was eight years old. She was sad about her mom, and I wanted to remind her that no matter what, we would always be together."

"Of course I remember," he says. "I drove you to the store, didn't I?"

"Yeah," I say softly. "You did."

We turn back to our work. I scrub, and my father pours, and together we make my mother's grave the cleanest in the cemetery. And I know it's okay my mother's not here to forgive me. Because I never needed her forgiveness. She always loved me, no matter what. No matter what I did, no matter how I felt. Her feelings for me never wavered.

There's only one person from whom I need forgiveness. Myself.

My head aches. My eyelids feel like they're weighed down by sandbags. But I don't take a nap when I get home from the cemetery. Because my mother left me her journal for a reason, and I need to figure out why.

I crawl back into bed and prop myself against my pillows. She was exploited and raped by her high school teacher, but this isn't about sharing her secret. "Oh dear god, it's happened again," she wrote at the bottom of Lil's entry. "I'm close to getting proof," she encoded in her message to me.

Twenty-five years later. Another student, another explicit photo. A cycle of exploitation repeated. What does it mean? How does it all add up?

Part of me wants to duck under the covers and pretend I never found the journal. But it's too late now. I can never turn my back on her, ever again.

So I flip to the beginning of the notebook and read it again, searching for clues. Looking for answers I missed the first time around.

I find it in the fourth entry. Sitting up straight, I reread the passage.

It's like my own delicious secret—OUR delicious secret, mine and his—and somehow this makes what we have even more special. Our love is on a different plane, above and beyond what is felt on this world and so there's no need to share it with anyone.

They wouldn't understand, anyway. They can't because they don't know how he makes me feel.

With him, I feel like I can fly without wings. Breathe underwater. Defy gravity. That's what his love does for me.

It makes me invincible.

The strange words were familiar before, but the alarm bells were ringing too loudly then for me to pay much attention. I frown, racking my brain. I've heard these words before. Not from this journal. Somewhere else. From somebody else. Where . . . Who . . .

When the answer comes to me, the notebook slips through my fingers and falls to the floor. It looks like I'm going to have to tell Sam, after all.

Because it's not just a cycle that's being repeated. Twenty-five years later, my mom's predator is still around.

And he's after Sam's sister, Briony.

Chapter 32

"Let me get this straight." Sam's eyebrows shoot above the frame of his glasses half an hour later. "You're saying your mom's sexual predator is dating my sister?"

"Not just any predator, either," I say. "Maybe also a murderer."

I didn't want to tell Sam about the contents of the journal, but I had no choice. Briony's life—or at least her integrity—is in danger. I can't sit back and let the predator have his way because I'm skittish about sharing information. I'm just going to have to trust that Sam is true to his word—that he's not going to hurt people in order to get a good story.

Ha. Easier said than done. I may have kissed the boy; I may even be falling for him. Doesn't necessarily mean I can trust him.

Around us, the parking lot of the public library is empty, unless you count the bushy-tailed squirrels chasing each other up a tree. In Lakewood, nine a.m. on Saturday is like the crack of dawn anywhere else. Dead as the corpses in Kassel's funeral parlor. I would know. I spent enough hours there to last a lifetime.

I take a deep breath. There's that pesky trust issue swimming laps around my stomach again. "I don't think my mom committed suicide," I force myself to say. And once I start talking, the words continue to roll out, almost at their own volition. "I think she stumbled across her former predator and threatened to expose him and his pornography ring. And then he killed her to keep her quiet."

He frowns. "What about Tommy Farrow?"

"He was lying, pure and simple."

"And you think my sister's involved in this? Oh, jeez." He rubs his temples, as if that alone can protect him from what I'm saying. "I don't get it. She *told* you she wasn't seeing an older guy. She said it was disgusting."

"Maybe she was trying to throw me off track. Who knows? The thing is, she used the same words to describe her boyfriend. Not the same idea—but the exact same words. What are the chances? Both she and my mom must be repeating what this asshole told them."

I hand him the journal, open to the fourth entry. I've given him a summary of the other entries, but this part, he needs to see for himself.

"I don't actually remember what Bri said," he admits, after running his eyes over the page.

"Did you bring the silver cuff?"

"Yeah." He fishes the wide metal band out of his backpack. "She's going to kill me when she finds out I took it from her room."

"Just return it before she wakes up. Read the inscription on the back."

He turns the bracelet over. My midsection flutters, like it's taking a few test jumps before attempting to fly out of my body. What if I'm wrong? God knows, I'm working on zero sleep. Maybe it's messing with my memory.

The squirrels scrabble up one side of the tree, kuk-kuk-kuking at one another. And then down the other side.

"It's the same," he finally says, and my stomach unclenches. "But could they both be repeating a famous quote? Or, I don't know, song lyrics or something?"

"I did a search on the Internet. Nothing popped up."

He sinks onto the curb, gripping his head between his hands. I know what he's feeling because I've felt it, too. The world turning into quicksand, pulling me under with no branch, no hand, no help in sight.

"You know what this means, don't you?" I ask softly, sitting next to him. "You can't run your story about the shed being used as a rendezvous point, not if we're going to have any hope of catching this guy."

He looks up. "Why not? What does a secret tryst have to do with what you're talking about? My deadline's in three days. Plus, I've got that ridiculous auction tomorrow night, and I still have to write my profile for it."

"What if it's them?" I ask. "Briony and her boyfriend have to be meeting somewhere. It's possible they've been using the old shed. If you publish the article, he'll know we're on to him. And we lose every advantage we've got."

He chews his lip, and I press forward. "For the same reason, you can't write anything about my mom's journal."

"What would you have me do, CeCe?" he bursts out. "I have to write something, or they'll fire me."

"You could write about our tour of the hotline."

He squeezes his eyes shut. "It's so boring, they'll fire me anyway."

"You told me a week ago that you weren't going to hurt anyone," I whisper, my heart swelling like one of those polymer toys that grow in the water. "You said you chose this career to help people, not to kick them while they're down. Well, I'm telling you right now, if you share the contents of my mom's journal with anyone, you will hurt me."

I wait, hardly daring to breathe. Who am I? A girl he met mere weeks ago. How can I hope to compete against a dream he's been working toward for years?

He opens his eyes. "I'm not going to hurt you, CeCe. At least, not on purpose. And I'm also not going to endanger Bri."

I want to breathe a sigh of relief, but I can't. Because words only mean as much as you let them. Besides, he's not finished talking.

"I'm not going to give up on writing a kick-ass article, either," he continues. "Which leaves us with one option . . ."

"What's that?"

"We're going to have to figure out who this asshole is before my deadline." He nods toward the gray, cinder-block building. "I think the library's open now. Let's go."

We walk inside. The smell of stale popcorn and musty books hits me, and I'm transported back to my childhood, when story hour was accompanied by treats cranked out by the old-fashioned popcorn machine that still sits in the corner. My mom would curl up on the orange and yellow plastic cushions with one of her fat romance novels, and I would systematically work through the books in the children's section, shelf by shelf.

A decade later, the library still looks the same. The same kids' corner, the same colorful cushions, even the same librarian.

Sam heads straight to the shelves behind the racks of newspapers. "The yearbooks are back here."

"How do you know?" I ask, taking two steps for every one of his.

"After your mom's topless photo was posted, I came here to see if I could figure out who might've been around twenty-five years ago. But I didn't get very far because it could've been anybody—a fellow student, a member of the administration, a volunteer at the school. But now that we know we're looking for a teacher, it narrows the search considerably."

"You're such a reporter, aren't you?" I ask.

His hand drifts to my chin, and for a moment, I think he might kiss me right there in the library. But then, he lowers his hand and looks at the shelves. "Your mom graduated in 1991. Should we start there?"

My shoulders droop, but it's silly to feel disappointed. We're here on a mission, not a date. "Maybe a few years in either direction, just to be safe." I find the proper volumes and toss him a couple. "Here."

We turn pages in silence. Some of the yearbooks are pristine; others are covered with inscriptions and handwritten notes. They must've been donated to replace the library's damaged or missing volumes.

The carpet feels scratchy even through my jeans, and the sunlight streams through a window and highlights a column of dust particles. Presently, Sam pushes an open yearbook toward me. "Your mom was popular."

I look at the photo. Yep, it's Mom, all right, her eyes bright, her full lips parted in midlaugh. She's sitting on the hood of a sports car, surrounded by what looks like the in crowd. A blond guy with a chain around his neck has an arm looped around her shoulder, his dimples winking at the camera. On her other side, a girl crosses her slim thighs beneath a short skirt, her teased brown bangs partially obscuring the face of the kid behind her.

"Yeah, that's her," I say and wait for the inevitable comments. How beautiful she is. How stunning.

But he says none of those things. Instead, he glances from me to the photo, as if he's seeing the seventeen-year-old Tabitha for the first time. "There's a similarity. But from what you said, I would think the resemblance would be much closer."

"That's because you haven't seen me naked," I blurt out. And then my ears, my neck, even my toes boil. Oh god, what is wrong with me?

"You're right. I haven't." A smile plays on his lips. "Tell you what. Once I do, I'll give you another opinion, okay?"

He returns to the yearbook, studiously flipping pages as if our conversation weren't anything out of the ordinary. As if—dear god—I hadn't practically propositioned him.

I press a cool hand against my neck and follow his example. After paging through four years' worth of yearbooks, we find seven staff members still working at the school today. Three of them are women. One of them, the history teacher, is nearly seventy—a short, squat man with white hair and a paunch. I can't imagine him being attractive even twenty years ago.

That leaves three suspects. Mr. Swift. Mr. Willoughby. And Principal Winters, although he wasn't the principal back then.

"It could be any of them," Sam says. "They're all in their late forties or early fifties. Reasonably good-looking. Well-liked by the students."

I turn back to the photo of my mom sitting on the hood of

the car. My eyes drift over the faces of the students and then the inscription scrawled across the top of the page.

And a flash of electricity zips over my skin. Orange permanent marker. Block script with squared-off corners.

"I think we can rule out Mr. Swift," I say shakily. "I'm pretty sure we're looking for someone whose name starts with a W. Take a look at this."

I point to the message and read the words along with him.

It doesn't get any better than this! —W.

"The phone number on the doctored hotline posters was written in this same block script, with the same orange marker," I say, the excitement bubbling up my throat. "Plus, we received an arrangement of flowers at my mother's funeral that said, 'I will never forget you,' signed by the same W. It's got to be our guy."

Sam checks our list of suspects. "So that narrows it down to Mr. Willoughby or Principal Winters." He taps his fingers on his knees. "But an inscription in an old yearbook isn't proof. We need something more."

"And I know where to get it. Tommy Farrow. If he's lying about my mom having sex with him, he had to have a reason why. And I'll bet you anything it has something to do with our predator."

"There's only one problem," he says. "Tommy won't talk to you."

I take a deep breath. If my mother could survive sexual abuse from a man she thought she loved, well . . . what I'm about to do is kid stuff. "Which is exactly why I'm going to win a date with him at the auction tomorrow night."

Chapter 33

The next evening, I squeeze through a sea of neckties, flouncy dresses, and mascaraed lashes to get to the end of the registration line. I've never seen the hallway outside the school auditorium so packed. Or well-dressed.

Someone thrusts a program into my hands, and a high-pitched giggle cuts through the racket. I stiffen. Is everyone looking at me? Wondering why Cecilia Brooks is standing in line to get a bid number?

Whisper, whisper. Snort. Full-on belly laugh. They can't even bother to hide their amusement.

But when I whip around, no one's even looking at me. *Good god, CeCe. Get ahold of yourself. Nobody even notices you're here.*

I lean against the wall and skim through the program. My stomach bounces around, and I'm glad I didn't have any of the taco salad I made for my dad. Ah, there he is: Sam Davidson, page four. Glasses, of course. Sheepish grin. Tousled hair that makes my fingers itch to brush it off his face.

How could you *not* bid on him? If I weren't on a mission, if I didn't care what other people thought, I'd empty out my savings account to win a date with Sam.

I'd emptied out my savings account this afternoon, all right. If only the $522 tucked in my backpack were for romance.

I read the profile underneath Sam's photo.

Name: Sam Davidson

Class: Senior

Soliciting bids from: Girls

Perfect match: Someone who is compassionate and brave. She goes out of her way to help others, even if it costs her. She stands up for what's right and searches for the truth.

Turn-ons: Black high-top sneakers. No, seriously, I like a girl who is confident in her looks. She doesn't need to dress flashy or be flashy. She knows that in ripped jeans and a ponytail, she has more allure than anyone else.

Perfect date: I like adventure. Maybe we're sneaking somewhere in the middle of the night, with the full moon as our only light. Or maybe we're kissing against a tree, as a delicious cover in a secret mission. One thing's for sure: Nothing's ever boring when she's around.

My cheeks burn. He's describing me. The ponytail, the black high-top sneakers. Our "date" the other night.

But what about his answer for "perfect match"? I'm not brave. Far from it. And only recently have I started searching for the truth.

Is he telling me I'm *not* the one for him? Or does he see something I don't?

I reach the front of the line and receive a paddle with the number 107. My hand trembles as I sign the form, and my signature swims before me. Can I really do this? Can I bid, in front of the entire school, on the boy who everyone believes slept with my mother?

"Hey, CeCe! I didn't expect to see you tonight." Liam approaches me, his arms loaded down with wires and microphones. He looks like one of those wire-frame snowmen you stick on the front lawn. Plug him in, and he could light up a neighborhood.

"How are you, Liam?" I ask, smiling because he's so darned cute. I haven't seen him since Wednesday, when I leaped into his arms after being freaked out by the flickering lights. Just a few days ago, but so much has happened, it feels like a lifetime. "What are you doing here?"

"Principal Winters roped me into making sure all our dates are properly miked." He peers at the paddle in my hands. "Are you bidding on someone at the auction?"

"Oh." I blush and shove the paddle into my jeans pocket. Something in his tone tells me he knows Sam is a candidate.

Just tell him, a voice inside me urges. *Tell him you and Sam are together. Let him know that your relationship with him is purely platonic.*

But when I open my mouth, I can't. "I haven't decided," I say instead.

He shifts the equipment in his arms and steps closer. "You want to grab a bite to eat after the auction?"

"Oh, um." I yank the paddle out of my pants. What do I say? How do I respond? And what exactly am I supposed to do with this oversized number on a Popsicle stick? "I was supposed to meet up with my friend, so I'm not sure . . ."

He frowns. I want to bury myself under the microphones and wires in his arms. This is so awkward. Liam never said he was interested in me. And yet, from the way he looks at me, from the undeniable chemistry swirling in the air between us, it's obvious his thoughts toward me are more than just friendly . . .

"Okay, some other time," he says. "The anniversary of my dad's death is coming up, and I could use someone to talk to."

Oh. My heart squeezes, and I reach out and pat his hand among the maze of wires. "I'm sorry, I can't tonight. Rain check?"

"Sure thing." He gives me a sad smile and shuffles away.

The heaviness sinks through my body, nailing my feet to the ground. Didn't I just swear by my mother's grave that I was going to be a better person? That means not being self-centered. That means thinking about other people. Liam is my friend, and he's hurting right now.

And yet, I don't run after him. I can't. This is my only chance to talk to Tommy, and I'm not going to squander it. I'm just going to have to be a bad person for one more night.

Alisara walks up to me. “Who’s that? He’s cute. If a bit over-accessorized.”

“His name’s Liam. He, um, wanted to talk, but I had to put him off.”

She flutters her fake eyelashes at me and begins guiding me toward seats inside the auditorium. “And why, darling girl, would you do that?”

We settle into the middle section of the middle row. My favorite spot. I bite my lip, wondering if I should tell her. Oh, why the hell not? She’ll see for herself before the night is over. “I’m planning on winning a date tonight.”

“Oh really?” She whips out her program and turns to Sam’s profile. “You’ve been holding out on me. Black high-top sneakers, huh?” She taps her platforms against my shoes. “So romantic.”

“No!” I yelp and then cringe, lowering my voice. “You know I don’t do public relationships. I’m bidding tonight for another reason.”

I glance around the auditorium to see if anyone noticed my outburst, and then my breath catches. In the first row of the right section, Justin Blake sits, his long legs sprawled in the aisle.

My pulse races, and my palms instantly break out in sweat. Other than the glimpse of his look-alike rounding the corner, I haven’t seen him since the bonfire. What’s he doing here? Has he seen me yet?

Oh god. I can’t bid on Tommy in front of him. I can’t. Justin will crucify me. I don’t know what I ever did to make him hate me so much. But all those reasons will come rushing back to the surface now. He’s back in his old school, back on the grounds where he was a prince in Tommy’s kingdom. He won’t hesitate to unleash his cruelty, and this time, I may not survive the blow.

I lurch to my feet, about to run out of the auditorium, but then the lights dim, and Alisara pulls me back down. She can’t possibly understand the battle waging inside my head, but she looks at me with her pretty almond-shaped eyes and nods, as if to say: *You’ve got this. I am your friend. You are not alone.*

I swallow the panic, and my breathing slows. I'm doing this for Mom. She would've emptied the oceans for me, scoop by scoop, and all I have to do is stick a paddle in the air. Easy peasy. Right?

Principal Winters struts onto the stage, cornily handsome in a tux, top hat, and cane.

My stomach flips. This is the first time I've seen him since my research at the library, and I scrutinize him carefully, certain that something will leap out at me. Some telltale detail that will confirm or deny that he was my mom's sexual predator.

But there's nothing. He's the same jovial principal he's always been.

"Welcome, students. I'm so pleased to see so many of you here in support of literacy. Our nation's youths will thank you for your generosity, your pocketbooks . . . and your raging hormones," he says, with an exaggerated wink.

The crowd laughs.

"I've been backstage and wowee! If anyone can inspire you to dig deep, it's this group of gorgeous girls and guys. I guarantee, you'll be most impressed by their . . . extensive vocabulary and reading skills."

The audience titters again. He's always been a popular principal. Warm, engaging, magnetic. But is he enticing enough to attract a student? Are those hands cruel enough to shove a girl's head into his crotch?

"And now, without further ado, here comes our first date," he says as a junior girl bounces onto the stage. "I don't need to tell you boys what a catch this young lady is. But I will. Gloria's perfect match is . . ."

I only half-listen as the first few dates are auctioned off. And then Sam walks onto the stage.

My toes squeeze together in my black high-tops. He's wearing a pair of slacks instead of his usual jeans, and they actually cover his ankles. His broad chest stretches the knit shirt—in the best possible way—and he gives the crowd an easy smile and waves. He looks so . . . so . . . *Sam.*

Immediately, a couple of paddles pop into the air, even though the bidding hasn't begun, followed by catcalls and whistles.

Principal Winters ties a blindfold around Sam's eyes, as part of the tradition of the evening. The person on stage won't know who wins his date until after the auction.

That's exactly what I'm counting on.

In the front row, a girl stands and makes her way to the aisle. She wears a stunning cherry-red dress that drapes in all the right places. Probably designer, most definitely expensive. Who else but Mackenzie?

She poses for a moment, as if giving her many fans a chance to take her photo. And then she drops her paddle, steps on it, and crosses her arms across her chest. The message is clear: Bid on Sam Davidson and face her wrath.

The paddles that had been wagging in the air hesitate and then slowly lower.

And when Principal Winters opens the floor for bids, there's no response. Not a single one.

I can't breathe. I pound my fist against my chest, and still, I can't dislodge the air stuck inside. I should've known. Mackenzie Myers doesn't forgive and she doesn't forget. Sam humiliated her on the first day of school, and she hasn't done anything to retaliate.

This is why. She's been waiting for precisely this moment to get back at him. Hell, she probably convinced the auction committee to select him to be auctioned off for this exact reason.

"Anyone?" Principal Winters scans the room. "Look at this boy! Why, I'd bid on him myself, if I could. What do you think, Ms. Hughes?" He looks at the front row, where the school secretary sits. "Is some young lady about to get lucky?"

Ms. Hughes smooths her French manicure over her white-blond hair. "For sure."

But the seconds tick by. And nobody moves. Nobody.

Sam's smile freezes on his face, no longer easy, no longer impervious. He can't see anything but he can hear. Oh god, can he hear the silence permeating the auditorium. And I can't stand it anymore.

I don't think about Justin. I don't care about Mackenzie. I jump to my feet and wave my paddle in the air. "Fifty dollars!"

Every head in the auditorium turns and looks at me. All four hundred students, plus a dozen or so staff. Maybe they're noticing my ponytail and my black high-top sneakers. Maybe they're wondering why the social pariah is bidding on the new guy. Maybe they're whispering this is the only way Cecilia Brooks will ever go on a proper date.

But it doesn't matter. Because anything is better than seeing Sam's rival-the-sun smile turn to ice.

"Fifty dollars to bidder number 107." Relief runs in rivulets down Principal Winters's voice. "Do I hear sixty dollars? Sixty dollars for this fine young specimen?"

A paddle shoots up next to me. "Yes, bidder 83! Sixty dollars! We're on a roll now. How about seventy?" He looks at the other side of the auditorium, where one of the catcalling girls waves her paddle. "Yes!"

And the auction is off.

I sink into my seat. Alisara lowers her paddle and winks. "Don't mean to encroach on your property, but what can I say? He's such a fine young specimen," she says in a deep voice, imitating Principal Winters. "Not to worry, though. It's not like I can compete with your black high-top sneakers."

I squeeze her hand. "Thank you."

I hope she understands it's not just for this. It's for baking a coffee cake with me in the third grade. Regaling me with meaningless gossip for hours. Never giving up on me when everyone else did. "I should be so lucky to compete with you."

She grins and bats her eyelashes, and even Mackenzie and Justin watching me from across the auditorium can't take the moment away.

In the end, a vivacious junior girl wins the date with Sam, at a very respectable $130. Her friends hug her and squeal, and her smooth brown skin glows under the stage lights.

I drop my eyes before I notice anything else. It's only one date. What can happen on one date? The scenarios run rampant in my mind. I'm not able to push them aside until Principal Winters announces the last date of the evening. The one for which we've all been waiting.

"Well, girls, get those purses ready, because we're in for a very special treat," the principal booms. "He's been the star of this auction for three years running, and just because he's graduated doesn't mean we've forgotten him. In fact, we'll see if absence really does make the heart grow fonder—or the pockets sag deeper. Boys and girls, may I present Tommy Farrow!"

Tommy swaggers onto the stage, his hair curling charmingly over his handsome face. The bidding begins fast and furious, with four or five girls hardly waiting for a bid to be acknowledged before throwing their paddles back into the air once again.

And then Mackenzie stands. The bids slow and then stop as she saunters to center stage. Even Principal Winter halts his spiel.

The bidding girls collapse in their seats, defeated. They know what's coming. We all do.

Every year, Mackenzie's father gives her $500 to bid on the boy of her choice. Not a dollar more, not a dollar less. Invariably, the chosen date becomes Mackenzie's boyfriend and can look forward to catered dinners at the Myers household and tennis lessons at the country club.

So no one's surprised when Mackenzie lifts a bedazzled paddle and announces, "Five hundred dollars."

The audience cheers. A whistle slices through the air. A row of students begins to drumroll their feet.

I move as if underwater, pushing myself to my feet and lifting my paddle in the air. I feel the scorch of Justin's eyes thirty feet away. I know I'm crossing a line that I'll never be able to uncross. But I leap over it anyway.

"Five hundred and twenty-two dollars," I say.

The noise cuts off like a power outage. It's as if no one can believe what I just did.

Least of all me.

Chapter 34

"Congratulations," Raleigh chirps, like she's auditioning to be a camp counselor. She consults her clipboard and hands me a piece of paper. "Your date's waiting for you in room 222. You can leave for your night out from there. Thanks for supporting literacy!"

I thank her and turn, thinking I'm about to get off easy. Before I can leave, however, my former friend digs her long, red fingernails into my skin.

"Why'd you do it, CeCe?" She opens her eyes wide, so that she looks even more like a plastic doll. "Dissing Mackenzie, and for the boy your mom slept with! Can't you see how this looks?"

I try to retract my arm, but her nails seem to have grown spikes.

"You know what they're saying, don't you?" she fake-whispers. "They think you're the one who altered the photos. That you put your head on your mom's body because you couldn't look enough like her. And now, you're going after her high school boy toy!" She relaxes her grip, and a trail of half-moon indentations decorates my forearm. "If you can't be yourself, there are better people to imitate. Let's face it. Your mom was never going to win any prizes in the morality department."

I stare. "My mother washed your pajamas, underwear, and sleeping bag when you wet the bed at my house, Raleigh. She did it that very night, so you wouldn't have to tell your mother and get in trouble. Do you remember? Sounds like a decent person to me."

She flushes and drops my arm. I skirt around the table and squeeze between the barrier of chairs before anyone else can talk to me. No one's allowed past the barricade other than the dates, the winning bidders, and the auction committee. Thank goodness. That means I won't have to deal with either Justin or Mackenzie.

I shiver, even though the air inside the hallway is hot and stuffy. I defied the school princess in front of an auditorium full of people. Not once, but twice. If she attempted a school-wide humiliation of Sam after he cut her down in the locker corridor, what's she going to do to me?

I swallow hard. I can't think about Mackenzie, not now. Not when I have another nemesis to confront.

I enter the classroom. Tommy's facing the bulletin board. I scuff my feet through the confetti hearts Raleigh and her committee sprinkled on the floor, probably hoping the decor would push the auction participants into paroxysms of lust.

At the sound, Tommy turns, his eyes widening. "You!"

I wipe my palms across my jeans. "You've been avoiding my phone calls, Tommy."

He stumbles backward. Scared? Of me? Now that's a new one. "I don't have anything to say to you."

"You did the other night," I say, with a confidence I don't feel. "At the bonfire, you had plenty to tell me. Plenty I 'deserved to know,' if I remember correctly."

"I was drunk. I didn't know what I was saying."

"Well, you're not drunk now. And by my estimation, $522 should get me at least an hour of your time. So start talking."

"I don't have to do this," he rasps, scanning the room for escape. "I'll tell Principal Winters. This was false pretenses. This was entrapment. This was—"

"Me winning the auction, fair and square. I paid a lot of money for your company, Tommy. So you can tell Principal

Winters you don't want to support literacy, and they'll give me my money back. Or you can talk to me for a few minutes."

He sizes me up and then nods, reluctantly, as if I've cornered him with two bad options.

And maybe I have. But what choices has he given me? When you accuse a woman of sexual exploitation, where does that leave her daughter? Did he ever think of that?

I perch on the edge of a desk. "Tell me about my mom."

He holds up a finger and tilts his head, as if he is straining to make out something in the hallway. I listen, and then I hear it, too. The slightest squeak of rubber against linoleum. A breathing so light I can't tell if it's real or imagined. The same breathing that haunts my dreams every night. The same breathing I thought I heard inside my house.

Somebody is outside the classroom. And he or she is listening to our conversation.

My heart rate cranks up. Justin Blake. It has to be. Tommy's watchdog has somehow made it past the folding-chair barrier, no doubt by turning on his sleazy charm for that airhead, Raleigh.

Tommy creeps to the door. I follow him, but when we're halfway there, I slip on the stupid confetti hearts.

"Oooofff." I muffle the sigh as best as I can, but we hear the thup-thup-thup of footsteps scampering away.

He opens the door, and we look up and down the hallway. I think I catch a glimpse of black curls disappearing around the corner. Briony? Nah. I remember all of a sudden that she's on the auction committee, but why would she be skulking around the hallways? I probably didn't see anything at all. Probably it was just a wavering shadow.

"Nobody's here," Tommy says.

"Not anymore. Some of your buddies checking up on you, perhaps? Do you need their permission to use the bathroom, too?"

His neck turns red. "Justin can be a little . . . overzealous. But he means well. He's a good friend."

I raise my eyebrows. That's the last phrase I would use to describe Justin Blake, but the clock's ticking. Now that the eavesdropper is gone, I need information. "My mother."

"Right." He sighs and grabs a scalloped heart with a love poem printed on it off a desk. "What do you want to know?"

"Anything. Details on how you met. The nature of your relationship. Why you liked her. That kind of thing."

"It's not anything you want to hear."

"Not true," I say. "At this moment, there's nothing I'd like to know more."

He sits down, holding onto the paper heart as if it were a life preserver. This is the most we've talked since my mom's death. In fact, other than the night at the bonfire, he's gone out of his way to avoid me. I thought it was because of how intimately he knew my mother. But maybe I had it wrong. Maybe it's because he never knew her at all.

"The police are reopening my mom's case," I lie. "They found fingerprints on my mom's body. Semen, too. The detectives are wondering if maybe you had a lover's spat. If maybe the spat escalated and turned into murder."

He leaps to his feet, knocking over the chair. "Murder? What are you talking about?" His Adam's apple bobs like a buoy at sea. "I've got nothing to do with that. I never even touched her, I swear!"

I narrow my eyes. "You never touched her? Now that's interesting, Tommy. If you never touched her, then how on earth did you have sex with her?"

He stares at me, his mouth opening and closing. Then, he picks up the chair and sits back down. He drops his head into his hands, crushing the paper heart.

"It was only a rumor." His voice is so low I can't tell if he's talking to me or the poems. "I never testified in any court. I never swore it was true."

I suck in a breath, but it's too little, too late. The confession washes over me like a mammoth wave, and I'm coughing, sputtering, spitting out the salt water of deception. "Everything you said about my mom . . . was a lie?"

"I didn't know she was going to commit suicide," he says miserably.

"But why? What was in it for you? Did you hate my mother so much?"

"Listen, I didn't know your mom, okay? I've got nothing against her." He looks about how I feel. Tortured, exhausted. As if he were dumped on the River Styx six months ago and has been trying to row his way back ever since. "I was blackmailed. If I didn't do what he said, he was going to expose my sister's photos."

I go perfectly still. "Her photos? You mean to say—"

He laughs, and it's like he swallowed a mouthful of rusty nails. "Yeah, you'd know all about that, wouldn't you? Topless photos, see-through lingerie. The kind of pictures you never, ever want to see of your kid sister. Especially when she's only fourteen.

"He said all I had to do was say this one thing, and the photos would go away. Otherwise, he'd e-mail them to every inbox in the school, post them on social media. And my sister's life would be ruined."

I breathe out slowly. If I can make my breaths even enough, maybe this will all turn out okay. But part of me knows that all the yoga classes in the world can't erase this kind of evil.

"Ruined? Kinda like my life. Kinda like my mother's. Except her life isn't just ruined. It's over."

"I'm sorry, CeCe." He takes my hand and pulls it to his chest. "I've relived that moment a million times and wished it had come out differently. Wished I'd been able to think of another way. Wished my sister weren't stupid enough to get involved in that mess."

I pull my hand away. Like Tommy, I wish things had come out differently, too. But the past is past. And I'm not ready to forgive.

Because part of forgiving is giving up. And I won't do that. I won't let my mother's killer get away.

"Who, Tommy? Tell me. Who made you do this?"

He picks up one of the poems and begins to shred it. "That's the thing. I never met him in person. We communicated purely through text. And his phone number was from a prepaid cell, so I couldn't trace it." He piles the bits of paper into a small mound. "I've been doing nothing these last few months but look for this guy. My grades are suffering for it. Nearly all my friends have dropped me because I never want to party anymore. The night I saw you at the bonfire was an exception, and I only went because I finally admitted to myself, once and for all, that I was never going to find this guy. That's why I got so drunk."

I frown. "Did you talk to your sister? What did your parents say?"

"My sister won't talk. He must still have some hold over her, or maybe she's afraid he'll release the photos, after all. He sent me the negatives when I told everybody about my supposed affair with your mom, but that doesn't mean anything. He could still have copies."

Tommy smashes his fist through the mound of paper, and the ripped-up bits flutter in the air. "My parents are divorced, and we never see our dad anymore. Lila refused to confess to my mom, and she said she would deny everything if I told her. The only way I could've convinced my mom was to show her the negatives, and I wasn't about to do that. Having one sexual deviant for a child is enough."

"Wait—your sister's name is Lila?" My tongue is as dry as sandpaper. "Her nickname wouldn't be Lil, would it?"

He attempts to pick up the scraps from the floor, but the pieces are too small, and his fingers are too large. "That's what I used to call her as a kid, but I don't think anyone's used that nickname since. Why do you ask?"

"No reason," I say, mind whirling.

"That reminds me, though. The only thing Lila let slip was

that the guy called himself 'Phoenix.' Didn't help in my investigation any, though."

My blood runs cold. Phoenix. As in, the bird who always rises from his ashes. The legend who never dies. The predator who always wins.

Well, not this time. Not if I have anything to do about it.

Chapter 35

"Hey, CeCe," a varsity soccer player snickers the next morning at school. "Who did Tommy prefer, you or your mom?"

A few feet later, a girl from the drama club rolls her eyes. "I know Tommy's hot, but to use your mother as an 'in' to the relationship? That's sick."

And then, before I can make my escape into the classroom, the student council president clasps my hands in her clammy grip. "I'm so glad you took Mackenzie down a notch. She thinks she runs the school, and frankly, that's my job."

I'm drained by the time I crumple into my seat in psych class. At least this morning, I don't cower in the face of these comments. Instead, I give the soccer player a withering look, tell the drama girl *she's* sick for letting her mind go there, and smile and thank the student council president. In each case, the commenter blinks, as if he or she didn't expect me to respond, and then hurries away.

I could get used to this standing-up-for-myself thing. And I think my mother would approve. I have her leather-bound journal in my backpack. Maybe it's risky bringing it to school. Riskier than a measly old printout of my mom's call entry. But having the journal close to me gives me a shot of courage, which I'm going to need in order to track down Phoenix and confront him.

If only my partner would get to class already.

I wanted to text Sam last night. The second I left Tommy, I

wanted to go straight to his house. But he had a date, with a pretty junior girl with glowing brown skin. And he didn't bother to call me. For all I know, he was so preoccupied with his date, he's forgotten my name, much less our mission.

So I passed the time running Internet searches on "Phoenix," looking for a connection with either Mr. Willoughby or Principal Winters. But Tommy was right. I didn't find anything remotely useful, and by morning, the only thing I had to show for my efforts were the bags under my eyes.

And now Sam's late.

He beats Mr. Willoughby through the door by half a step.

"I waited for you to call all night," he says as he dumps his books on his desk. "I was worried about you, but I didn't want to intrude on your date. And this morning, I slept through my alarm. So how did it go? Did Tommy tell you anything?"

I flush. He was worried? Maybe he didn't forget about me. Maybe this is just a case of both of us being insecure. "Tommy told me he was blackmailed to lie about my mom," I blurt out. Class is going to begin any second, and we don't have much time. "The guy threatened to expose his sister's topless photos if he didn't comply. The guy called himself 'Phoenix,' and Tommy's sister's name is Lila. Do you think she could be Lil?"

"Maybe. It would make sense." Sam frowns. "Phoenix. The same name that's in your mom's journal. And now that I think of it, the entity that posted your mom's photo was 'PX1990.' Nineteen ninety. As in the year the journal is dated. It has to be the same person."

Before I can respond, Mr. Willoughby calls the class to order. I face forward, clenching my jaw. I've waited all night to talk to Sam. And now, I'm supposed to sit through a boring lecture about god-knows-who researcher doing god-knows-what experiment? It's not fair.

I hunch over, positioning my textbooks in a wall around my desk. My backpack gapes open, the corner of the leather-bound journal sticking out. I take the notebook out so that I can reposition it more securely inside.

Sam watches me put back the yellowed pages, and then he bends over his own desk. A moment later, my phone vibrates.

A text message from Sam: *It's got to be a code name. What could Phoenix stand for? There's the capital of Arizona.*

I quickly respond. *Yeah, And the mythical bird. A basketball team, a bunch of newspapers. What other phoenixes can you think of?*

Sam: *Some comic book characters are named Phoenix.*

Comic books? Mr. Willoughby is a comic book fiend. Could that be the connection?

I peek through my fortress at the psych teacher. He's flipping through bar graphs on the interactive whiteboard, and threads of silver shoot through his light brown hair.

I turn back to my phone. Before I lose my nerve, I type: *How was your date last night?*

A fly buzzes through the air. Raleigh flips her hot-roller curls over her shoulder. Someone opens their lunch, and the smell of bologna wafts through the air.

Finally, Sam responds. *Fine.*

Fine? Lots of things are fine. My class schedule, for example, or the frozen Hot Pockets Gram eats for her dinner. That's the best he can do to describe his date?

Me: *She's pretty.*

Sam: *She's not you.*

I try, and fail, to blot the smile from my face. I could dwell on that statement for hours—probably will, in fact, when he's not around.

A shadow falls over me. All of a sudden, I realize the room is silent. Oh, crap. How could I forget where I am? What I'm supposed to be doing?

"Ms. Brooks, would you like to contribute your thoughts to the class discussion?" Mr. Willoughby asks.

I wince. "Sorry. I guess I wasn't paying attention."

"Apparently." Quick as a hummingbird, he swoops down and plucks the cell phone out of my hands. "You can have this back at the end of the day, after you've had a chance to think about your actions."

And then, he carries my phone, with its revealing texts about Phoenix, back to his desk.

Mr. Willoughby can't read the texts. By the time he looks, my phone will have locked up with my security code, right?

Still, I worry. I worry all the way through sines and cosines, through the lunch I can't eat, through conjugating verbs in Spanish class.

But when I arrive in Mr. Willoughby's office, my phone seems to be the last thing on his mind. He taps his feet as if late for an appointment, and a musky scent emanates from him, something I've never noticed during class. Plus, he's freshly clean-shaven. As in: His cheeks weren't this smooth earlier today. Did he sneak a razor into the faculty restroom?

"Hot date, Mr. W?" I blurt out.

He fiddles with a string bracelet around his wrist. When I look closer, I see images of The Avengers woven into the bracelet. "Of course not. Where would you get that idea? I've got a tutoring appointment."

As long as we're pretending, I plaster on a smile. "I mean, you're a teacher, but you're human, too. How come you don't date more? Good-looking man like you?"

"I appreciate the vote of confidence, Cecilia. But it's just not a priority in my life right now." He fishes my phone out of his briefcase and hands it to me. "I'm willing to overlook this infraction, since you're normally such a good student. And I know there's been upheaval in your life lately. But will you give me your word you'll do a better job paying attention in class?"

I nod, trying to appear contrite. He's not acting like he saw the texts—thank goodness. But he looks like he's about to fly out the door any moment, and I can't let this meeting end without finding out if he's Phoenix.

I pinch the inside of my arm until tears well in my eyes. "To tell you the truth, I've been having a rough time lately."

He glances at the clock, as if calculating how much time he can spare. Then, with a sigh, he gestures to the sitting area. "Would you like to talk?"

Gotcha.

I sit in the same folding chair I did a few weeks ago, twisting my hands together. "You know about the topless photo, of course."

"Yes, and I'm surprised you haven't come to me before. I hope you know I'm always here for you." His voice is gentle and sincere. It's hard to believe this man could be capable of abusing my mother—or anyone, for that matter. But as Gram says, we always think we know someone. Until we don't.

"The photo made me realize how little I knew my mother. At least, how she was at my age," I say. "But you did. What was she like when she was your student? She was in the first class you taught, right?"

For some reason, this makes him pick up the pewter frame containing the photo of his dead wife. "Your mother was an extraordinary person, Cecilia. Beautiful and popular. The girl all the boys wanted, the one all the other girls wanted to be. But life wasn't always easy for her. Sometimes, I'd see sorrow on her face, behind that fabulous smile. Maybe she was depressed even back then. Who knows?"

"All the boys?" I press. "Even you, Mr. Willoughby?"

The hand holding the frame trembles. Then, he places the picture facedown on the coffee table. "What? Well, no. I mean, she was gorgeous, of course. Anybody could see that. But I was her teacher."

"Some people wouldn't let that stop them," I murmur.

"I suppose. I'm not one of those people."

"What about later, Mr. Willoughby, when she was your colleague? Did you ever want to ask her out?"

He laughs, but it stutters and stalls in his throat like a car with a bad engine. "This isn't a very appropriate line of questioning, Cecilia."

"I guess I'm trying to collect as many different viewpoints of my mother as possible."

The lines in his face relax. "That's fair. I guess you could say I had a crush on her. It wasn't the way she looked, but the utter passion she had for life. When she was around, I felt like I could jump out of an airplane without a parachute and not get hurt. She made me feel like I could do just about anything."

I stiffen. This is essentially what my mother said in her journal, right? I struggle to recall the words she'd written. Something about defying gravity and flying without wings. So not exactly, but close. Too close. Uncomfortably close.

He clears his throat. "I don't know what happened those last few months of her life. If she had sexual relations with that boy, it was highly inappropriate. But she doesn't deserve to be vilified the way she has."

"That doesn't sound like a crush," I say carefully. "You sound like you were in love with her."

He rubs the heel of his palm against his chest. "Maybe I was. But she was always married, so I didn't bother to find out."

Chills run up my spine, and I lace my fingers together to prevent my hands from shaking. What, exactly, did Mr. Willoughby just confess? He was in love with my mother, sure. But for how long? Was he her sexual predator? Has he been obsessed with her all these years?

"Mr. Willoughby, did you send a flower arrangement to her funeral? A glass cube with an all-white arrangement, with a card signed, 'W.'?"

"It's possible I did, Cecilia. To be honest, I don't really remember." He glances at the clock. "I hate to cut this short, but I'm late for my appointment. Perhaps we can schedule a time to talk next week?"

"Sure." I stand, my mind whirling. I pick up my backpack, holding it zipper-side down. While it's unzipped. Pens, note cards, textbooks, and paper spill everywhere. "Oh, crap! I'm sorry, Mr. W., I'm such a klutz sometimes. Please, don't let me keep you. I know you've got that appointment to make."

He checks the clock again. "Are you sure?"

"Oh, yeah." I wave my hand. "Go. I'll be out of here two minutes after you."

With one last glance around the room, he leaves. I count to ten and then dash over to his desk. I don't know exactly what I'm looking for, but there's got to be something incriminating here. A planner. Manila files with blank college applications. Next week's lecture notes.

And then I see it. On the corner of his desk, beneath a stack of junk mail, I find a glossy X-Men comic book, featuring a voluptuous woman in a skintight green costume, complete with gold sash, gloves, and thigh-high boots. Flaming red hair—strikingly similar to my mom's—falls down her back. Her name, according to the cover, is Jean Grey.

And her story is told in the Dark Phoenix Saga.

Chapter 36

The ocean roars in my ears. I gulp and gulp the air, as if I've just swallowed a mouthful of seawater. Oh good god. Mr. Willoughby is Phoenix. I can't believe it.

But I'm staring right at the evidence, and it makes perfect sense. Who else would name himself Phoenix other than someone obsessed with comic books? Someone haunted by Jean Grey—and other voluptuous, redheaded women like her.

It can't be a coincidence. Not when I've spent the last day searching for a connection with Phoenix.

My knees turn to rubber as I remember my last image of Mr. Willoughby. Clean-shaven, smelling of musk. Rushing off to a "tutoring" appointment.

If he's Phoenix, it can only mean one thing. He's meeting a girl. Maybe Briony. Or the student I saw in the parking lot—what was her name? Ashley, Amber? Maybe that's his MO. Start with late-night meet-ups, and then escalate the relationship by taking the sessions off school premises.

This could be the meeting where an innocent student turns into prey.

I drop to the floor, shoving my spilled stuff and the comic book into my backpack. I don't have a moment to lose. I've got a sexual predator to stop.

I fly down the hallway. How much of a head start did Mr. Willoughby have? Three minutes, four? I couldn't have been in his office very long. If he stopped to talk to someone, if he took a detour back to his classroom, I can still catch him.

I jump into my car and drive to the faculty lot, scanning the vehicles for either the Bug or the Prius I saw the other night. There! On the far side of the lot, I see a familiar silver car. Exactly the type of vehicle Mr. Willoughby would drive.

Hunkering down in my seat, I pull out my phone and call Sam. It goes straight to voice mail.

Oh, that's right. He told me he was going to turn off his phone and work on the article, since his deadline's first thing tomorrow morning. If I need him, he said, call his home phone.

Well, if there was ever an emergency, this is it. I root around my backpack for the slip of paper with his contact information, but when I call the number, there's no answer.

I frown. Where could he have gone?

Before I can think of someone else to call, Mr. Willoughby strides out of the building, the momentum swinging his arms like a pendulum. He dumps his briefcase in the backseat, gets in the car, and pulls out of the parking lot. I throw my phone down and follow him.

We wind through town. There's never much traffic in Lakewood, but I manage to keep a couple of cars between us. He then turns onto a road that will take us into the country, and the few vehicles evaporate.

Crap! I grit my teeth and hit the brakes, dropping even farther behind. The pavement disappears. My car bumps and thuds on the dirt, and clouds of dust billow up with each rotation of my tires.

I glance at the gas gauge. It's been hovering on "empty" for a while now. And the farther we get out of town, the more my palms slide on the steering wheel. What am I doing? Why am I following a sexual predator to the middle of nowhere? I should turn around. Go to the police, or at least wait for Sam to come with me.

But what about the girl? If I abandon my tail now, it might be too late for her. She could end up like my mom—or worse. Tightening my grip on the steering wheel, I keep going.

An eternity later, the Prius slows and turns into a long driveway. I pull onto the side of the road. The crickets chirp over each other in a cacophony of music, and the sun flirts with the horizon, its final rays lighting the leaves on fire. Shadows creep up the trees like insidious smoke.

I rub my bare arms, which the air has pebbled into goose bumps. Slow down, heart! Apparently, it still thinks we're going forty-five miles per hour.

I take a deep breath and make my way up the side of the driveway, using the dense shrubbery for camouflage.

The branches scratch my arms, adding blood to the raised pattern on my skin, and the leaves tangle in my hair. Presently, I come to a small creek lined with rocks. Hearing voices, I perch on one of the rocks, wrap my arms around a tree for balance, and peek around the trunk.

Two people stand on the front porch of the tucked-away house. Mr. Willoughby. And a girl with her back to me.

She's wearing tight jeans and red Converse sneakers, her hair a waterfall of white over the deep black material of her shirt. The hair looks familiar. Straight, shiny, and white-blond. I've seen it before, I'm sure of it. But I can't remember where.

The girl reaches up and pulls Mr. Willoughby into a passionate kiss. My psych teacher cups his hands around her bottom and lifts her against him. Her feet leave the ground, and she wraps her legs around his waist.

Hot, smoldering coals burn in my stomach. Mr. Willoughby may be on private property, conducting his personal affairs, but I don't care. He made it my business when he decided to prey on a student. I couldn't help my mom when she needed it. But I can do something now. The question is: what?

As I watch, he puts his hands on her head and presses his fingers on her scalp.

A line from my mother's journal floats across my mind. *He dug his nails into my scalp, so hard it felt like real metal nails being hammered into my head.*

The coals turn into redhot sparks shooting through my entire body. I can't stand here any longer, observing. Helpless.

Sam may not be home, but there are other people who answer the phone all the time. I fumble the phone out of my pocket and dial 911.

A female voice comes on the line. "Please state your emergency."

"There's a teacher, a sexual predator, who lures girls to his home and takes advantage of them," I whisper. "I'm watching them right now."

I've barely uttered the last word when I slip on the rock, and my feet plunge into the creek. I manage to stifle a scream—but there's nothing I can do about the splash of the water.

As if in slow motion, Mr. Willoughby and the girl break apart and turn toward the noise. For the first time, I see the girl's face clearly.

Even as I hear the operator asking me for the address, the phone slides through my fingers and joins my feet in the water.

Because the girl is not a student, after all.

Instead, she's our school secretary, Ms. Hughes.

Chapter 37

Ms. Hughes. A consenting adult. Not a student.

Not a student. Not a student.

I was wrong.

My chest tingles, my throat's thick. I'm about to throw up all over my wet feet. How could I make such a mistake?

And I almost reported him. I almost gave the operator his address. His life would've been over. Even if my accusation was later proven false, the taint of scandal has a way of lingering. I should know.

The clouds spin as the ramifications hit me. The branches are suddenly on the ground, the creek in the sky. I sway, swinging my arms to catch onto something, anything. But there's nothing but the deep, pervasive knowledge of my shame.

"Cecilia, is that you?" Mr. Willoughby's voice breaks into my haze. "What are you doing here?"

Great question. I'm following you because I'm an idiot? Because I thought you were about to prey on a student? Because I was sure you killed my mother? Somehow, none of these answers seems appropriate.

I sink to my knees, and while I'm there, I fish my phone out of the creek, where it's nestled between two rocks. When I climb out, my socks weld to my toes like blocks of wet cement. Good. I deserve nothing less.

I step around the bushes and stop ten feet from the porch.

"I'm so sorry," I choke out. They can't know the truth. That

I almost ruined his career—no, his life—is bad enough. No one can know how badly I messed up. "I, uh, followed you home because you dropped something." My mind whirls. The comic book! It's in my backpack. I could pretend I'm returning it to him. "But then I saw you had company, and I would've turned back. Except my car ran out of gas. And I'm not sure my phone's working." I hold out my dripping phone, warming to my story. "I was hoping I could use yours."

Ms. Hughes raises her eyebrows. They're the same white-blond as her hair. How could I have forgotten? Nobody else has hair that color. "Your car ran out of gas. Right in front of Mr. Willoughby's house."

"Oh, yes. You can check my gauge, if you don't believe me."

She doesn't say anything. A gust of wind blows her blouse open where two of her buttons are undone, and she quickly fastens them.

"Your hair's different," I add lamely.

"I wear it up at school. More professional." She confers with Mr. Willoughby with her eyes. "You might as well come in."

I chew on my lip. "I don't want to interrupt."

"I'd say you already have."

I trudge onto their porch and take off my socks and shoes, so that I don't leave tracks in the house. But there's nothing I can do about my footprints on the wood. They stare at me like blemishes, the marks of my shame. Hester had her scarlet letter, and I have my wet feet.

"What did I drop, Cecilia?" Mr. Willoughby asks as we go inside.

"An X-Men comic book," I say. "The Dark Phoenix Saga."

As I say the words, part of me dares to hope. Maybe I'm not as foolish as I thought. Maybe he is Phoenix. Just because he's hooking up with Ms. Hughes doesn't mean he's not preying on students as well.

"Not sure where that came from," he says. "I haven't read that comic in ages."

Maybe not. He can't very well be obsessed with Jean Grey if

he never reads her story. Unless he's lying. But how would he know to lie about something so inconsequential?

My chest deflates. Too many maybes. Too many ifs. If there is a case against Mr. Willoughby, it's full of holes.

Ms. Hughes ushers me into the kitchen and hands me a cordless phone. I stare at the black device. Who should I call? Sam? I don't have much choice. I don't have any phone numbers memorized, and I can't scroll through the address book on my waterlogged phone. So I grab the slip of paper from my pocket and dial his home number. No one picks up. Again.

"It's me," I say to the dial tone, rather than explain my predicament. "My car ran out of gas. Could you meet me and bring a gallon of gas, please?" I rattle off the country road and then hang up.

"Well, thank you so much," I say, channeling my inner Raleigh. "I'll go wait in my car now. Bye."

"Not so fast." Ms. Hughes crosses her arms. "I'd like to talk to you."

Mr. Willoughby starts to say something, but she presses a hand on his arm. "Let me handle this, honey."

He nods. "Okay. See you at school, Cecilia," he says, and leaves the room.

"Can we make this quick?" I mumble. "My ride will be here any minute."

"You didn't make a phone call, Cecilia." Her voice is small and tight. Completely unlike the friendly secretary I know from school. "I could hear the dial tone from where I was standing."

Oh. Just when I thought I'd hit creek-bottom. Crap, crap, crap!

"I decided to walk." My words fall out like the rounds of a machine gun. "I remembered my friend lives near here and—"

"You don't have to do this. I know why you're really here."

This stops me. "You do?"

"Mr. Willoughby is a good-looking man." She sighs, as if it's taken her months to come to terms with this fact. "Many of his students have crushes on him."

My mouth drops open. "I don't have a crush on him. I was . . ."

But I can hardly tell her the truth. That I suspected him of exploiting my mom. That I was seconds from reporting him to the police. A water's splash from destroying his life—and mine. What's left of it, anyway.

"It's okay. I'm not going to call your grandma or dad." Her tone softens. She's not quite at the lollipop-offering stage yet, but she's getting close. "Just don't follow him again, okay?"

I nod, staring at the floor. It's the same yellow laminate that's at our house. Maybe the hardware store was having a sale. And maybe, if I keep my mouth shut, I'll be able to show my face sometime in the next century.

"Now I would appreciate it if you could do something for me," she says. "Nobody at school knows about Ty and me. And we'd like to keep it that way."

"What's the big secret?" I blurt.

"He has his reasons." She rubs her neck. "It's a long story, and it mostly concerns his wife."

"Who's been dead for over twenty years."

"Twenty-six years, to be exact," she says, her tone suddenly weary. "But who's counting?"

I twist the straps of my backpack. I should get out of here before my poor judgment gets me in even more trouble. And yet, part of me is curious. Even before I found the comic book, I suspected Mr. Willoughby. And there's a reason. He acted suspicious. He did his best to keep his relationship with Ms. Hughes a secret. Why?

"Could you tell me the story?" I ask haltingly. "I know it's none of my business, but I'm curious. Mr. Willoughby is such a mystery. Maybe I wouldn't have followed him if I knew more about him."

She studies me so closely she could be counting my eyelashes. "All right, I'll tell you. But only because I think you're right. This secret hurts more people than Ty realizes."

She walks to the sink, where she runs water over a stack of dirty plates. I don't think her need to wash dishes is so urgent, but like my backpack-twisting, it keeps her hands busy.

"Maria was Mexican," she says. "Ty met her during one of his semesters abroad in college, and they eloped to the States when she was eighteen. Immediately, she was diagnosed with a brain tumor and died six months later. It's a tragedy, to be sure, but he could've moved on from it. He should've moved on."

Her nails scrape across a plate. "Problem is, her family blames him. They feel she wouldn't have died if he hadn't taken her away. And a large part of him agrees. It's completely irrational, of course, but he feels tremendous guilt. So much that he's brought her entire family here to live, and he won't go public with any relationship. He feels like it would disrespect his late wife's memory."

Guilt. Yes, I can understand that. I've felt the way it wraps its tentacles around me, squeezing so tightly I can hardly breathe. And if this monster has infiltrated Mr. Willoughby's life, it would explain why he's never openly dated anyone.

But I still have to ask. "And you're sure he's not seeing anybody else?"

She looks up, her gaze sharper than the knife in the drying rack. "Cecilia, I love this man. And he loves me, even if he doesn't realize it yet. I'd stake my life on his faithfulness."

She's so certain. So positive. We always think we know someone . . . until we don't. But even I have to admit it's looking less likely that Mr. Willoughby is Phoenix.

"Thanks for telling me," I say. "And, uh, sorry about the intrusion. I'll let myself out."

I leave the house and hurry to my Camry. It may only be a hundred yards, but after the hour I had, it feels more like a hundred miles.

Come on. Hold it together for a few more minutes. A few more minutes, and then you can collapse in the safety of your car.

I reach the Camry, and I almost cry as my hand closes around the door handle. But my relief is short-lived. Because the car won't start.

I groan. My lie has become truth. I'm out of gas.

Chapter 38

I trudge into town.

Fool, my mind chants as one foot after the other stirs up the dusty road. *You FOOL,* it screams when I reach the gas station. *Fool, fool, fool,* it plays on repeat as I pace in front of the refrigerated drinks, waiting for a mechanic to give me—and my gallon of gas—a ride back to my car.

What was I thinking? Honestly, what was going on in my EMPTY brain cells? Following Mr. Willoughby, barging into his house. All on the basis of a comic book. Unbelievable.

But how could it be a coincidence? a little voice asks. *Finding that comic was too fortuitous to be a coincidence.*

Shut up, I snarl at the voice. If it had a physical presence, I'd slam the voice against the wall until it was knocked unconscious. *It* was *a coincidence, so shut the hell up. You've already made me the biggest fool in Lakewood, if not the entire world.*

Nothing new there. I always suspected I was a fool. Now I have irrefutable proof.

When I get in my car again, and it actually starts, I'm not sure where to go. Part of me wants to sit in the bathtub and cry, so much that you could use my tears as bathwater. The other part wants to see Sam.

I don't want anyone to find out what happened—but Sam doesn't count. He's different. He won't judge me. If anyone or anything can make me feel better, it's Sam.

Decision made, I drive to his house. Mrs. Davidson appears in front of the screen door when I knock. Her hands are covered in clear plastic gloves and bits of white meat. And a large purple bruise stretches over her left cheek.

"Good to see you, CeCe." Her words are weak, with almost a translucent quality. As though they exist only because they're propped up on the aroma of carrots, celery, and garlic in the air.

"Mrs. Davidson, are you okay?" I venture. Something is wrong. That much is obvious. I'm just not sure what.

She holds up her gloved hands, indicating the shreds of meat like they are poison. "I'm making a chicken pot pie. Sam's favorite. I thought we could all use a bit of comfort after this afternoon."

"What happened?" I ask softly.

"My ex-husband. If Sam weren't here, I . . . I don't know how far it would've gone." Her voice cracks, but she straightens her spine and walks into the kitchen, gesturing for me to follow her. She attacks the cooked chicken breast on the counter, shredding the meat as if her life—or at least her dignity—depends on it.

"No one got hurt, so don't worry. The fight involved more raised voices than fists. But Sam's been upstairs since his dad left, and he says he's not coming down until he finishes his article. He's taken over the whole floor—I've heard him stomping in the hallway for the last hour."

I lick my lips, not sure what to say or do. If it were my mother, I'd take her in my arms and stroke her hair as though our roles were reversed. I'd lay her bruised cheek on my lap and hum the lullabies she used to sing me at night.

But she's not my mother. She's a stranger I've only met once, and with whom I've barely spoken. I don't know how to comfort her without prying. I don't know how to put myself out there, to risk being shot down, when I've proven, without the slightest doubt, what a fool I am.

"Is that why you didn't pick up the phone at four o'clock?" I ask instead. "I called, and then again half an hour later, and no one picked up." I pull the slip of paper out of my back pocket. It looks like it's been through the wash. And no wonder. Between the dip in the creek and my anxious grip, it's had rougher treatment than the spin cycle. "Sam gave me your home number, since he turned off his cell."

"No, no. My ex-husband was gone by then." She looks over her shoulder and frowns. Three lines slice across her forehead. "That's strange. I was here the whole time, and I never heard the phone. Would you mind checking to see if it's broken, CeCe? As you can see, my hands are full of chicken."

She wiggles her fingers in the air. I lay the slip of paper on the counter and pick up the phone on the wall.

"There's a dial tone," I murmur. "I wonder why it didn't ring."

Frowning, I press some buttons to navigate the menu, searching for the "missed calls" log. I hit the wrong button and enter the "dialed calls" log. I'm about to exit when I see something.

"I got it." Mrs. Davidson squints at the slip of paper. "You were calling the wrong number. His 'seven' here looks like a 'one.' "

But her words are a long-distance buzz in my ears. My vision is fuzzy, and my lungs feel like they're being squished between two metal plates.

I blink. And blink again. But no matter how hard I try, I can't erase what I'm seeing. On September 18, before Sam and I became partners or friends, there are six calls to my cell phone number. Six calls on the same day the hotline posters were doctored.

I didn't recognize his home number when he first gave it to me. But there's no denying *my* phone number on this screen.

There has to be an explanation. Was he legitimately trying to call the hotline? He never mentioned it when I told him about the doctored hotline posters. Did Briony make those calls? Doubtful. With her uncanny ability for friendships, she doesn't need to pour her heart out to a stranger.

Without meaning to, I begin to build the case against Sam.

He knew my call counselor schedule—so he knew exactly when I would be at the hotline. He was the one who suggested anyone's head could be Photoshopped onto an image. He was the only person I confided in about Phoenix. And my mom's journal. And my suspicions.

Throughout this entire investigation, Sam always seemed to know things about me before I had a chance to tell him. He knew my mother had died in the old shed, for example. And the fact that I was a call counselor. I thought it was because he was a good reporter. But maybe it's because he's been engineering my harassment from the beginning.

I place the phone back in its cradle. My hands were gripping the handle so hard my fingerprints shine on the surface. It's not that I think Sam is Phoenix. That would be ridiculous. He's my age, and he wasn't even in town when my mom committed suicide. Clearly, he's not preying on any young girls and convincing them to take topless photos.

But maybe he wanted to write a good story so desperately he was willing to manipulate the situation to get what he wanted. Maybe the harassment was designed to send me running straight into his arms. Maybe all those kisses were a way to get close to me, to discover tidbits about my mom I never would've otherwise confided.

Well, it worked. If Sam is actually behind the harassment, I'm an even bigger fool than I thought.

"Are you okay, dear?" Mrs. Davidson stirs the roux on the stovetop, her eyebrows knit together. "You look pale all of a sudden."

I bare my teeth in what I hope passes for a smile. I'm not going to jump to conclusions. I did that with Mr. Willoughby and look what happened. "I'm fine. Is it okay if I go see Sam now?"

"Go right ahead. You know where his room is."

I move into the hallway like a moth flitting around, not sure where to land. I walk up the stairs to the second floor. The entire hallway is strewn with Sam's school supplies. His worn navy backpack with the broken zipper. A calculator jumbled with a protractor and some graph paper. His black-and-white composition notebook.

And papers. Lots and lots of crumbled-up papers, possible early drafts of his article.

Without fully understanding why, I pick up a ball of paper, smoothing it out and skimming my eyes over the words.

A headline marches across the page: Secret Journal Reveals Sex Suicide's Sexual Past.

I stumble backward and sag against the wall as I read. And then my legs give out entirely, and I collapse to the floor.

The article lays it all out, in black and white. How seventeen-year-old Tabitha Brooks began dating her teacher. How she became increasingly isolated from her friends. How she was made to perform oral sex under a wooden desk in a classroom filled with students.

Sam's memory for details is uncanny. He remembered the names of Tabitha's best friend and even the boy with whom she was supposed to double-date. He described her outfit down to the thong. He even included a few quotes that came directly from my mother's journal.

How did he remember all that? I'm not sure I even gave him all those facts.

It's almost as if he had the journal right in front of him.

No. That's impossible. The journal has been in my backpack the entire day. Why, I haven't even taken it out since first period . . .

A chill runs over my spine. Oh my god. Sam watched me adjust the journal in my backpack. He knows I brought it to school. He could've taken it when I wasn't paying attention.

My heart drilling holes in my ears, I pick up Sam's navy backpack and look inside. Sure enough, my mother's yellowed-page, leather-bound journal lies inside.

There's no mistake. Sam Davidson stole from me.

I clutch my chest, a sharp pain spearing the very center of me.

When I thought my mother betrayed me, a blade lodged in my heart. And now it's being twisted and turned, shredding and destroying.

Until there's nothing left.

And the worst part? The hand that wields the blade belongs to Sam.

The boy with whom I was beginning to fall in love.

Chapter 39

I hover at the entrance to Sam's room. He hunches over his computer, his fingers flying over the keyboard. An empty mug sits on his desk, next to a faint coffee ring. More crumbled-up papers fill a wire-mesh trash can, and he's muttering to himself.

Any other time, I might have admired his discipline. Now, it takes all my strength not to drive my fist through the computer screen.

"You ass," I say. "How could you do this to me?"

He cocks his head like he's trying to hear something. A whisper on the air, maybe, or his conscience. If he even has one.

After a moment, he continues typing. That's when I realize he's wearing headphones. The words are a refrain inside my brain; my throat's clogged with lies and betrayal. I don't want to say the words again, and the fact that I have to makes the anger flame even higher.

I march into the room and slam my mother's journal on his keyboard.

"CeCe!" Sam jumps and removes the headphones. "When did you get here? Did you get your phone back from Mr. Willoughby?"

I blink. Mr. Willoughby? Oh right. Sam still doesn't know what happened. "He's not Phoenix," I say flatly. "He's in a serious relationship with Ms. Hughes and doesn't have time to mess around with young girls. But that's not why I'm here."

I jab my finger at the journal.

He studies the book as if he hadn't stolen it. As if he weren't planning to betray me. No—like he hadn't already betrayed me. "This isn't what you think . . ."

"You used 'sex' twice in your article headline, did you know that? Isn't that a 'no-no' in journalism, repeating words in the same headline? Or maybe there's an exception since sex sells. Sex wins awards and gets you scholarships. Isn't that right, Sam?"

"I'm not going to submit that article to my editor." He takes off his glasses and scrubs a hand down his face. I see a laceration on his temple, where his glasses might have cut into his skin if he had been knocked around. A dark purple bruise is beginning to form on his cheekbone.

My knees go weak. This must be from the fight with his dad. I want to trace my fingers along his skin, kiss him until the pain goes away. But I can't feel sorry for him. I won't. He doesn't deserve my sympathy, this bastard who was using me.

"The draft you read was just a warm-up exercise, CeCe. Something to get the words flowing. I wouldn't let them run something like this."

"And yet, you wrote it," I say. "You stole from me. After I trusted you, after everything we had together, you felt okay sneaking into my backpack and taking my mom's journal. A backup plan, in case you couldn't come up with anything better."

I whip around and pace the room, in a line between his bed and dresser. "How could you, Sam? I thought you wanted to be a journalist. A serious investigative reporter, standing up for the little guy, protecting what's right."

He stands and steps directly in my path. I could veer around him, but he's too big and the room's too small. "I do, and that's not why I took the journal. I have a contact who knows Tommy Farrow's sister. The girl with the striped tights, the one I helped on the first day of school? She's friends with Lila and is arranging for me to have a meeting with her. I thought if I showed her the journal, it would convince her to talk."

I stare at him. It all sounds so reasonable, so believable. But

I'm done trusting Sam Davidson. "If that's true, why didn't you tell me?" I whisper. "Why didn't you ask?"

"Because I knew you wouldn't let anyone else see the journal."

My anger flares again. "Damn straight. You knew that, and you didn't care. You decided to invade my privacy and steal my property, anyway."

He shoves his hands in his hair. "Don't you see you're not helping anything by hiding this? If the police knew, maybe they would reopen your mom's case. Maybe they'd be able to find Phoenix. And maybe it would all be over by now. Before anyone else gets hurt." His voice is soft now, as fine as steel wire. And just as strong. "Before this scumbag gets his hooks even deeper into my sister."

"Is this what this is about? You're publishing this article about my mom's journal because you think it's my fault this guy is on the loose. You're punishing me because you're pissed about your sister."

"Of course not." His chest moves with the force of the breath. "I told you already, it was a writing exercise. I never intended to publish it." He seizes my hands. "You would know that if you even trusted me a little bit. But that's our problem. You don't take what we have seriously."

I yank my hands out of his. "The hell I don't! I've given you more of myself than I have to anybody else."

"For god's sake, CeCe," he explodes. "You wouldn't even tell anybody we were together. Anytime we were at school, you were always looking around, making sure no one saw us. You wouldn't even bid on me at the auction."

"What are you talking about? I did bid for you." And then I remember the blindfold. He has no idea what Mackenzie did. No idea I stood up for him.

He continues, as if I haven't spoken. "You knew I was dreading it. And yet, you didn't care enough to save me from a date with a stranger. Did you read my profile in the program?" He steps forward, his eyes bright with an emotion I can't identify.

"That was me on my knees, asking you to come forward with our relationship. To announce to the school what I meant to you. Because how you felt about me was more important than what other people say."

I shake my head. "You knew I had to bid on Tommy that night. He wouldn't talk to me otherwise."

"We could've found another way." His voice is bitter, so bitter it leaks acid onto my tongue. "In all the years of their marriage, my mother never brought up my dad to anyone outside of the family. It wasn't that she didn't talk about the abuse. She didn't talk about him, period. She was ashamed of him, CeCe, ashamed of their relationship. It was as if she could make that shame go away if she pretended he didn't exist." He draws himself up to his full height. "I've told you this before, I have no interest in being in a secret relationship. I don't need to be with someone who's ashamed of me."

Heat rushes to every appendage of my body. "Don't you dare turn this on me. You'd do anything to win that scholarship, even if it means selling me out. Even if it means setting me up. I know about the phone calls, Sam. I know you dialed me six times the day the doctored posters went up. What were you trying to do? Rattle me so much, I'd run to you and confess everything?"

He gives me a blank look. "I don't know what you're talking about. I never called you until after we kissed."

"It's right there on your call log, Sam!"

He shakes his head. "It wasn't me."

"I don't believe you," I say.

"Well, I don't believe you, either, so I guess we're even."

We stare at each other. His face is hard, immobile. A statue carved out of marble. If I touched it, the cold would spread like a virus through my body, paralyzing me, too.

There's nothing more to say. Nothing to fix this breach between us. Nothing to make things return to the way they used to be.

That's the tragedy of life. Nothing good ever lasts.

When I can't stand it anymore, I turn and walk away from the new guy. The one who was different from everyone else. I thought he saw past the surface. I thought he knew me for who I really was.

He's different, all right. More than Tommy Farrow, more than Justin Blake, he aimed straight at my heart. And blew it to smithereens.

Chapter 40

I don't go to school. I don't draw. I don't even do my dad's laundry. Gram's on her trip to Vegas, and my dad floats between his job, the cemetery, and the den. If he notices there's no dinner on the table, he doesn't complain. For once, I can't bring myself to care. I lie around in my pajamas and eat cereal out of the box and take that bath I wanted.

But I don't cry. Somehow, it seems indulgent to cry when I brought this on myself.

After the first day, Alisara calls. I don't answer. The second morning, a stuffed dog with floppy ears and ridiculous spots arrives at my house. A balloon tied to his wrist proclaims, "Fly away with me."

I read the message from Alisara—"Call me!!!"—and hug the puppy close. My chest burns. It's like the unshed tears are piling up. As they cram tighter, their temperature increases. At some point, the tears will boil over. But not yet.

I send Alisara a quick text to thank her, but I don't call. The moment she hears my voice, she'll come over and take up vigil by my bedside. But I don't deserve that. Nobody died. The only thing I'm mourning is my own stupidity.

The only time I rouse myself is to call Liam at the hotline. I leave a message at the administrative number, telling him to assign my shifts to somebody else. He calls me back immediately.

"I'm leaving the hotline," I say, my voice echoing back at me, dull and colorless.

For a moment, all I hear is the honk-honk-honk of the crazy geese on the lake. "Did something happen?" Liam asks quietly.

"Yes." My voice cracks, and colors begin to leak back in. Except they're the colors nobody wants. Mud-puddle browns and rainy-day grays. The crayons that remain pristine in the box while every other stick is used-up and broken. "I almost accused someone of something really bad. But I was wrong. My judgment was off. I have no business counseling other people. I'm really sorry, Liam. I thought I could do this, but I can't. It would be better for everyone if I stopped involving myself in other people's lives."

"I'm here for you, CeCe," he says. "If you ever need to talk, if you need anything at all, just say the word. Let me help you. Please."

It's tempting, so tempting. Liam isn't Sam. He doesn't make me laugh the way Sam does. He doesn't electrify a room with his passion and personality. But maybe that's good. I was never able to show Sam the darker parts of myself, not the way I could with Liam. I was afraid he wouldn't accept me. I thought he was too good.

Turns out, Sam's goodness was nothing but a lie. Nothing but one more deception to add to my collection of betrayals.

Liam hasn't lied to me. I appreciate his kindness and understanding so much. Maybe someday, I'll be able to show him how much. But at the moment, I'm just too worn down to trust anyone else.

"Not today," I say. "I need to be by myself. When I'm ready for company, you'll be the first to know. But right now, I just . . . can't."

He gives me his personal cell number, and I dutifully jot it down.

And then I go to bed. And I stay there. Because with my last act—quitting the hotline—my texter has won. He got exactly what he wanted. Me, back in my turtle shell. Where I belong.

On the third day, Gram comes home. She bursts into my room, shopping bags in her hands and pockets bulging with casino chips. I haven't brushed my hair for days. Empty cereal boxes lay strewn across the carpet, and my shades are drawn tighter than the curtains inside a hearse.

"Good lord, girl!" she says. "I haven't even been gone a week. Did something die in here?"

I shake my head and clutch the spotted dog closer to my body.

"Where's your father?" She drops the bags and strides around the room, snapping open the shades. The late evening sun streams through the window, and I squint. "Have you seen him today?"

I don't answer, but she doesn't expect me to. This is our pattern, after all. She asks questions; I nod and pretend she cares. And then we can both go away believing she's done her duty.

"I've got something for you." She empties her pockets and holds out two handfuls of casino chips. "It was a good week, CeCe. A real good week. You can add these to your bank account."

For some reason, the pile of chips is my undoing. I launch myself at Gram and burst into tears.

"CeCe, I . . ." The chips spill onto my bed. She doesn't embrace me, exactly, but I can feel her hands hovering above me, as if she's not sure what to do with them. Finally, they land, butterfly-light, in the middle of my back.

That tentative touch releases the words I've been hoarding. "I can't do this anymore," I sob. "I tried to do what's right, but I don't know who to trust. I don't know who's telling the truth. I don't know anything anymore."

She strokes my hair more certainly. "We can only do our best, child."

"But my best isn't good enough. I screwed up so badly, Gram. I almost ruined someone's life."

"But you didn't, did you?"

"No," I whisper. "I almost accused someone falsely. But I didn't. I realized my mistake before it was too late."

"It happens, child. I almost ruined someone's life, too. But we have to keep striving forward, because there's always the chance we'll rectify our past."

I lift my head. Her designer blouse is splotchy with my tears. "What do you mean? Whose life did you ruin?"

She sighs and removes her chunky gold earrings. Without the baubles, her earlobes look long, stretched-out. Old. "It can be hard to attribute the way a person turns out to any one event, but I see life as a string of dominoes. A single tile can set off a chain of events that leads to the present. I believe I was that tile for your father.

"You've heard me say I'm not cut out for children. I thought my big mistake was deciding to keep the baby." She rubs her ears, as if erasing the red marks can rewind the years of her life. "But I know now that wasn't the mistake. My mistake was not raising him properly. If I'd been a better parent, maybe he would've had a clearer idea how to handle you. Maybe he would've understood he needed to keep a piece of his heart intact, if not for himself, then for his teenage daughter. Instead, he completely fell apart when your mother passed."

My eyes strain against my swollen eyelids. "It's not his fault, Gram. He loved her. We all did."

"And I don't want you to think for one second I'm belittling their love. It was, and still is, beautiful to see." She attempts—and fails—to finger-comb my bramble of hair. "But she's gone now, and you're still here. You need him, not the other way around. That's why I moved here. Sure, it disrupted my career. It meant living in this nowhere town in the sticks. But it was my shot to make up, in a small way, for my failures with your father. I may not be doing such a bang-up job, but I'm trying, CeCe. By god, I'm trying."

"Oh, Gram." I move toward her, and this time, she lifts her arms immediately to embrace me.

"And my next job," she says, "is to make you go to school tomorrow."

I stiffen, and she laughs. "Don't act so shocked. Your father may not know how to talk to you, but he does notice when you skip school three days in a row. He's trying, too, the best way he knows how."

"I don't want to go. I can't face . . . him," I mumble into her shoulder. But even as I say the words, I'm not sure who I mean. Mr. Willoughby. Or Sam. Maybe both. The article comes out tomorrow. Whatever information Sam decides to print will be laid out for the world to see. And I have Mr. Willoughby for first period. I wouldn't mind never meeting his eyes, ever again.

"It's always a boy, isn't it? Do you want to talk about it?"

I shake my head. Maybe someday, I'll be able to confide in her. Someday, it won't hurt so much and I'll be able to tell her everything. But not now.

"Well, I'm sorry, kiddo." She kisses my forehead, something she never does because it wrecks her lipstick. "Life's not easy, but you still have to live it. Maybe, like me, you'll get the chance to fix your mistakes. But that's not going to happen if you stay in bed."

She pulls me to my feet. "Come on. Alisara called me with your assignments, and the janitor's waiting at school to let you into your locker."

I gape at her. "You want me to do my homework while I'm in the middle of a crisis?"

She gives me the fierce don't-mess-with-me look she usually saves for the poker tables. "I certainly do. And while you're at it, here." She pulls a manila folder out of one of her shopping bags.

I take the folder. "What is it?"

"An application to Parsons." The words drift through the air like perfume, scenting and changing everything. "Your father printed it out during one of his sleepless nights. He wants you to apply, CeCe. He wants you to continue living, with or without him." She pauses. "With or without your mother."

Chapter 41

The janitor meets me at the back entrance of the school. I catch a whiff of beer on his breath, and he sports a full week's scruff on his chin. He's the same janitor who came running when the sophomore found my mother's body. The same one who covered her with a blanket and called the police. He's never acknowledged me in any way, but ever since my mother's death, the floor in front of my locker is always so slick and shiny that I nearly slip.

He does a double-take when he sees me and then covers his surprise with a scowl.

"It's a good thing I live around the corner," he grumbles as he unlocks the door. "I hope your little 'emergency' is worth pulling me out of the recliner."

I wince. "Sorry. It's not really an emergency. My Gram can be a bit dramatic."

He grunts. "Shoulda told me that before I left." But then he holds the door open—and keeps holding it until I'm all the way inside the dim lobby. "You want me to come in with you?" he asks, his voice gentle now. "Awful dark in here."

"No, no. I'll be fine. You go back to your recliner. I'll just grab my stuff and go."

He lingers, his hand propping open the door. "Okay, then. If you need anything . . . call. The door will lock behind you."

The door closes, and I swallow hard. The janitor's right. It is dark in here. And the corridors look different at night. The banners stretched across the ceiling have morphed into indecipherable shadows, and each corner hides a potential threat.

It even smells different. The lemony chemical scent of industrial cleaners masks the regular stench of sweat and body odor. The sterility of it bothers me. It's like someone tried to wipe out the student population—and didn't quite succeed.

I rub my arms and make my way down the hallway. This is the second time in a week I've been on school property after hours. Only this time, I'm inside the building. Alone.

I turn a corner, trying to muffle my footsteps. It's as quiet as a tomb, and the slightest noise is magnified tenfold. I hold my breath, the way I do when I first enter a cemetery, as if too violent an exhale will wake the sleeping corpses.

Maybe I should stop being so morbid.

A slight breeze blows against my neck. A breeze? Inside the school? Wrapping my arms around myself, I scan the area, looking for the source.

Ah. There. I walk through the open door of the girls' bathroom. The highest window has been cranked.

That window's *never* open. It's too high, too inconveniently located. Plus, the weather's getting chilly, as we dive more deeply into fall. Did the janitor leave it open to air out the school? Or is there an intruder inside the school?

The hair stands at the back of my neck, and every nerve comes to life. I'm being ridiculous, of course. The window could be open for any number of reasons, none of which have to do with breaking and entering.

I climb on the radiator and shut the window. And then I force myself to start walking down the hallway again. I haven't gone ten steps when I hear a tap and then a shuffle. I pause. Did my shoe slap too loudly against the floor? Nope, there it is again. That's not me.

Someone else is here.

My heart launches into my throat, and I look wildly around the hallway. My muscles bunch, in anticipation of a sprint, but the problem is, I can't tell from which direction the sound is coming. Even if I wanted to run, I wouldn't know where.

It's a teacher, I tell myself firmly. *They must have their own keys to the building. Maybe Mrs. Hopkins is hanging up posters for the fall musical. I should give her a hand, as long as I'm here.*

But even as I think the words, I know, at the very core of my being, that it's not Mrs. Hopkins.

Tap. Shuffle. Slap.

There it is again. I take off, as quickly and quietly as I can. Down the hall, left at the corner, toward the senior locker corridor. Toward the front entrance of the school. Toward freedom.

Get to my locker. Get my homework. Get out of here. Fast.

I'm almost at the senior corridor when I realize a light is blazing, while the rest of the school is dimly lit with emergency lights.

Oh god, oh god, oh god. Whoever the intruder is, I've run straight to him.

I press myself against the wall, my breathing quick and shallow and frenzied. Now what? Do I run back the way I came? Is there another way out of this school?

Slowly, I ease down the hall, away from the senior corridor. But then I hear it again.

Tap. Shuffle. Slap.

I freeze. I recognize those sounds. A footstep. The shuffle of papers. A slap against the wall with a piece of tape.

What on earth is the intruder doing? Every muscle in my body begs me to run, but I can't leave now. I need to see. Oh dear god, I need to see.

I take a deep breath. Count to three. And peek around the corner.

A decidedly female figure tapes a flyer to the wall. She wears black clothes and a ski mask, looking remarkably like Sam and I did almost a week ago. Dozens of papers line the hallway, like moths preparing for flight.

The acid spurts up my throat, and all my fear morphs to anger. Not this. Not again.

I grit my teeth and grab the paper closest to me.

Sure enough, it's another picture with my head on it. Only

the body I'm on isn't just nude. This time, it's doing grotesque sexual acts with a dog.

My rage grows wings and breathes fire. "HEY! What are you doing?"

The masked figure takes one look at me, drops a sheaf of papers, and runs.

I sprint after her. I slide on the scattered papers, but I don't go down. The figure's got a head start, but I ran track in middle school. I'm a little out of practice, but adrenaline takes the place of muscle training, and I run faster than ever.

We tear down the hall. She dashes out the double-glass doors. The door swings and begins to close. I slap my hands against the glass, forcing it open again.

My lungs burn, my legs ache, but I refuse to notice. We're outside now. I whip my head around, searching for the fleeing figure, but there are too many shadows. Maybe Sam was onto something with the black clothes, after all.

Come on, come on. Where are you?

There! The figure scampers through the parking lot, giving up her advantage. Stupid. No cars to weave between. No obstacles to hide behind. Just a wide expanse of open space. I've got her now.

I pour on a burst of speed and begin to close the gap.

Twenty feet.

She looks over her shoulder, which takes time, energy. I stare straight ahead, slamming one foot in front of the other.

Fifteen feet.

She's slowing. I can feel it. I can almost taste it. Sweat—grueling, salty, and harsh.

Ten feet.

Where is she going? Her car? Out of the corner of my eye, a silver bullet of a vehicle gleams in the moonlight. She'll never make it. I won't let her.

Five feet.

It's like fishing in a barrel now. I've got her on a hook; it's only a matter of reeling her in.

Four, three, two . . .

OOOOFF.

I crash into her body, and we go flying across the pavement. Even though I'm on top, the breath's knocked out of me as we hit the ground, hard. My bare arms skid across the parking lot, tearing up my skin. My knees join the bloody slide, rubbing bone against asphalt.

Still, I don't think. I don't feel. A split second after we stop, I straddle the figure and yank off the ski mask.

And look right into the eyes of Mackenzie Myers.

Chapter 42

The parking lot tilts. If I weren't straddling Mackenzie, I might slide right off. I should've known it was her. I definitely suspected. But now that she's under me, caught like the rat she is, my mind's not computing.

"You. It was you, this entire time?"

Mascara streaks down her face like tangled roots, and her lower lip trembles. All of a sudden, the slight gap between her two front teeth makes her look very young.

My shoulders collapse. "I thought it was Sam, but it was you, all along."

"I couldn't let you tell them about me," she moans. "I had to stop you."

"Tell them what, Mackenzie?" I jiggle my head, trying to clear it. "I don't know anything about you, other than you're a spoiled, rich bitch. But everybody already knows that."

"So you don't know my secret?" The air rushes in and out of her mouth, picking up speed like an out-of-control train.

"I have no idea what you're talking about." I ease off her torso. Given how hard she's working to breathe, I highly doubt she's going anywhere. Plus, I've already identified her. Even if she takes off now, the damage is done.

She sits up and drops her head between her knees. The stars glitter in the black sky. My elbows are a smear of blood and gravel. Knees, too. Wincing, I extend my legs. Very likely I'll need a gallon of antiseptic, not to mention stitches.

A few minutes later, Mackenzie's breathing resembles a human's again. "Why did you want to talk to Tommy so badly? Wasn't it to dig up dirt about me?"

"So I could find out about my mom," I say. "Not you. What do I care about your business?"

"Oh." Her voice is small, like I might forget the words if she says them softly enough. "I . . . uh, guess I shouldn't have listened to Justin and hung up those photos of you."

You think? "And you shouldn't have doctored the hotline posters with my phone number. And sent me a bunch of creepy text messages. I didn't deserve any of that, either."

She shakes her head. "No, I didn't do any of that. And neither did Justin. After the bonfire, he was pissed that you embarrassed him, and I didn't want you talking to Tommy. So we decided to teach you a lesson. You really did see him in the hallways that morning, but I lied and said he was out of town. But that was the only thing we did until tonight. I swear it."

I wouldn't trust Mackenzie to file my nails, but I believe her. Because she has no reason to lie. Because the other harassment was about getting me to stay away from the hotline, and all Mackenzie cares about is Tommy. Because the timing makes sense. The posters went up the Monday after the bonfire. She was even the one who first showed them to me.

I rub my temples. What does this mean? If Mackenzie and Justin are only responsible for the posters, who did the other stuff?

"I thought you got the message because you seemed to back off," she says. "But when you won that date with Tommy, I knew I had to step it up."

"Step it up? More like launch it out of this world. Mackenzie, that dog . . . that dog was in her *crotch*. Where did you find that photo?"

"It wasn't easy." She shudders. "Some of the photos I saw, I'm going to have nightmares about for a long, long time. But I was desperate."

"What could Tommy possibly have on you that's worth this?"

She clasps her hands over her knees. Even her nails are painted black. Trust Mackenzie to color-coordinate her vandalism get-up. "I guess you deserve to know." She licks her lips. "You see, in all the months Tommy and I dated, we never slept together. I was more than ready to take the next step, but he never seemed to pick up on my hints. Finally, I sent him a sexy photo of myself, thinking it might pique his interest." She ducks her head. "Nothing like your mom's photo, of course. Just me in some lingerie. But instead of getting excited, Tommy completely blew up at me. Next thing I know, he's telling everybody he's sleeping with your mom. And I knew it had to be because my ass is too big and my tits are too small."

"But that's ridiculous," I sputter. She doesn't know about Lila's explicit photos, so of course she wouldn't understand Tommy's reaction. But, still. Mackenzie Myers, insecure about her looks? It doesn't make sense. "Every boy in school is dying to go out with you."

"Because of my money. I'm like the emperor with new clothes. I pretend I'm hot shit, and everyone's happy to go along with that fiction. At least for now. But I knew once you told everyone how Tommy was disgusted by my photo, they'd admit to each other how ugly I really am."

Your personality's ugly, maybe, I want to say. *Nothing more.* But I can't. As awful as she's been, I can't bring myself to her level. "He wasn't disgusted. He was probably just, um, surprised to get a picture like that from you. You're not ugly, Mackenzie. Far from it."

"Easy for you to say. You and your mom, you both look like supermodels. I'd give anything to have a body like yours."

I stare. "You want Justin Blake to stick his tongue between his fingers every time you walk by? Oh, and how about harassment from the resident mean girl? How would you like your head to be plastered on topless, disgusting photos?"

"I guess I never thought about it that way before." She lays her hand on my arm. The bloody knuckles and black nails blend with my elbows, and for the first time since grade school, Mackenzie Myers and I don't seem so different after all.

She pulls her hand back and twists her rings around her fingers. Black opals. Surprise, surprise. "Please don't tell anybody about me sending those photos to Tommy."

"Not my business to tell."

She rotates the rings again, faster this time, like she's trying to corkscrew them off. "But what about the posters? They *are* your business. Are you going to tell Principal Winters what I did to you?"

"Would you deny it?"

"No." Her fingers fall to her knees. "I messed up. Even if you really were threatening to expose me, I shouldn't have done that. So, whatever punishment's handed down, I'll take it."

"Then I won't tell." I close my eyes, wondering if I'll regret this in the morning. Not sure Sam would agree with my decision. But he's not the person I thought he was, and so many people have already been hurt by the lies Tommy spun. It won't make me feel better to hurt Mackenzie any more.

I crack open my eyelids. "As long as not a single one of these new photos gets out."

She stands up, brushes the dust off her vandalism pants. "Come on, then. Let's go take down those posters."

"There's only one problem," I say, my limbs turning into lead. "The doors lock automatically behind us. And I closed the window in the girls' bathroom."

Her eyes widen. "Which means there's no way for us to get back inside?"

"Not exactly." I sigh. "Looks like I'll need to call the janitor once again."

Chapter 43

In the end, Mackenzie took charge of contacting the janitor. Using an old tissue I found in my pocket and some spit, she wiped the mascara off her face. And when she gave the janitor a winning smile and tucked a twenty-dollar bill in his pocket, he didn't even grumble about being pulled from his recliner a second time. What's more, he left us at the door, once again—which meant he only had time to shoot me just one or two sympathetic glances.

It took an hour and two broken nails to remove all the tape and flyers, and yet, when I get to school in the morning, groups of students huddle together, buzzing excitedly about something.

Did we leave one of the photos up by mistake? Or is it Sam's article? It was supposed to come out this morning. Did he go with the harassment angle, after all?

I peer at my face in the small mirror inside my locker, as if I can find the answer there. My skin looks like stale Wonder Bread, and I know it's Sam's article. It has to be. He could have printed everything in my mom's journal. I took the notebook back home with me, but the damage was already done. He had hours to reproduce every entry, every word. It's all fodder for an article that will mark his start as a rising star.

Should've known better. He's a reporter, for god's sake. His job is to unearth the truth. He never hid his purpose from me. He never made any promises. It was my own fault I trusted him.

My own naivety that I thought he would place my feelings above his future career.

I slam my locker door closed, leaving my books inside, and lean my forehead against the cool metal. I can't do this today. Can't have them gawking at me, like I'm an exhibit at the zoo. Can't listen to the whispers, with a few choice words rising to the level of hearing. Words like "slut" and "serves her right" and "shoulda known."

Shoulda known. Shoulda known. Shoulda known.

I shouldn't have trusted Sam. Shouldn't have dug up the past. And I really, really shouldn't have fallen in love in him.

I'm about to escape to the girls' restroom when Alisara's colorful bangles jingle to my side.

"Did you hear? Mr. Swift's been suspended. Everyone's going crazy with the news."

"What?" I straighten, my heart racing down the hall, around the faculty lounge, into the school's darkroom. So, not about me, after all.

"Principal Winters got an anonymous tip this morning to check out the darkroom. And guess what he found in Mr. Swift's personal drawers? Yearbook photos of girls in our senior class, blown up to poster size. What a sleazebag."

Something clicks in my mind. Something Sam told me a week and a half ago about my study hall teacher. "Wasn't he using the photos for a class project or something? I heard he asked the yearbook staff for those photos."

"A project involving his penis, maybe." She leans closer, and I can see she's used five different shades of eye shadow to match the bangles. "There's more. Apparently, Principal Winters also found a bunch of candid shots of a senior girl, which were clearly taken from a distance. Guess who it was?"

"Who?" Please don't say me. Please don't say me.

"Raleigh! She's strutting around the halls like she's some kind of goddess. Like it's a compliment Mr. Swift was stalking her. Personally, I think it's creepy as hell."

Not to mention gross, disgusting. And something Phoenix would do. "Was he involved with Raleigh? Or any of the others?"

She shrugs, pushing the bangles up her arm as if they were sleeves. "I don't think so. Raleigh says this is the first she's heard of his fixation, and I believe her. But one of the photos is a close-up of her cheerleading bloomers, as she bends over to tie her shoe, so the school's turned the case over to the police. You can bet they'll start interviewing the girls whose pictures he had."

She cocks her head, watching me reopen my locker and retrieve my books. So long as the gossip isn't about me, I guess I'll go to class, after all.

"Maybe he's the one who Photoshopped those posters," she says softly. "I mean, it kinda breaks pattern, because the other photos were untouched. But you never know."

"Maybe," I say noncommittally.

But for the first time in days, I'm able to breathe deeply again. Because the police have Phoenix now. And I didn't have to tell my side of the story. Didn't have to explain about my mom. Didn't have to put myself out there and risk the world's censure. Once they start investigating him, surely they'll uncover his underage pornography ring. From there, they should be able to uncover clues that will lead to his guilt as my mother's murderer. And if they don't, I can point them in the right direction by leaving anonymous tips, so that they don't discount my allegations.

My hand tightens on my textbook. An anonymous tip. Didn't Alisara say that an anonymous tip led to the discovery of the photos? Who could've tipped off Principal Winters? And why?

I suppose it doesn't matter. All that matters is that the police have him. I push the unease away and walk down the hall feeling like I have balloons tied to my body. For the first time since I mistook Ms. Hughes for a student, I think everything might be all right. The police will stop Phoenix, and I'll go back to being invisible. No grand romances, no silly laughter with friends, no reason to believe anything I say or do makes a difference. My mom's name still isn't clear, and her murder hasn't been brought to light, but that's okay. It's only a matter of time before they will be.

When I enter the classroom, Mr. Willoughby nods at me but thankfully doesn't try to talk. I hurry to my seat. Sam is already sitting at his desk. The article. It must have come out, but nobody's talking about it. Nobody is darting glances at me. So whatever he published must have been innocuous enough to disappear under the news of Mr. Swift's suspension. That doesn't mean I forgive him.

I sit down and refuse to look at him, although he tries to catch my eye throughout the entire class period.

I weaken once. I just want to see how the sun falls on the smattering of freckles across his nose. That's it. But as soon as I look, his gaze grabs onto me like a hook and holds on tight. "Phoenix?" he mouths. "Mr. Swift?"

I duck my head and refuse to be drawn in. In the world of lures, his bait is a shiny, neon-glowing fish with iridescent scales. I fell for it once, and I'm not going to again.

I still don't know what he wrote in that article, and I'm not going to care. I'm *not.* My classmates are leaving me alone. That's all I can ask.

After school, I get in my car. The radio's still broken, and the scratches on the leather interior still look like a treasure map. But for some reason, it feels . . . lonelier than usual. I should be celebrating. Punching the air because my ordeal is done. I've stopped Phoenix. He can't hurt anybody else.

And yet, I'm still lost. As bereft as I was in the weeks following my mother's death.

A knock rattles my window, and I jerk, the key scraping across my palm. It's Sam's sister.

I roll down the window and fashion my lips into a smile. Her black hair is tucked into a knit hat pulled all the way to her eyebrows, and she's holding a newspaper. "Hi, Briony. How are you?"

She must be devastated. Not only was her boyfriend arrested, but he was caught with photos of other girls. I don't know how that feels, but I'm no stranger to betrayal. If she needs to talk, I'll listen all night.

But she doesn't seem at all upset as she thrusts the paper at me.

"Sam's article came out in the *Lakewood Sun,*" she says. "Did you see it?"

I shake my head. I was saving it for, oh, sometime like never. But she waggles the daily at me, folded open to the right page, and I have no choice but to take it.

"Read it," she demands.

I scan the article. A brief summary of the hotline's history. General quotes about the importance of connecting from Mr. Willoughby. Statistics from crisis call centers around the country. Even a throwaway sentence about the vanilla air fresheners the hotline uses—which has to be an inside joke for me. And that's it.

I sag against the steering wheel, my arm hitting the horn. BLEEEEEP. The sound of tension being released from soul, body, and spirit. I knew the contents of the article couldn't be scandalous—but that's nothing compared to seeing the bland words for myself.

"He thinks he's going to get fired over this." Briony's voice jabs holes in my relief. "And if he does, he can kiss that Winkelhake scholarship goodbye."

I hand the paper back to her. "Why are you telling me this?"

"Because you care about him. Or at least, you used to. He's hurting right now. I thought it would matter to you."

My chest feels like the air inside a sauna, saturated and moist. It does matter. It matters a lot. But I'm not sure how I'm supposed to feel anymore.

He never intended to publish the scandalous story, he said to me. And here's the proof. He opted for a subpar story, knowing he was risking his scholarship. And with Mackenzie confessing to the photos, and Mr. Swift under investigation by the police, what exactly am I still holding against him?

The six dialed calls. The stolen journal. When it comes down to it, he still betrayed me.

"I don't know what happened between the two of you."

Briony pushes the knit hat up an inch. "But my brother hasn't been himself lately. He hasn't been bugging me for rides or trying out some crazy new gadget. He seems to think . . ." She pauses. "He thinks you're ashamed to be seen with him. Is that true?"

"Of course not. Sometimes you don't want other people to know about a relationship. But that doesn't make your feelings any less real."

"Doesn't it?" she murmurs.

The alarms ringing faintly at the back of my head turn into sirens. She's not acting devastated. She's more concerned about her brother's relationship than her own boyfriend being arrested. What's going on?

"Why do you say that?" I ask.

"No reason." She adjusts the knit cap again, pulling it over her eyebrows. "It's just, my boyfriend and I are in love. And I want everyone else to feel that way, too."

Still in love. Still her boyfriend. So she isn't suffering from a breakup?

And yet, her voice doesn't sound like she's in love. Instead, it's high-pitched and squeaky, and each word rear-ends the following one. As if she's trying to convince herself. As if she were my mother, in the final entries of her journal.

"Briony," I say carefully. "Did you call my cell phone, the second week of school? Did you call me six times?"

"Oh." Two bright spots show on her cheeks. "Um, I don't think so. I mean, what reason would I have to call you?"

"I don't have the slightest clue."

"Yes, well. Listen. I need to get going." She shoves the hat toward her hairline and backs away a few feet. "But if you care about my brother—and it sounds like you do—tell him. When he was with you, he was happy. He hasn't been this happy since . . . well, since before my dad started beating up my mom. And that was a looong time ago. So, think about it, okay?"

She turns, and a gust of wind lifts the hat right off her head, blowing it to the asphalt. She lunges after the hat and struggles to put it back on.

"Oh, jeez. Bad haircut," she babbles. "I've got an appointment at the salon to have them even it out."

But I don't respond. I can't. I'm too busy staring. Briony's once-lustrous, wild mane of hair has been lopped off near the base of her neck. In choppy, jagged cuts. As if by a butcher knife.

I've seen that haircut only once before. On my mother, in the police photos of her dead body.

Chapter 44

I get back to my house in record time, but an hour later, I still haven't made it off the front porch. If I haven't worn a rut in the wooden slats yet, it's not for lack of trying. How could Briony have the same haircut as my mom? How?

I close my eyes, conjuring up an image of my mother the last time I saw her. Even with the funeral parlor makeup, she was beautiful. So beautiful. The eyelids creamy and rounded, her lips closed and relaxed. Her hair short, the jagged edges trimmed. But the hairstylist didn't get rid of the jutting angles. He must've thought they were part of my mom's personal style.

There's only one answer, really. Only one thing Briony and my mom could have had in common.

Or should I say: one man.

Phoenix.

Briony stated over and over again she wasn't dating an older man. And no matter how weird she was at the end of our conversation, she's not acting like a girl whose boyfriend was just busted for having blown-up photos of girls in our senior class.

Whoever her boyfriend is, it's not Mr. Swift. And if it's not my study hall teacher, that means the real sexual predator is still out there. That means Phoenix is still on the loose.

I reach the railing, spin around, and am about to stalk up my porch for the hundredth time when Sam scoots up my driveway. He ditches the metal contraption by the bushes and bounds up the steps, safety pads and all.

"I thought you'd retired that thing." My hands go to my hair, my shirt, my jeans. I don't know when I was expecting to see him on my porch again. Certainly not this soon. Not now, when I haven't figured out how I feel.

"I know you're still mad, but you've got to help me," he says. "It's about my sister."

I stop pacing. "Briony? I just saw her an hour ago. What's going on?"

"She left for the night. She told my parents she was staying at a friend's house, but I ran into Amber at the coffee shop. Without Bri. She admitted Bri went off with her boyfriend and was using Amber as an excuse." His feet tap a staccato rhythm on the porch. "She won't pick up my calls, but a few minutes ago, she texted me this."

He hands me his cell phone, the tips of his fingers brushing my knuckles. I try not to feel the tingle, try not to notice the broad chest hovering over me as I read:

Sammy, don't judge! Amber said I was so busted. But you won't tell Mom, will you? You know I'd do it for you. You and me against the world, remember? Love you.

I hand the phone back, my mind whirling. So she's with Phoenix right now? After he cut her hair the same way as my mother's? What can it mean?

"Am I overreacting?" Sam's eyes pierce into me, making me breathless and achy, all at the same time. "What should I do? If Mr. Swift is Phoenix, then she's probably with some guy her own age. Should I leave them alone?"

I've never seen him like this. As confused as a boy lost in the woods, when he's normally the one who holds the compass.

I take a deep breath and tell him everything. Briony's strange behavior. The jagged haircut. My suspicion that Mr. Swift and Phoenix aren't the same person.

"My god! We have to find her. We have to get her away from that monster before it's too late."

"They're still in the happy stage of their relationship," I say, even as I remember the high-pitched, squeaky voice. "Maybe he hasn't moved on to the exploitative parts yet."

"The very fact they're together is exploitative," he moans. "He's got her to himself for the next twenty-four hours. A lot can happen in twenty-four hours."

As much as I'd like to, I can't disagree. "Do you have any idea where they could be?"

"No clue." Despair edges his voice like the spiky remains of a broken window. "I quizzed Amber, hard. But she says she doesn't know anything. Bri told her she wanted privacy. So they could have uninterrupted time and space to revel in their love. Whatever that means."

"Text her," I suggest, pulling my own phone out of my pocket. "I'll try calling. Maybe she'll pick up if it's me."

But the call goes straight to voice mail. "Briony, it's me, CeCe," I say. "I've been thinking about what you said. About Sam. And I'm so confused. I really need to talk to you. Please call me." I hang up.

"I sent the text," Sam says, a funny look on his face as if he overheard someone talking about him.

Oh crap, he did. My voice mail message. What was I thinking? Not about who was standing next to me, apparently.

"You and Bri were talking about me?" he asks.

"I was trying to get her to call me back. I would've said anything."

"But you did talk about me," he insists. "What about?"

"She showed me your article. The one that came out this morning." I could leave it at that. In fact, I probably should.

But the only thing his "feature" article featured were some dry statistics about crisis call centers. He wrote about vanilla air fresheners, of all things. For me.

"Oh Sam. Your story . . . it was awful. Truly awful."

He blinks. "That bad, huh?"

"It was one of the most boring things I've ever read."

His lips twitch, and he takes a step closer to me. "I told you I'd never print anything that would hurt you."

"Thank you," I whisper.

I don't know if he closes the gap, or if I do. But all of a sudden, our mouths smash together, and our limbs wind around each other. Our tongues tangle and then sigh and then tangle again.

But just as quickly, it's over. This time, I know exactly who moved, because my lips are still hanging in the air.

The look he gives me yanks my heart into long, sticky strands of taffy. "I wish you could've done that before the article came out," he says. "I wish you could've trusted me to do what I said."

I drop my eyes. "I can't even trust myself, let alone anybody else."

He walks to the other end of the porch, as far from me as he can get on the wooden slats. "I guess I can't blame you. I did steal your journal. And I'm not sorry I did. I told Lila Farrow the gist of your mom's history over the phone. I didn't read her lines from the journal, I didn't give her unnecessary details. But I did tell her. And because of that, she agreed to meet with me. When they suspended Mr. Swift this morning, I thought the meeting was no longer necessary. But now that we know that Phoenix is still out there, that he's holed up with my sister, we need Lila to confess, more than ever."

His voice hardens, and I can see the fifteen-year-old boy who stepped in front of his mother to save her from his father's fists. "I'm sorry I violated your trust, CeCe. But if it means saving my sister, I'd do it again."

I squeeze my eyes shut. I try to summon the red-hot fire of betrayal, but it doesn't come. Nothing's changed—and yet, everything has. I can't forget what he's done—but I can't continue to be mad, either.

If we were reading from a script, the next lines couldn't be clearer. *It's okay, Sam. I'll forgive you, if you'll forgive me. I'm sorry I kept our relationship a secret. I'm not afraid to shout it across the lake. To TP the school's front lawn with our initials. To kiss you in the middle of the locker corridor.*

The words march across my tongue, trampling on my taste buds, and yet I don't say them. I can't. I want to reach through this wall separating us. Dismantle the bricks and smash them on the ground. But I'm battling more than just mortar and concrete. I have to fight against doubt and insecurity and distrust. And I'm just not equal to the task.

"When's your appointment with Lila?" I ask hollowly.

He looks at his watch. "I have to leave in a few minutes."

"Let's keep looking for Briony, then. You check Twitter and Instagram. I'll take Facebook and Tumblr."

He nods. Without a word, he turns and props his phone on the railing. A sudden gale shakes the trees, and the leaves shiver. I shiver, too. Will he ever talk to me in that light, teasing tone again? Or are we forever doomed to this businesslike interaction?

I rub my arms and pull Facebook up on my phone. And almost drop the battered device onto the floor.

"Sam," I say. "Take a look at this."

I hand him the phone. His face turns pale as he reads his sister's updated status:

The weather is beautiful—the perfect evening for a photo shoot.

Chapter 45

A photo shoot. A nude, explicit photo shoot, just like my mother's.

We're too late, we're too late, we're too late.

Sam staggers backward. "How could they be at this point already? You said they were happy."

"I didn't know." Nausea clenches my stomach. The cycle's repeating twenty-five years later. And it's all my fault.

"It's because of me," I whisper. "After I almost accused Mr. Willoughby, I dropped the investigation. I retreated into my shell. I did everything Phoenix wanted me to do. He must've seen that as a triumph. It must've given him the confidence to move on to the next phase of his plan with Briony. With me off his trail, it gave him the opening to do what he wanted."

"And what he wants is to destroy my sister." Sam's voice is dull, defeated. With the hopelessness of a guy who spent a year setting up a house of playing cards, only to have it tumble down one card from completion.

You did this, something inside me shouts. *You were too scared to stand up for what was right. Too scared to put yourself in the spotlight. You let what other people think dictate your life. You let your fear of their judgment cause you to make the biggest mistake of all. There was nothing you could do to save your mother. But now, you've endangered another girl just like her.*

The emptiness inside calls me. The one that just claimed three days of my life. The one into which I've disappeared for months at a time. It would be so easy to stop fighting and sink, sink, sink. To let the nothingness claim me as surely as quicksand.

But I can't. Not this time. Because Briony needs me. And I'm not going to let her down once again.

"We have to find Phoenix," I say, not recognizing my own voice.

Sam gets to his feet, and the familiar set of his shoulders returns. "You said you eliminated Mr. Willoughby. And we've just determined Briony can't possibly be dating Mr. Swift. That leaves Principal Winters, right?"

"Maybe." But my stomach swirls like a washing machine. Something's not right. It can't be a process of elimination. We're missing something. Someone. But what? "I want to go back to the library. Check out the yearbooks again."

Sam nods. "Okay. I'm going to meet Lila. Maybe I can convince her to tell us who Phoenix is."

I fish my keys out of the stuff I dumped on the steps. Sam and I are about to separate, to go our different ways, to pursue two distinct leads. And yet, despite our disagreement, despite the lingering betrayal, I feel closer to him than ever before. "Good luck," I say. "Partner."

Something I can't read crosses his face, and he nods once. "Partner."

Families gather on the sidewalk outside the public library. A little boy yanks his sister's pigtails, and kids run around in circles, chasing each other. The moms look on, weighed down with diaper bags and red-and-white-striped boxes of popcorn, with varying degrees of exasperation.

"What happened?" I ask the least harried-looking mom.

She rolls her eyes and sticks a pacifier into the mouth of a wailing toddler. "They canceled story hour. Power's out."

"They closed the library?"

She gives me a sympathetic look, like she would give me a pacifier, too, if it would make me feel better. "You can still go in there. They're open, but it's dark."

I thank her and walk inside. It's dim and cave-like, the only light coming from the late afternoon rays slanting through the windows. The librarian sits at the reference desk, her face shadowed.

She grimaces when she sees me. "They say I have to stay here. Can you believe it? Power should be back in an hour, but if you can't wait, take one of these." She hands me one of the half dozen flashlights on her desk.

I switch it on, and the light, as flimsy as candles on a birthday cake, cuts through the shadows. Spooky. Steeling my shoulders, I make my way to the shelves behind the newspapers and kneel in front of the yearbooks. I find my mom's senior yearbook. Holding the flashlight with one hand and turning the pages with the other, I go through the yearbook slowly, looking for anything I may have missed the first time.

Prom queen, student council president. My mom was everywhere her senior year. Looking at her red hair and her even redder lips, the brilliant smile and the straight posture, I'd never guess that seventeen-year-old Tabitha was anything less than perfectly happy. But I of all people should know how deceiving appearances can be. This is the girl that everybody sees. The girl in the mirror. The real Tabitha is hidden somewhere inside this beautiful face, so deep that the only people who glimpsed her might have been my father and me.

Tears suddenly rush to my eyes. *Don't worry, Mom. I'm going to find Phoenix. I won't let him hurt anyone else, and I'm going to show the world who you really are. Not the bimbo teacher who slept with a student. Not the weak woman who abandoned her husband and daughter.*

But the mother who loved me beyond measure. The woman who made her husband come alive. The teacher who cared so much and so deeply that she set up a crisis hotline so no student would ever feel as lost as she did. That's the real Tabitha Brooks. And it's time for her to resume her rightful place in our memories.

Quickly, before the tears can begin a fresh assault, I turn to the photo of my mom sitting on the sports car next to her friends. Here. This is where I get that niggling feeling. This is where the dots need connecting. But how?

I bob the flashlight, and for a moment, all I see is the front bumper of the car. The car. I was so focused on the people before, I didn't bother to look at what they're gathered around. I've seen this car before. I know it.

I squint at the yearbook. The photo is black and white, but the shape of the car is so familiar. And then there's the racing stripe down the center . . . Oh my god. The racing stripe. If this car were orange, it could be Liam's car.

Liam's car. I don't get it. He couldn't be involved. Right?

A flashlight shines in my eyes and then moves away. An instant later, Sam drops down beside me, panting. "Lila wouldn't give me a name, but she admitted they met through the hotline." His words tumble over each other. "She called to talk about her parents' divorce, and he was her counselor. After a few calls, he suggested they meet, and the relationship progressed from there. What do you think? This helps, right?"

As he talks, the kernel of dread in my stomach unfurls. No. It has to be a coincidence. A sick twist of life. I won't believe it. I won't.

Wordlessly, I hand Sam the yearbook and tap my finger on the bumper. I have to swallow twice before I can speak. "What kind of car is this?"

"An old Firebird. The same kind Liam drives."

A blast of ice hits right at my core. "Did you say 'Firebird'? As in, another name for Phoenix?"

We stare at each other, and I watch the realization move across his face.

"Holy crap. It's the same car." Sam brings the flashlight closer to the page, as if the light will reveal more answers. "I don't get it. Liam's only a couple years older than us. What's he doing driving a car from this picture?"

My eyes dart around the faces in the photo, snagging on the blond guy next to my mom. The one with a strong cleft chin and dimples. The one with a chain around his neck. The one who looks just like Liam.

I can't breathe. It's like a vise has been placed around my lungs, squeezing, squeezing, squeezing until there's no air left. Sweat drenches my forehead, my neck, my lips, and the carpet sways beneath my knees. I can't deny the truth anymore, but I don't understand. Liam was my friend. He listened to me. He held me in his arms and comforted me.

I try to organize my thoughts, but they fly away, chasing each other like wind inside a tornado.

"Look." Sam points out the name in the caption. Sure enough. William Kessler. I'd thought the blond guy with his arm slung around my mom's shoulder was a student, but it says right there, in black and white, that Mr. Kessler was the photography teacher.

"It's his dad. His dad is 'W.' " I can't believe I'm saying these words, but as I talk, the puzzle pieces begin falling into place. "His dad must've been the guy who preyed on my mom, but he passed away a couple years ago. Liam inherited his car and the cabin by the lake, which was their summer home. He told me . . . Oh god. He told me he was going to do everything in his power to pick up his dad's torch."

Sam's hand closes in a fist above the photo. "Including prey on young girls he meets through the hotline. The more vulnerable the better."

"Did Briony call the hotline?"

"Yes, right when we moved to town." He takes a shuddering breath. "At the end of the last school year, my dad hit my sister for the first time. She wasn't too hurt—nothing like the bruises he would leave on my mom—but it was enough to prompt my mom to do what she couldn't do for herself. She left him, and we came to Lakewood. Both my mom and I thought Briony would benefit from talking to someone, and she didn't want a therapist, so the hotline was it. Talking to the counselors seemed to help her a lot. That's one of the reasons I leaped at the chance to write a story about the hotline. Because it helps people."

My heart aches. Once again, I misjudged. Once again, I made assumptions based on someone's appearances. I'd thought Briony had so many friends she had no need for a crisis hotline. I couldn't have been more wrong.

"Liam must've been following his father's MO," I say slowly. "Down to the very lines the original Phoenix used to woo his girls. That was our mistake. We were looking for someone twenty-five years older. We completely discounted Liam, even though everything leads back to him."

Sam doesn't speak. He doesn't have to. His thoughts are identical to mine.

Liam. It's been Liam all along.

Liam, whose name is short for William. Liam, whose pendant displayed a picture of a bird. And not just any bird, I realize now, but a phoenix. Liam, who saw me discover my mother's wall-papered box. Liam, who knew exactly when I would be at the hotline. Liam, to whom I confessed that I was retreating back into my shell. Liam, who wasn't old enough for Briony to consider "old."

Liam, Liam, Liam. Always there, but so good at turning on the charm, I never suspected him. Not once.

"Now what?" Sam asks. "How do we find them?"

"Don't worry," I say as the chatter of geese fills my ears. "I know exactly where they are."

Chapter 46

"I've never seen you wear anything like that," Sam says, his eyes drifting to my cleavage. But not because he enjoys the sight. The opposite, in fact, if his frown's any indication.

"I blend with the bushes." I tug at my shirt. "Isn't that what you said we should do, when we were breaking into the shed? Blend?"

His eyes haven't left my neckline. "This wasn't what I had in mind."

He has a point. Instead of robber-black, I'm wearing a snug forest-green top that dips into a low V, a birthday gift from Alisara last year. What I said was true—it's the same color as the greenery—but I'm not wearing it for camouflage. Rather, I want to be prepared.

We peek through the foliage at one of the cabins along the lake. The sun's fiery orb skims the edge of the water, and the geese honk as if they're stuck in a traffic jam. It was the crazy birds that clued me in. From our first conversation, Liam has complained about the birds waking him up every morning. And while the geese utilize the entire lake as their playground, they converge on the south side where their shelter is.

Once we narrowed our search, it was a simple matter of driving along the south side of the lake looking for the Firebird. We found the car in the third driveway we searched, a few cabins from Bobby Parker's house and across the lake from the hotline.

"I don't like this," he says. "You dangling yourself as bait."

"I'm not crazy about it, either. But do you have a better idea?"

"We could call the police."

"And say what? That your sister's dating a twenty-year-old guy? If they haven't had sex, then there's no crime." I take a deep breath, remembering the scathing looks the detectives gave my dad when he came to them with one of his theories. The way they didn't even bother to hide their snickers. But I'll endure all that, and more, if it means Liam won't be able to hurt anyone, ever again. "By the time we explain the whole story, it will be too late. We'll call them as soon we get Briony out of there. I promise."

He nods, adjusting his glasses. "Do you think he'll fall for your plan? My sister's a sure thing. Why would he let her leave?"

"He needs to expand his pornography ring. And I'm positive he was grooming me to be his next victim." I blush, thinking of the way Liam flattered me with his attention. The way he made me feel special, like I was the only girl in the world. If I hadn't had Sam, how close would I have come to getting sucked under his spell? "If I give him an opening, I don't think he'll turn it down."

Sam squints at the cabin. Not a flutter of the curtain, not a stray cat meowing on the deck. "I guess there's only one way to find out."

I settle on the ground, put the phone on speaker, and dial Liam's personal cell number.

He answers on the fourth ring. "Hello."

In the background, we hear a faint but familiar shrill of laughter.

Sam almost falls over. "That's her," he mouths.

"Liam, this is CeCe," I say, trying—and failing—to sound coy. How on earth does Raleigh pack so much coquettishness into her words? "I was hoping we could talk."

"Sure, go ahead."

Not what I'm looking for.

"Could we talk in person? I'd like to see you."

He pauses. "This isn't a good time, CeCe. Maybe tomorrow?"

"Oh." I don't have to fake the disappointment in my voice. "I'd really like to see you tonight. You said, anytime I wanted to talk, just say the word. I wasn't up to company a few days ago. But now that I've had the chance to mull things over, I think I'm ready."

I glance up, and Sam's right there, knees touching mine, face inches away. I look right into his eyes as I continue, "Sometimes, I think you're the only person in this world who understands me."

The seconds pass. Liam clears his throat, and static snakes onto the line, as if he's moving the phone into another room. Did I lay it on too thick?

"Okay," Liam says finally. "Come by my cabin in half an hour."

I grin at Sam, and he lifts his hand for a high-five. Instead, I lace my fingers with his. Because it makes less noise and because I want to.

Liam gives me the address—the address of the very property on which we're sitting—and I hang up.

"And now," Sam says, squeezing my hand. "We wait. The second she comes out, we'll grab her."

We crouch behind the bushes, watching the front door for Briony to emerge. We wait and we watch. We watch and we wait. And then we wait and watch some more.

But there's no sign of Briony.

I glance at my watch. "Almost thirty minutes have passed."

"What's he thinking?" Sam shoves his hands through his hair. "That Bri will stay in the other room while he hooks up with you? Or does he have her tied up? Or—oh god—what if that wasn't her we heard, after all? What if he's already hurt her or drugged her or—"

"Sam!" I grab his arms. "We don't know. We're not going to know anything until I go inside."

He lowers his forehead until it's touching mine. The frame of his glasses jabs into my skin, but I don't back away. Not a single inch. "You knew you were going in," he says dully. "That's what the shirt is all about."

"I hoped I wouldn't have to."

He pulls back, and the glasses are crooked on his face. I reach out to straighten them, my heart full of resolve and anticipation and fear—and something else, too. Something only Sam evokes in me. If it's not love, then it's pretty damn close.

"Be careful, CeCe," he says.

"I'll try."

Chapter 47

Liam answers the door seconds after I knock, dressed in jeans and a hoodie zipped halfway up his bare chest. He smiles when he sees me, a smile that reaches his eyes and broadcasts his sincerity.

Not once does he look at my cleavage.

Man, he's good. If the evidence hadn't been staring at me from the yearbook, if Lila hadn't confessed that she met Phoenix at the hotline, I never would've suspected him in a million years.

"You're here," he says, giving me a hug.

For a second, I go statue-still. I've hugged him before. Hell, that day the lights flickered at the hotline, I spent a good five minutes in his arms. But that was before I knew he was a sexual predator. Before I knew he very likely killed my mom.

You're supposed to have a massive crush on him, remember? Act like it.

I wind my arms around him automatically. I feel like I'm hugging a snake. Those limbs slithering across my back. The cool, minty breath against my cheek. Even his chest, where it brushes against my skin, feels too smooth. Too silky.

A column of flame burns up my chest. Instant heartburn. Oh god. I hope I don't throw up over us both.

He moves back and grins. "I'm so glad you came."

"Me, too." I let the nerves leak into my voice. That's appropriate, right? If I were visiting my crush at his cabin for the first time, I'd definitely be nervous.

He tucks me into his side like a doll, and we walk past the kitchen and into the living room. So far, the layout looks like the hotline's. If the pattern holds, the bathroom will be down the hall, the basement office a few steps below that. The most private area of the house. The perfect place to stash a girl to keep her out of sight.

"You wanted to talk?" He gestures toward a dark leather couch and pours me a glass of water from a pitcher sitting on the end table. It even holds thin slices of lemon.

"That was an excuse. I wanted to see you." I look at him through my eyelashes—a move I've seen Raleigh perform dozens of times. I must do a decent job because he smiles and sits next to me.

"I must say, I'm surprised. That night at the auction, I got the impression you were interested in someone else."

I lick my lips. "I've always liked you. But you were older and so good-looking. I thought *you* would never be interested in me."

He narrows his eyes. "And yet, you turned down my dinner invitation. You chose Tommy Farrow's company over mine."

My pulse hammers in my throat. Oh god. He doesn't believe me. What can I say?

And then it comes to me: the truth. As Gram taught me, the most believable lies are based on an element of truth.

"You're the one I want," I say. "My date with Tommy wasn't romantic. I bid on him so that I could talk to him about my mom."

His hands clench. "Ah. Did you, uh, get the information you were looking for?"

I make myself look straight in his reptilian eyes. How could I ever have thought he was handsome? The eyes give it away. Small and cruel, a blue so cold it could freeze water. "He gave me a tip, but it didn't pan out. Like I told you on the phone, I made a mistake and almost accused the wrong person." I stare at my fingers. "I was silly. Playing detective, when I don't know the first thing about tracking down a criminal. I guess you could say I learned my lesson. From now on, I'm leaving the investigating to the professionals."

The words come easily. As they should. This was exactly how I felt before I saw Briony's chopped-off hair. But does Liam buy it?

I count four breaths, in and out, and then he squeezes my shoulder. "Why don't I give you a tour? We can start upstairs. With the bedrooms."

Gotcha.

"I'd love a tour," I say. "But first, could I freshen up in the bathroom?"

"No problem." His fingers slide under my short cap sleeves, both a caress and a promise. "It's right down the hall."

Giving him my best seductive smile, I sashay away. Once I'm halfway down the hall, I glance over my shoulder. He's nowhere in sight. Good.

My heart scampers, my mouth dries. This is it. My chance to find Briony and get us the hell out of here.

I blow past the bathroom and trip down the stairs, making sure my footsteps are muffled by the carpet. Opening the door, I walk into a photo studio. I scan the room. An expensive-looking camera on a tripod, professional spotlights, a big white backdrop. A four-poster bed with fluffy pillows. Slinky red boa. A bucket of ice.

And standing in the middle of the set is Briony.

"CeCe!" Her eyes take up half her face. "What are you doing here?"

Her feet are bare, and her body is wrapped in a black silk kimono. She's wearing a wig of sunset red hair, shot through with flames. I've only known one person who has hair that color.

One person from whom the wig could've been made.

The room pitches, and I wrap my hand around the bedpost to stay upright.

But there's no time to faint. I grit my teeth, fighting the dizziness. "We've got to get out of here. Is there a back door? A window we can climb through?"

Her eyebrows crease. "What are you talking about? I'm not going anywhere. How'd you find out about Liam, anyway?"

"Briony, listen to me. Your boyfriend is a sexual predator." Convince her. Quickly. "He runs an underage pornography business, and he lures girls into falling in love with him so he can take their pictures."

She glances at the photo set, with its bed and props. "He said they would be for his personal enjoyment. He said I was so sexy he couldn't get enough of me, and this way, he'd be able to enjoy me all the time."

"You haven't taken any photos, have you, Bri? Oh please. Tell me I got here in time."

Her hands go to her waist, tightening the belt of her kimono. "We were just about to get started when he got called away on business."

"I was his business. I called and asked to come over, and he leaped at the opportunity to convert me into one of his victims." I take a deep breath. "While you were down here waiting, he was upstairs, flirting with me."

"I don't believe you." She shakes her head, and the red strands swing in the air. So bouncy. So lifelike. "He loves me."

We don't have time for this. Liam will be here any second. He's probably looking for me now.

I grip her shoulders. "The wig you're wearing. It's made from my mother's hair. She was investigating his pornography ring, and when she got too close, he killed her. Only he chopped off her hair first, just like he chopped off yours. You're wearing a dead woman's hair, Bri. That's the kind of monster he is. Now do you believe me?"

She pales, and my hands slide to her forearms. I've got her now. "Come on. We've got to go."

But it's too late.

The door creaks open, and Liam stalks into the room, his white teeth glinting in the overly bright spotlights.

Chapter 48

"Hello, ladies," Liam drawls. "I see you've found each other."

His hands are empty. That means no weapon. Not yet. There's two of us. One of him. We can take him. We can get out of here.

But only if my second is willing to fight.

Briony shakes my hand off and walks to her boyfriend.

"It's not true, is it?" she says. "CeCe's been telling me all these crazy things. You're not really a child pornographer, are you? You didn't kill her mom?" She pulls the wig from her head and lets it drop to the floor, shuddering. "This isn't the hair of a dead woman?"

His eyes widen, his mouth drops—the very picture of an innocent man accused. He's not just a good actor; he's a goddamn psychopath.

"Of course it's not true." He strokes her blunt, jagged locks, as though he's a parent soothing a toddler. "CeCe's unstable. You must've seen it."

"Liar!" I burst out.

He talks right over me. "That's why Mr. Willoughby recommended she volunteer at the hotline. He thought we could help her. Instead, she fell in love with me. Which, incidentally, is why things didn't work out between her and your brother. She'd say anything to get rid of you. Anything to have me." He caresses her lips, her chin. "But she won't come between us, will she, my love? Because you're the only one for me. Now and forever."

He drops his hand from her face and winds it around her waist. She sighs and leans into him.

"Briony, don't listen to him." I rise on my toes. I have to make her understand. "He's lying. He's a madman and murderer. You can ask your brother. He'll tell you. He knows the truth."

But she no longer hears me. She closes her eyes, and he grins at me over her head. Smug. Triumphant. I want to take the bucket of ice and dump it on his head.

"Let me handle this, darling," he says to Briony. "Go wait for me upstairs, and I'll be along shortly. Okay?"

"Okay." She glances at me over her shoulder. An expression I can't read flits across her face. "Please hurry."

Seconds later, she's gone, the door banging a few times against the jamb.

Liam turns to me, a sneer twisting his features. "For once, I thought I'd found my equal. I thought you would be the one to understand the complicated nuances of my relationship with my father. We could've been good, you and I. But, no. Just when I thought we had a shot, you had to go poking around where you had no business."

"What are you going to do?" I plant my feet, even though my knees tremble like a kite in the wind. Don't quiver, dammit. Look him straight in the eyes. Be strong. "Kill me like you killed my mother?"

"I warned you, didn't I? I told you to get back in your shell. But you didn't listen. You just had to dig up your mom's past. You just had to get to the bottom of her supposed affair with Tommy." He walks to a set of drawers and pulls out a pair of scissors. Shiny, metal, blunt. "I have to admit, I'll enjoy reenacting her suicide scene. So much better than reliving the memory with only a wig. I'll cut your hair, overdose you on pills, and drag you to the crisis hotline. What do you think?"

"You're insane," I whisper.

"Maybe. But your hotshot reporter boyfriend will love it. Can you imagine? It will be the story of the year! Daughter follows suicidal mother's footsteps."

"Like you tried to mimic your dad?" I ask. The scissors are open now at pointed at me. I've got to keep him talking. Got to find a way to distract him. "He was quite the loser, you know. Taking advantage of his student like that."

"He was in love." Liam snaps the scissors closed. "It was your mother who broke his heart. Your mother who betrayed him and turned him into a hard, bitter man. It was a moment's flirtation for her. Just another instance of her acting like the slut she was. But for me? It meant a lifetime of punishment and cruelty, of being shot down again and again for not being good enough. She made him that way. And so, she had to pay."

My eyes widen. "That's why you killed her? She flirted with one boy, Liam. Twenty-five years ago. Your dad was already messed up. It had nothing to do with her."

"It had everything to do with her!" He's panting hard now, and the scissors tremble in his hand. He takes several long, deep breaths, as if struggling for control.

"I didn't set out to kill her," he says more softly. "After my dad died, I went through his papers and found what I thought was an unfinished manuscript he was writing. Only it wasn't fiction. It didn't take me long to figure out that the names of the places and people were real. That was when I learned how Tabitha Brooks destroyed my father's life. So, I moved to Lakewood and volunteered at the hotline to get to know her better. And then, something unexpected happened."

He straightens his shoulders and inclines his head. Right in front of me, he seems to grow two inches. "I discovered power. When I was on the phone with these callers, they listened to me. They deferred to me. They hung on to my every word, and they wouldn't have dared take a step without my permission. I realized not only could I finally live up to my father's expectations, I could surpass him. He had one high school girl; I would have a dozen. He took explicit photos for his own enjoyment; I would post my photos for the world to see."

He flashes his teeth. This must be the smile he gives when nobody's looking. When he doesn't have to be anybody but himself. "If my dad could see me now, he would approve, don't you think?"

"But you didn't expect my mom to find out," I say. "You didn't count on one of your victims calling the hotline and tipping her off. You didn't know she'd be able to connect you with your father."

"It worked out." He opens and closes the scissors, and the blades click as they rub against one another. "She died before she could do any real damage."

I lick my lips, staring at the scissors. Keep him talking. Just keep him talking. "There are a few things I don't get. How did the six missed calls get on Sam's home phone? And how did the Jean Grey comic book get in Mr. Willoughby's office?"

Liam walks closer. He's an arm's length away now. "Easy." He grins, and I'm not sure which is more menacing. The scissors, or his gleaming, white teeth. "Briony. She'd jump off a cliff for me. It was a simple matter to ask her to call you and to eavesdrop on your conversation with Tommy. She told me you were hot on Phoenix's trail, not that she understood what it meant. That's when I put that comic book in his office."

That's right. I remember the glimpse of dark curls disappearing around the corner. Tommy and I checked for eavesdroppers before we started the conversation, but we never looked again. Briony could've come back. She could've heard us talking, and Liam's savvy enough to make up a believable story to explain why he was asking her to do these "favors."

"What about the Photoshopped pictures, the ones that Mackenzie put up?" I ask. "When you texted me, you made it sound like you were responsible. Were you in league with her?"

"Nah. I was just lucky that rich bimbo Mackenzie was out to get you. It fit perfectly into my plans. Any other questions?"

He loves this, I can tell. He loves sharing his brilliance, and it doesn't matter what I know, anyway, because he thinks I'll end up dead.

"Mr. Swift!" I say. "Was it also just a coincidence that those photos were discovered in his darkroom this morning?"

"I may capitalize off coincidence, but I don't rely on it." His grin is quick and arrogant. "I knew you had ruled out Mr. Willoughby. You all but confessed that to me when you told me you almost made a false accusation. I needed another scapegoat, so I planted the photos in Mr. Swift's darkroom and left an anonymous tip for Principal Winters."

Out of the corner of my eye, I see the door move. A fraction of an inch. Is it my imagination? Or maybe the wind? "So he's innocent?"

"As innocent as your mother. The photos weren't his, but I'm sure he's had a lewd thought or twenty. Who doesn't?" Liam shoots his hand out, wrapping my hair around his fist. "But that's enough talking. Time to get down to business." He closes the scissors, and a hunk of my hair floats to the floor.

He opens the scissors, about to take another chunk, when the door flies open. Briony bursts into the room, a frying pan in her hands. She smashes the pan over his head, her muscles bulging, and he pitches forward.

"Run, CeCe, run!"

We tear up the stairs and down the hall, Briony a few steps ahead of me. My head roars, my lungs burn, but I'm only focused on one thing.

Get out, get out, get out.

There! The front door. She fumbles with the knob once, twice, and then manages to get it open. We dash down the sidewalk, but as we step off the flagstone, she twists her ankle and goes down on the gravel.

I yank her torso, trying to haul her up. She almost comes to a standing position. I almost get my arm underneath her. But then she puts pressure on her foot, yelps, and collapses onto the ground once again.

"I'm so sorry, CeCe," she sobs. "I never meant to hurt you or anybody else. He convinced me that I was just looking out for my brother. That I had to spy on you to make sure you were the right girl for Sam . . ."

I try to pull her up once more. "It's okay, Bri. Don't worry about that right now. We're so close. We just have to get to Sam, and he'll help us. We're almost there. Almost there . . ."

"Not soon enough."

My heart sinks to the gravel beside Briony. Liam strides out of the cabin, blood trickling down his forehead and a weapon in his hands. Only this time, it's not a pair of scissors—but a gun.

"Get back in the house. Both of you. Or you're both dead."

"But she's hurt," I say. "She can't stand—"

"Then maybe I should shoot her like the bitch she is." He strides over to Briony and hauls her up, pressing the gun to her temple. "She's no use to me lame. And she knows too much. Yes, I think I'll kill her right now and turn this sordid affair into a murder-suicide. You think good old Sam will still get his rocks off on this story?"

Briony whimpers in pain. It's more than a sprain. A glistening white bone pokes out of her ankle. Even if I can pry her from his grip, there's no way she'll be able to run away.

"Count with me." He jabs the gun deeper into her skin. "One . . ."

I look frantically around the front lawn, looking for a weapon, a way out, any kind of exit strategy. But there's nothing. Just the log cabin and forest-green grass and the densely planted trees Sam and I were hiding behind. Where the hell is Sam? Why isn't he out here helping me save his sister?

"Two . . ."

My mind spins. Forget Sam. Forget any other help. I'm on my own here, and I can't let him kill her. I need to distract him. But how? How? How?

"Thr—"

"Wait!" I shout. "You don't have to do this. Because you can have something to hold over me. To hold over both of us." My eyes, my hands, my entire body go still. Never, in a million years, would I have believed it would come to this. But now that the moment's here, a strange calmness overtakes me. This is the way it's supposed to be. Maybe the way it was always supposed to be. "I'll pose for you. Right here, right now. I'll take off my clothes, and you can take as many pictures as you want."

He takes the gun from her temple and lowers it an inch. He's thinking about it. Good.

"Once you have the photos, you know I'll never betray you," I say. "I would never risk being judged like that. You know me. You know it's true. Please, Liam. Don't kill us, when there's another way."

"That's a very interesting proposition." He lowers the gun all the way, so that it's pointing at the ground. "Why don't you take off your shirt, and then we'll see—"

BANG!

My heart stops.

Not literally. A moment later, it beats again. And continues beating. I'm still here. Still thinking. I don't feel any pain.

I glance at Briony, expecting to see blood on her body, but she's okay, too.

It's Liam who's crumbled on the ground, red blossoming around his kneecap. What on earth?

And then chaos.

A dozen police officers storm the lawn, and my dad is running toward us, Sam at his shoulder.

My dad reaches me first and sweeps me in his arms. "Oh god, CeCe. My little girl. I thought I'd lost you." He sobs. "I love you, sweetheart. I've always loved you. I just didn't know how to show it."

My brain starts working again. The police must have shot Liam. They must have been waiting for an opening, and when Liam lowered his gun, they took their opportunity. I have no idea how they got here. No idea who called them. No idea what's going to happen next.

All I know is I'm safe now. And exactly where I'm supposed to be.

In my father's embrace. Hearing the words I never thought I'd hear again.

I love you, too, Dad. I love you so much.

Epilogue

I stand in the middle of the locker corridor. My palms are sweaty, but I refuse to wring them. My stomach turns, but I refuse to run.

The hallway begins to fill. Alisara leans against her locker, shooting me supportive smiles. Mackenzie lounges at the end of the corridor, hip cocked in her trademark I-couldn't-care-less pose. But if she didn't care, she wouldn't still be hanging around. Especially after I made her get up an hour early to help me this morning.

A lot has happened in the last two weeks. Liam Kessler is in jail, awaiting his trial. The prosecutor has sworn to bring him up on charges of everything from murder to child pornography to statutory rape. Once they know what they're looking for, the Lakewood police, it seems, aren't half bad at their jobs. Of course, it didn't hurt that Liam is a psychopath and a pack rat, to boot. A simple raid of his cabin uncovered my mom's hair, as well as albums of his victims' pornographic photos.

Mr. Swift hasn't been back at school, and rumor has it that he's looking for jobs in another town. I don't blame him. He may be innocent, but it's hard to live down even a whiff of scandal in Lakewood.

I'm more grateful than ever that I didn't actually accuse Mr. Willoughby. Especially after he brought me the contents of my mother's wallpapered box. It seems Liam neglected to bring me all of her possessions. In addition to the snow globe, my mother also left a letter in a sealed envelope. Not THE final letter, but my birthday letter, the one that she writes me every year. I guess she wrote it a month early last year, and her words are as special as ever. Even more special because I know, once and for all, that this is the last letter I'll ever receive from her.

My dad and I have been going to my mom's grave site together on the weekends. I've convinced him to cut down his visits to once a week. Sometimes we talk, and sometimes we work companionably in silence, cleaning the bird poop off the slab of marble. I still cook dinner every night, but he does his own laundry now. And last Sunday, he whipped up a batch of biscuits the way he used to when my mother was still alive.

New York is no longer off the table, even though I haven't settled on a subject for the Parsons Challenge. My mom, perhaps. The way I've forgotten myself, maybe. Or something else entirely, something much less abstract. The application deadline is still months away, so I have plenty of time to decide.

As for the Davidsons, Briony has a big cast on her ankle. I ran into her in the restroom once, and she was sobbing her mascara down the drain. She wrapped her arms around me for five whole minutes and then left without saying a word. But later, I saw her in the lunchroom, surrounded by her friends, laughing or at least pretending to. So I hope—I pray—one day she'll be okay.

And Sam . . . well, he got his big story, after all. Reporters camped out on my front lawn, like they did six months ago. And like last time, I refused to talk to any of them. Except one. It was the least I could do, since he was the one who called both my dad and the cops after I didn't come out of Liam's cabin. I don't know if the exclusive will be enough to win him the scholarship, but at least now he's got a shot.

Which is more than I can say for us. Other than the interview, we've barely spoken. And I get it. We worked together to bring down a sexual predator and murderer, but I still haven't given him what he really wants.

Until now.

Every person who walks into the corridor stops and stares. At me, standing in front of Sam's locker. But mostly at the hundreds of papers taped to the walls. Under their glances, my knees tremble. My ankles shake. My toes shiver. But this is necessary. This is part of the plan. The more onlookers I have, the better.

When Sam arrives, a few minutes before the bell, practically the entire senior class is waiting.

He walks through the front door, in his elbow and kneepads, carrying his helmet. Did he ride the scooter to school today? Or has he discovered a new mode of transportation altogether? I hope I have the chance to find out.

The crowd parts, creating a path for him to walk straight to his locker. Straight to me.

"CeCe?" he says as he approaches. "What's going on?"

Instead of answering, I gesture to the papers Mackenzie and I taped up this morning. The drawings I did of him the first day we met. Of his glasses, his bare ankles, his broad chest. And a dozen more sketches I drew in the following weeks. Of Sam flailing on his rollerblades. Sam with a black robber-cap pulled over his ears. Sam smiling a moment after kissing me. Almost every memory I've had with him, I've drawn.

And now I've posted them all for the world to see.

"What's this?" he asks softly.

"This is how I feel about you." I don't bother trying to keep my voice quiet. The way my classmates are straining, they'll pick up every word, anyway. "These drawings are the very heart of me. You are the heart of me. And I don't care who knows it."

His deep, black eyes pierce into me. Like they did that first day. As I hope they'll do for many days and weeks and months to come.

"Do you mean it?" he murmurs.

In response, I crash my lips into his. He lifts me high off the ground, and I'm smiling and laughing and kissing at the same time.

The people whoop and clap and cheer. I know they're staring at me. I know, once again, I'm the center of attention.

But you know what? With Sam's lips warm on mine, all I can think is:

Let them stare.

A READING GROUP GUIDE

THE DARKEST LIE

Pintip Dunn

About This Guide

The suggested questions are included to enhance your group's reading of Pintip Dunn's *The Darkest Lie*.

Discussion Questions

1. At the beginning of the book, CeCe refuses to let Mr. Willoughby flip through the drawings in her self-examination journal, even if it means receiving a zero for the assignment. And yet, by the end of the story, she posts drawings of Sam in the senior locker corridor for the entire school to see. What changed? What lessons did CeCe learn—and how?

2. CeCe and Liam discuss how their feelings toward their parents can be a mixture of love and hate. Do you believe these two emotions can be experienced simultaneously, or does one always take precedence over the other? Have you ever felt this way?

3. Discuss the various ways that characters grieve in this story. Is there one correct way of grieving?

4. What does "scandal" mean? Does this definition change, depending on the size of the community? This story takes place in the fictional town of Lakewood, Kansas, with a population of 10,000, where many of the high school seniors have known each other since preschool. Would this story be different if it took place in a city? If so, in what ways?

5. CeCe seems to be the object of widespread harassment and bullying. Many times, she'll cite "the football team" or "Tommy Farrow's friends" as the perpetrators, but she really only identifies Justin Blake and Mackenzie Myers. What difference—if any—does it make if the harassment comes from two people or several? Is one type more devastating than the other?

6. What constitutes harassment? In the story, CeCe distinguishes between "stupid pranks" and something which should be reported to the authorities. Is there a differ-

ence? CeCe has her own reasons for not wanting to go to the police. Where should the line be drawn?

7. Sam states that bullies count on their victims being weak. Once the bullied takes a stand, however, the bullies lose their power. Is this true? Have you ever witnessed an example of this happening?

8. How does the Internet affect and/or change the nature of bullying? Some say the Internet can turn any place into a small community. Do you believe this is true? If so, does that mean the definition of "scandal" is affected as well?

9. Characters are manipulated in numerous ways in this story—whether it is through charm or fear or guilt. Is there a particular method that is more effective than the others? How can you identify when you are being manipulated? Or is that the very definition of being manipulated—that you don't know?

10. When CeCe and Briony talk about posing for explicit photos, Briony defends her boyfriend by saying that he promises the photos will be for his private use. Is this a valid defense?

11. There are a number of secret relationships in this book. Sam states very clearly that he has no interest in being part of a secret relationship, but is the desire for privacy necessarily wrong? Are there any good reasons for keeping a relationship secret?

12. CeCe states that when her mother was alive, she could use her mother's forgiveness to absolve her own guilt. But now that her mother's not around—and therefore cannot bestow her forgiveness—CeCe will have to do something much harder and forgive herself. Do you think this is true? Do we use other people's forgiveness as a way to erase our blame?